— KREWE FAVOR —

ADVANCE PRAISE FOR:

NOLA

"Pull up a chair for an immersive literary feast in New Orleans. Debut author, Molly Jo Realy, can really craft a story. The twists and turns keep readers guessing, while the atmosphere pulls them deep into the culture of the Big Easy. The romance will engage your heart as the mystery keeps you reading long past your bedtime. This is an author to watch and I can't wait for her next offering."

—EDIE MELSON, award-winning author and blogger

"Molly Jo Realy is a gifted novelist and her book, NOLA, is a superb romantic tale filled with love, betrayal, and forgiveness. I thoroughly enjoyed this book and highly recommend it."

—MARILYN KING, author of The Winds of Love Series

"With her debut novel NOLA, accomplished author and writer Molly Jo Realy bursts onto the fiction scene with a vengeance. Juggling complicated, complex characters, she weaves an intricate plot of romance and intrigue that will keep the reader turning the pages. Her love for this project is clear on every page, and her mysterious, tender characters are at once endearing and unsettling. Navigating New Orleans, a new and foreign city that is every bit as developed and intriguing as the characters in it, Penny must learn to trust, to heal in her new life. But knowing who to trust isn't as easy as she might have imagined."

—AARON GANKSY, author of *The Bargain*,
The Hand of Adonai Series, and *Firsts in Fiction*

"Pour yourself a glass of sweet tea and get comfy in your easy chair—you are about to enter The Big Easy. Writer Penny Josie only wanted to leave behind the shattered pieces of her old life in California. Her journey forward leads Josie on a journey inward the moment she eyes the swampy bayous from the airplane window. Alive and breathing, New Orleans with all her charm and mystery is as much a character as her people. When Josie befriends some of the locals, she finds herself thrust in the middle of a bewildering and alluring story that keep readers turning the pages. Much more than a romantic mystery, readers will fall in love with Molly Jo Realy's *NOLA*."

—BECKIE LINDSEY, Editor of *SoCal Christian Voice* and
author of the award-winning series *Beauties from Ashes*

"Molly Jo Realy pulls off a doozy of a story in her breakout novel with buckets of plot twists, and where nothing is as it seems ... until the very end."

—CHRISTOPHER J. LYNCH, author of the award-winning *One Eyed Jack* crime novel series

"Molly Jo Realy has found her voice. In her breakout novel, she charms us with humor, piercing insight, and one woman's high-stakes search for herself...all deftly wrapped around an edgy story of murder, betrayal ... and love."

—VICTORIA ZACKHEIM, novelist, playwright

NOLA

MOLLY JO REALY

the

past

never

stays

buried

New Inklings Press

NOLA
Copyright © 2019 Molly Jo Realy

Library of Congress Cataloging-in-Publication Number: 2019907388

PUBLISHED BY:
New Inklings Press
www.NewInklingsPress.com
www.MollyJoRealy.com

paperback ISBN: 978-0-9890725-5-7
ebook ISBN: 978-0-9890725-8-8

Cover and interior design by Domini Dragoone
Editor: Yolanda Smith
Cover images: house © GJGK Photography/iStock,
    woman © Evgeniya Tiplyashina/123rf

10 9 8 7 6 5 4 3 2 1

— MAIS, CHER! —
DEDICATION

To my daughter, Hannah, who constantly shows me what it's like to be brave in a world of unknowns. You are my breath, and I am honored with the blessed fragrance of your life.

To my mother, Sally, whose never-ending love of books influenced me since before I can remember. This one's for you.

— WHO DAT? —
ACKNOWLEDGMENTS

WRITING IS BOTH A SOLITARY AND COLLECTIVE event. Truth be told, I would not have finished *NOLA* if not for the Swarm of family and friends who continuously buzzed their support and encouragement during the writing process. From the professionals who took time to mentor me, to the ones who weren't aware I was watching from the shadows, but ultimately to the team who surrounded me day in, day out, and never let me fail.

Aaron Gansky, my friend and first writing mentor, and his wife, Naomi. My favorite faux family, and reason for making chili. You taught me perseverance, believed in me when I didn't, and talked me in from the ledge more times than I can count. This book, and my career, would not be here if not for your tireless support. Here's to magic, music, GIFs, and running into poles.

My quasi-technical advisor, Lindsay Reine, Ms. New Orleans 2014, and Ms. Louisiana 2015/2016. Without your input, *NOLA* would be a puzzle with pieces missing. You helped shape the story, and kept me going with tireless text messages. I can't thank you enough for your friendship.

Edie and Kirk Melson. What can I say? You are my friends closer than a brother, and I love you. Through all the ups and downs of writing and not writing, you are there. Movie marathons, game nights, and the occasional wrong turn always give us more to talk about. I heart you, sirs.

Beckie Lindsey. Just, wow. You did it, girl. I'm so proud of you. From our first moment at Starbucks. "I told you this would happen." And it did. For both of us. Thanks for being a part of my journey. You are my inspiration.

Yolanda "This is Just a Suggestion" Smith. You are by far the best editor I have worked with. You listened to my voice, and helped me recapture when I thought I'd lost it. Your expertise and knowledge, friendship and comradery, are off the charts. Thank you for being my book midwife.

Monica and Tania, my partners in crime. How often we get together to talk writing and just enjoy the moments instead? From Applebee's to Starbucks, any time, day or night, you have been my go-to girls and no one will replace the pieces of my heart and soul that belong to you. We girls just want to have fun, and you encourage me every day to remember that life is a happy place.

To my writing peeps with BRMCWC, HDCWC. To DiAnn Mills, Jim Rubart, Michelle Cox, Bob Hostetler, Steve Laube, Heather Kreke, Vincent Brent (George) Davis, Andy Clapp, Steven Cannell, Victoria Zackheim, and so many others from the writing community who have come alongside to let me know this crazy diagnosis of being a writer isn't a disease, but a delight. Your heartfelt acknowledgments and large coffees have won me over.

I definitely need to give a shout out to Visit New Orleans, the official tourism media of New Orleans. Without your continued resources, input, assistance, and encouragement, *NOLA* would be sadly lacking much of its personality.

Domini Dragoone, you are an amazing book designer. From cover to cover, you held my hand and helped me navigate these new waters. Your creative expertise, willingness to bend, and ability to keep me rooted has shaped *NOLA* into a product I didn't know was possible. Thank you from the bottom of my coffee cup.

Finally, no author can truly write without with support of their family. To my daughter Hannah, mother Sally, brothers, Mark and Matt, thank you. Thank you for endless jokes, wonderful calls, and a lifetime of memories. Fair warning: Someday y'all will be in my biography. Play nice, and put the bird book back on the shelf. I love you all.

Savor the journey,
Molly Jo

"*There will come a time when you believe everything is finished; that will be the beginning.*"

—LOUIS L'AMOUR

Lizzie,

THANK you for voicing
life into NOLA. your hard
work is greatly appreciated.

NOLA

Looking forward to
working together again.
Savor the journey.

Molly Jo
Realy

CHAPTER ONE

FUNERALS AND PLANES. NEITHER WAS A PLACE I wanted to be, but here I was, flying away after the burial and everything that reminded me of home. It was the first Monday in October and the year had already lasted a decade.

"Can I get you anything, ma'am?" the polite attendant asked.

"Decaf." I never could sleep on planes. Would the red-eye be any different? I was tired beyond tired, but also ... something else. Something I couldn't quite put my finger on. Could it be hope? Trying to fight its way up from the darkness? Would things be okay after all?

I pulled a fortune cookie out of my backpack, cracked it open and ate half as I read the tiny paper.

All friends start out as strangers.

They should call them statement cookies. They don't even include lucky numbers anymore.

The cursor blinked from the computer game I wasn't playing.

He'd had no right to show up at the funeral.

The seat thrust me forward as a young boy kicked once more. I viewed the worn-out mother over my headrest as she struggled to buckle him up yet again without dropping the infant she was precariously holding.

"You need to stop," she told him, and apologized loud enough for those around her to hear. It was the same apology she'd offered at the boarding gate an hour ago as several of us walked past her noisy brood. More than one of us had said a not-so-silent prayer to find seats away from the commotion.

My toes clenched and flexed—a relaxation trick I'd learned from my cat when I was seven. But this time, like all recent times, it didn't work. I'd not slept well for months, maybe years. The last three months were unbearable. The living trust, the medical bills, the blur of lawyers and arrangements. And Uncle Martin's death.

If I never heard another funeral song, or had to choose a flower arrangement, or sign legal documents, it'd be fine with me.

His leaving me a small inheritance and his house did little to make things better. He was my shelter, my friend ... but now he was gone.

Living in his house, alone, was excruciating. Ted never liked that house.

When Martin was sick, I'd wanted his suffering to end. When it had, I'd wanted him to be here again.

I felt guilty for always needing things to be different.

I wished I believed more in ghosts.

At what point would that house stop feeling like his and start feeling like mine?

I'd had to get away from all the concerns that hung on me

like an old, worn sweatshirt. As ugly as they were to someone else, they were familiar to me. But a change was needed. So, I left. I dumped some things in my finally-I-have-a-reason-to-use-it suitcase and found myself on an airplane in the middle of the night, flying away from a place I didn't want to call home, and a guy I didn't want to call family. I hoped the deputy and his wife would get why I skipped town.

Another kick jolted my memories away and I glared between the seatbacks. I wanted to whisper obscenities at the child but decided against it when I glimpsed his frazzled mother.

The boy settled back and stuck his tongue out. I returned the gesture with a tired smile before turning toward the window.

One. I began my mantra. I refused to spend mental energy counting sheep. Instead, I let my brain focus on one. Only one. One. I let it draw out. Ooonnnnne. Like a chant.

Inhale. Ooonnnnne. Look into the dark.

Exhale. Ooonnnnne. Look at nothing.

Inhale. Ooonnnnne. Look at the star. Stars. Look at all the stars.

Great. Now I was counting stars.

The baby was screaming in a rhythm that matched a revving motorcycle.

"WaaAAAHHHHaaaa!" its angry voice announced. It was rude to consider a baby an it, but since I didn't know if it was a boy or girl, and I had no intention of finding out, it would remain an it.

There were a few empty seats ahead. I'd always hated changing seats on a plane. If we fell out of the sky, would my body go unidentified because it wasn't where it was supposed to be? The gain outweighed the risk and I nervously moved up four rows and across the aisle, trying not to disturb the elderly man sleeping through the commotion.

The middle seat. Away from the aisle and window. Away from the distractions, which was a distraction in itself.

Oh, to be that baby. To be able to cry, scream, kick, and fuss at the unfairness of the world. To be young enough to be held and told everything's going to be all right.

Ted had taken too much of me, and most of what was left was buried with Martin. But I was free now. Whatever that meant. At least, for the moment, I could breathe.

I twisted the diamond ring on my right hand. I should have returned it when we broke up, but let's be honest. I didn't want to. Wearing it on the "wrong" hand seemed poetic, justified. Empowering.

Ted wasn't all bad. More often than not, he cared for me like no one else.

It was just the occasional misunderstandings.

And then the regular ones.

Still, the in-between times weren't terrible.

It was those in-between times I missed.

No longer listening to the screaming baby, I searched past my sleeping seatmate into the dark sky. What storms were brewing in the distance? The summer news had been full of inclement weather, and the mid-Atlantic was already up to Tropical Storm Madison. Leave it to me to fly toward the storm instead of away from it.

Six hours ago, I'd stood in LAX, staring at the flight board. The immediate destination choices had been New Orleans or Cincinnati, and Cincinnati held no interest for me. If I didn't buy a ticket right away, I might drive home. Home to my lonely, lifeless life in the desert. Or worse ... to him. So, I'd hopped the plane before I had a chance to change my mind.

Nearly two thousand miles later and right after the sun called people either to breakfast or bed, the plane circled above New Orleans and the Louis Armstrong International Airport. Ted and I had talked of coming here someday, for our honeymoon, or maybe on one of my writing assignments. Why didn't I remember that before I was in the air? Did his presence at the funeral bring it back? Was that why it was now looming beneath me? Maybe I wanted to prove I could keep my dreams without keeping him in them.

NOLA.

It wasn't what I expected. Swampy bayous, lush green and autumn-orange scenery greeted me through misty remnants of clouds. Most buildings resembled each other from above—concrete and tar roofs next to shiny steel, framed by gray sidewalks and streets. The cemeteries, shops, and quaint buildings I wanted to see called to me. My heart lurched with excitement.

It no longer felt like I was running away. Even though I was going somewhere I'd never been, it felt like I was heading home.

Not the empty, dusty-desert home I was used to.

This home was a place where movies, plays, books, and music were born. Like jazz beats and A Streetcar Named Desire.

Maybe the magic air could make something of me, help me find those missing parts I didn't know I'd lost. Or maybe I'd get caught in a natural disaster and force others to seek me out.

I'd take any kind of hope I could get, even the misguided kind.

There should be a storm. Someone or something should stop me. My common sense or Uncle Martin's ghost. Maybe some cosmic interference telling me to turn back. But nothing, and no one, did. I wanted to pray for guidance and direction. I wanted to ... but didn't.

At least I'd made it to New Orleans.

After the scramble at the baggage claim, the doors slid open and I stepped outside.

My "knowledge" of New Orleans wasn't sufficient. This was nothing like the TV shows or books. This was so much more.

The air was full of mystery, heritage, and romance.

The desert winter in Southern California was still months—or at least many weeks—away, and in my rushed packing I'd neglected a jacket, among other things. This New Orleans chill had nothing to do with weather. Was this morning dew or remnants of an overnight rain? It didn't matter. It refreshed my soul.

"Where to?" The gruff cabby greeted me. The door read "Yellow Cab." Funny, since the car was a strange orangish hue with tan interior.

"Beignets," I said with mock authority and blurted out a name I figured everyone was familiar with. "Café du Mode, Decatur Street."

A faded, oversized postcard taped to the dash welcomed me to the Crescent City with a collage of scenes. Greenish waters, a Mardi Gras mask and something resembling a werewolf were interspersed with neon drinks and names of streets I'd hoped to learn, to experience.

"Home or visiting?"

I met the cabby's gaze in the rear-view mirror. "Visiting."

"Been here before?"

I was tired and didn't want to talk. I also didn't want to be California-rude. "No." My tired lips curled. "Just time for a trip."

"It's a nice place, for the most part. Everybody likes it here. Except the ones that don't."

How could I respond to that?

The sun tried to greet us between the buildings and the clouds. The eclectic people and their movements mesmerized me. Was this another city that never sleeps?

A high billboard invited me to the next Saints game. Another promised a great deal on a new Chevy. On a third, a beautifully sad blonde woman beckoned, "Have You Seen Me?" and listed an 855-number.

Around the corner, the towering metropolis gave way to cracked pavement, cobblestones, and worn sidewalks. There was so much available in such short proximity. In the desert, heat and wind made walking a rare option. Here, people strolled on wet pavement, circled around puddles, met some people and avoided others.

"Well, welcome to the sometimes murder capital of the state, and quite possibly, the nation." The cabby dropped my bags to the ground and drove away.

I made my way through the crowd. Apparently, I wasn't the only person who'd thought this would make a good breakfast.

"What can I get ya, honey?" The counter girl was too perky for my exhaustion.

Beignets were a must. Café au lait or coffee and chicory? Caffeine was a post-flight necessity, and I ordered both to go. The tables were full, so I parked my bags outside, balanced one drink and the remaining beignets on my suitcase, and leaned against the wall.

As I experienced the sweet taste of beignets being drowned by warm coffee, I gave in, and gave myself over to just being. I'd heard about the plethora of New Orleans characters, and this could be a chance to redefine myself. To find myself. To be who I needed to be for me. Yes, there was an abundance of life here. I refused to feel guilty over my indulgence, and took another coffee-dipped bite.

It may have been the pull of Christianity and Voodoo conflicting with each other that grabbed me. There's a sixth sense in NOLA that emanates from everywhere. It's an understanding of history and the promise of a future. It's magical and mystical and doesn't care what we were taught when we were young. It's the idea of living for now. Of leaving the past in the past. Which means anything is possible for the future.

New Orleans made it okay to not have all the answers ... or any.

Gravity and fatigue pulled my body low. I closed my eyes, swallowed the chicory, and embraced the moment.

Cups clanked on saucers and feet pounded the rue as people chattered and noised their appreciation of the decadent flavors. The aromas of beignets and coffees curled their way around me. A trumpet blared its melody through the air, and my foot tapped along before I could think about it.

A hard jolt forced me to open my eyes.

"Hey!" Someone yelled with urgency.

My suitcase lay on its side. The black coffee dripped onto the ground. A beignet was slow-motion falling. A few feet away, a guy with stringy, black hair was running like the devil was after him—running away with my laptop.

I fell and scraped my hands on the coffee-infused sidewalk. "My laptop!"

Two men gave chase, and a woman helped me to her now-empty seat while another brought my suitcase and backpack close to me. The young bandit wove into the distant crowd. The chasing men separated, scanned, circled around, but it was no use. The street rat had vanished. And so had my laptop.

Strangers surrounded me, took photos with their phones, called the police, asked if I was okay. It was a cluster of active noise I couldn't understand. One of the women sat and put her hand on my shoulder. "You all right?"

My dirty palms shook, and my not-so-white tennis shoe was tinged with spilled coffee.

It was a personal record. In less than half an hour, I'd become a statistic.

A tall dirty-blond guy with an apron tied around his waist weaved his way to me with another coffee. He set it down and ran a hand through his hair.

Adrenaline wasn't needed, but focus was. I pretended to sip through tight lips.

He knelt next to me. "I'm Tim, the manager. Sorry that happened. Most times we keep them characters away. Any valuables in that case? Other than a laptop?"

Other than my laptop? It wasn't gold-plated, but it was the one thing I still was attached to. When Ted and I split, when Martin was sick, when I didn't know what I needed, I could turn on my laptop and find a world of my own choosing. Music, movies, photos. My writing. The escape could last for a few minutes, or days on end.

Tim stood and held out a damp rag. I wiped the dirt from my hands and off my jeans, trying to ignore the uncomfortable stares and smart phone cameras.

I gripped my suitcase handle with ghastly knuckles. *Let's evaluate.* I cursed Ted's words. The laptop was backed up to an external drive. There were no passwords stored, and I'd cleared the cookies and cache regularly. I didn't think my identity could be stolen.

That would be funny. I hadn't had my own identity in years. I was too wrapped up in being Ted's girl before being his ex and being Martin's caretaker. *If you find my identity, could you let me know?*

Tim patted my shoulder and tried to reassure me New Orleans wasn't always like this. I wasn't sure I should believe him.

The coffee didn't taste as good as the first one.

The crowd dissipated, and the woman next to me excused herself as two men in suits approached. One showed a badge to the two chasers and took them aside, as the other chewed a toothpick and approached me.

"'Scuse me, ma'am. I'm Detective Jackson. That's my partner, Detective Chase." He pointed to my suitcase with his pen.

"Understand your belongings was stolen. May I?" He pulled a chair from a neighboring table and waited.

I gave him a quick nod. "You respond fast down here."

He sat. "We were down the Square, there. I understand you were hurt. We take that serious. You like to make a report?"

"I'm okay." I used Tim's rag to wipe more invisible dirt.

"May I?" He slowly reached for my hand. I let him hold it open and inspect the scratches. They stung, and I involuntarily curled my fingers against the pain.

"You'll be fine, but I suggest better safe than sorry on making that report. Gives us more reason to stay on the case."

Tim motioned. "I'll get y'all some coffee."

Detective Jackson's skin was almost the same color as my café au lait. The stupid things a person notices at times like these. I didn't want reminders of how stupid I was. I shouldn't have let go of the case. I shouldn't have closed my eyes. I shouldn't have gotten on that blasted plane.

But I had done those things and more. And I was about to pay the price for it.

"BETTER SAFE THAN SORRY."

That's what the deputy had said back home in the desert. It'd only happened once before. Maybe twice. And I think, really, it was an accident. A misunderstanding. These things happen a lot, right? Especially when two people are exhausted and overwhelmed?

But this time, it wasn't any of those reasons. And on top of all the words, all the looks, all the frustrations ... it was over. It had to be.

But in order for it to be over, something else had to start.

They took my statement, some photos. And sometime later there was an order that said Ted couldn't come around for a while. Couldn't contact me. Couldn't be anywhere near me or my friends. Except I had no friends.

I had no one.

Except the officer and his wife. I was okay being alone in life as long as the deputy was with me in court.

But when court was over, and time dragged on, and Martin passed ...

I didn't invite him to the funeral. He just showed up. And against the caring advice of Deputy Friendly, I'd said hi.

We'd both burned that bridge, and there was no going back to who we were together.

I didn't even know who I was alone.

CHAPTER TWO

HAVING RUN—OR FLOWN—AWAY FROM HOME without a real plan, I thankfully found there was no shortage of available hotel rooms.

The detectives took statements from me, Tim, and a few witnesses, then helped me find a place to stay at a substantial discount. I had been ready to slightly slum it, but not anymore. Now I wanted comfort more than adventure. At least, comfortably clean sheets and a soft robe.

The clerk's badge read *Grace*. Funny. I drummed my fingertips on the counter as her clumsy fingers keyed my information into the computer. She reminded me of selfish, unmannered Violet from *Charlie and the Chocolate Factory*. Did her lips smack when she ate, too? "Name?"

I often wondered if my parents understood the hardship they thrust upon me when they named me Penny. How much better my life might have turned out if instead they'd named me something richer like Ruby or Tiffany. "Penny Jo Embers," I said.

She eyed my hair, which by now had frizzed out like a copper-colored pot scrubber. *That's right. Redheaded Embers.*

Whenever I lost my temper, which for this Irish-Italian girl was plenty often, Uncle Martin would call me his California copperhead. Ted would call me something else I never enjoyed repeating.

"But people call me Josie." I tugged the hair behind my ear.

Payment was traded for the keycard and a toothbrush. "Enjoy your stay. If there's anything we can do to make it better, don't hesitate to call the front desk." She turned to yesterday's newspaper before I could ask for the winning lottery ticket.

Detective Jackson escorted me to my room. "Need me, call me."

After the hotel-branded pen and flimsy notepad were stuffed into my backpack, I took in the surroundings: third-story balcony, oversized bed, travel-sized bottles of generic personal products on the overly clean bathroom counter.

After a refreshing shower, I was ready for another early afternoon decaf. My bare feet welcomed the balcony. Subtle rumblings accompanied close lightning as it illuminated the growing darkness, the heavy curtains waved in the breeze. The ethereal smell was like a familiar dream—a mix of fresh air and wet dirt. It didn't matter that the sky was plopping into my coffee. The rain rejuvenated me as each splat and thunderbolt announced their presence.

Lightning struck close, and the mug crashed from my startled hands as I bounced back into the room.

My body ached and pulsed with a sharp, wet pain.

My view traveled from the shard-covered balcony where the rain was trying to wash away the evidence, to the trail of tiny ceramic pieces and red fluid spotting the carpet, to my left foot needing some sort of medical attention.

I hobbled to the bed and tried to scratch the debris from the bottom of my foot as I picked up the phone.

"Front desk. This is Grace." She smacked. Would she remember to call me Josie and not Penny?

"I need ..." Embarrassment trapped me, so I blurted. "The lightning made me drop my mug."

"I'm sorry to hear that, Penny." She offered to send up housecleaning. "And would you like me to call a doctor as well?"

Was she serious or sarcastic? "No, thank you," I said with a touch of syrup. "I'm capable of applying a Band-Aid all by myself."

At least I remembered to ask for the Band-Aid. And a new cup.

Take two. Another decaf. I pulled on a T-shirt and capris, and stepped again onto the balcony. After glancing down at the cacophony of people, I realized it wouldn't matter what I wore. In "N'Orlins," as I was corrected when I first called it "New Orleens," no one, or rather everyone, stood out in a crowd. Especially during Happy Hour. Which was, apparently, every hour.

Exhausted, I stepped inside and changed into Ted's old T-shirt. It was big. Soft. Comfortable. And because I'd bought it for him, I'd argued, it should be mine. He didn't argue back. The rare color of grass. The Strumbellas band logo on the front. These things never meant as much to Ted as they did to me. So, I kept the T-shirt, and I kept that piece of Good Ted that came with it. It no longer held his scent, but I pulled it to my nose and pretended it did.

The aroma of recent rain wafted through the balcony door I'd left open a few inches, and I crawled into the plush bed.

The TV kept me company as I stared at the ceiling, my thoughts competing with game show contestants. I focused on a single spot, hummed my monotone note, and fought sleep out of habit. For an entire eight minutes.

The hazy sunlight greeted my cough as I perched on the side of the bed. Was this the beginning of a deadly case of asthma? I was never more alive.

Today's statement cookie encouraged me to try something new. That wasn't going to be a problem.

After an easy breakfast of eggs and biscuits, I took a stroll.

The abundance of smells mixed with each other. At times, sweet or savory. At others, pungent and offensive remnants of someone's (or many someones') over-indulgences.

I stepped aside to people-watch. Some pushed around others. A homeless woman discreetly searched discarded food bags for her daily salvation. A clerk swept the entry of his shop and greeted me with a nod. "Nice day," he drawled. I gave a slight acknowledgment.

The sidewalks and cobblestones attracted me. Each crack and chip. Each smooth section worn with age and use. What stories did they tell? Would mine ever be among them?

The path led me around a corner, into the midst of everything old and new. The collision of bright history and steely skyscrapers should have been expected. Yet here they were screaming against each other in a way that assaulted my senses.

Ted always loved pointing out how good I was at compart-mentalizing.

I turned my back on the large, modern city, shrugging it off like an unwanted touch, and continued deeper into the history of the French Quarter.

Throngs of people buzzed in every direction. What had their attentions? Nothing, and everything. This was life in the Crescent City. In mid-morning, people drank juleps, smoked cigars, and danced to sidewalk jazz. I salivated at the freedom of it all.

There was no division between day and night as people of all ages and inebriations mixed among suits and rags. Panhandlers and prostitutes called to the unlistening masses. The crowds gave money, stole food, shared company, and pushed forward to their next personal adventure. No map or tour book could have led me here. There were no real beignets in the desert.

GPS wasn't welcome for this organic experience. I bought a latte from a street cart and followed the path to Lafitte's Blacksmith Shop Bar. The building oozed history and alcohol.

A boisterous group of young men approached, loudly recounting the night they couldn't remember, and challenging each other to come up with better stories.

The old bricks hugged me as I let them pass.

"Sorry, ma'am," one said.

"He's getting married soon." Another pointed as two more laughed.

"Good luck." I raised my coffee.

"Thanks." The almost-groom blushed as his friends pulled him into the bar.

Decatur Street brought me to a capturing storefront of used books and apothecary bottles. I opened the door with gratitude. There's nothing like the experience of vintage paper bound in real leather.

"Welcome to Bits & Bones, for books and hoodoo," the counter woman greeted me. "We specialize in old books, new spells, and everything in between." She was tall, thin, and dark. I couldn't tell if she was just past young, or this shy of aged.

Her deep red, sleeveless dress accentuated her curves, and a long, gold tasseled chain dangled to her midriff. Her red lipstick made sure the hard-of-hearing would be able to read her lips. "I'm Momma Tristan, and this is my store. How can I help you?" What was that accent? Not foreign, but more than a southern drawl. She embodied her own hodge-podge motto.

"Just looking," I said.

"You keep looking," she said. "You'll find it."

Shelves of various bottles and a plethora of bins containing bagged herbs and spices filled the wall behind her. Candles of all colors were identified with specific spells—green for money, gold for success, white for clarity. Boxes and pegs displayed charms, paper scraps, feathers, and other fascinating items.

Aisles of books welcomed my perusal, offering an abundance of adventures. I chose a collection of New Orleans-based short stories, and a photographic tour guide.

Momma Tristan rang me up. "You new to the city."

"Visiting," I said.

Her drilling eyes were so intense I had to turn away.

"Mmm." She shook her head. "You're no visitor. But you know that." She put my purchase into a paper bag. "You a writer, yes?"

"No." Maybe once upon a time I played with the idea. But Ted didn't think it was practical, and when I needed to spend all my time and attention on Martin, I guess it proved him right.

"Yes." She squinted. "You have stories in you, stories to share." Her white teeth showed against her dark skin. "I make you a mojo bag."

Should I object? She was already turned to the counter behind her, lighting two candles. She faced me and spread her hands in front of the minute flannel pouches. "Which color for you?"

My hands started to pulse. Maybe this magic wasn't dark. Maybe it wasn't real, only ambiance. "I like the red."

Her lip curled. "You have a touch of the gift."

"What? No. It's ... I like red." She could keep her free voodoo chants. Did I even want the books anymore?

Her raised hand motioned me to be still. I froze. Should I move? *Could* I move? I decided to wait her out.

She murmured quietly, took a red flannel pouch and filled it with an assortment of dried herbs and a silver charm. She tied the pouch, sprinkled it with a liquid and held it out.

Her hands pushed the bag into mine, and she curled her fingers tightly. "Tiny pieces, a starter of what you desire. It attracts more. It's not the black magic. It's hoodoo. It will not fight against you if you're good to it. Now don't you be sharing this with anyone, and don't you be showing it, either. It's for you, and only you. You keep it safe, dry, sheltered. You give it a name, you give it life. You protect it. It's not your slave. It's your essence. And it's not for luck." She waved her hands toward the ceiling. "It's for power. If you believe, and we all believe in power. You need to believe in *your* power. He believes in you. *You* believe in you. Tell your story. Trust your ending. You'll find it. That will be your beginning."

How was I supposed to feel about this, my first voo-doo-hoodoo experience? God shouldn't be mixed with spells. He's not a magician or a genie. But there were no lightning strikes, no earthquakes. No voice telling me to walk away. Maybe God didn't care how we called on Him, as long as we called.

I reached for my books.

"You keep that mojo bag on you at all times for at least a week," she said.

"On me?"

"Under your shirt. Near your heart, near your soul."

I searched for a safety pin or something on the bag. There wasn't one. I turned back to Momma Tristan, and she held out a thin, black lanyard.

"Two dollars." She grinned.

Two blocks from the hotel I found Fleur de Fanci.

"Hi there, sugar." A sweet voice enticed me to enter the boutique. The woman had delicate blonde waves, and a touch of steel in her eyes. She was simply exquisite, in a dress that could go from day to night with a change of shoes and acces-sories. "Can I help ya find something?"

She had a thick bracelet on each wrist, overflowing with charms that rang as she moved through the rack next to me.

"That dress in the window. Do you have it in my size?"

She studied me. "I'd say you're about a size—"

"You don't have to say it out loud."

She grinned and moved to another rack. "Well, now. That's not a N'Orlins accent."

"Southern California. I'm Josie." We shook hands.

"What's the occasion?"

I shrugged. "Nothing in particular." Other than I forgot to pack some things, I have no idea what I'm doing, and oh, by the way, I ran away from home.

"That's a nice, fine dress in the window, Josie, but I think I might have something better for you." She pushed the clothing aside after eyeing each piece. "I been to California once. In the summer. I'm Toni. That's short for Antoinette, but don't you be calling me that, now. Only my momma and daddy call me that, and now and then my gramma when she has a mind to visit."

"Which part of California did you visit?" I'd heard the South was a friendly place. Back home, people kept to themselves. At the very least, I owed her reciprocal courtesy.

"Los Angeles, mostly," she said. "Spent a week out there for a business networking conference. Didn't get to see much, unfortunately."

"Except the beach and Disneyland, right?" Everyone goes to the beach and Disneyland.

Toni chuckled. "Still got the ears on my shelf." She excused herself to help another customer, and in her void I spotted a black shell jacket.

The real leather felt good under my hand. I slipped into it with ease and turned as Toni returned.

"Try this." She held out a black dress. Something about it attracted me more than the dress in the window. This one reminded me of Audrey Hepburn or Bette Davis. Classic. Simple. Long. Elegant. Amazing. This was a dress to get noticed in.

Toni held it against my shoulders. "I bet it'd be awful fine on you." She led me to a fitting room and waited as I changed.

The promise of the sequined straps and flow of the soft fabric gathered me in its fantasy.

"Perfect fit," she said as I shimmied in the dress and jacket. "One to keep you warm. One to make you hot."

CHAPTER THREE

THE JACKET AND DRESS HUNG THEIR PROMISES in the hotel closet, and the books beckoned from the chair. Restlessness and hunger caught me, so I made my way back to the sidewalk.

"Hey, Cali-Girl." Toni approached from her storefront. "Where y'at?"

I chewed my lip.

"Aw, it means how you doing, whatcha up to?"

I wasn't used to telling strangers who I was, where I came from, and what my plans were. But something in the New Orleans air made it almost okay. "Um, lunch."

"Fantastic. What do you say to an authentic N'Orlins plate?"

"Don't you have to work?" I pointed toward the boutique.

"Sweet of you to be concerned. But I have three full-time employees and an assistant manager. I go in two or three afternoons a week to check on things and sign payroll. Now. How 'bout that food?"

Before I could resist, she took my arm in hers. "Oh, don't you be worryin'. We'll walk, and if you don't like the company,

24

you can leave. How's that? Besides. You and I are going to be great friends now, aren't we?"

I was strangely at peace, and for the second time in a day, allowed someone else to call the shots. More of that New Orleans voodoo-hoodoo.

When I couldn't decide between a steamy shrimp jambalaya and a po-boy, Toni ordered both and more. Soon our table was populated with an abundance of tantalizing aromas and flavors.

The world outside our window begged for me to notice it. "It's so busy and colorful. Is there some event going on?"

"Honey." She smiled. "This is our normal. Any time of day, any day of the week, you can be sure we'll find something to celebrate. This is N'Orlins. Place of unspoken debauchery and grand forgiveness. We can do it all by midnight and repent before breakfast."

Two men in business suits tossed coins into a street musician's open guitar case. A weary mother held onto a stroller with one hand and a large coffee with the other. Three young adults in collegiate shirts sat at a café table across the street and ignored their open text books.

"Those three there," Toni said. "They act like locals but they ain't. They're only here for what they can get out of it, not give. Then they'll leave. For the rest of their lives they'll tell their families about the time they lived in N'Orlins, but it won't be honest. Others, well, you can live here ten years and not be a local, or you could show up yesterday and fit right in." She studied me with this statement, and I understood.

I gained a quick appreciation of southern sweet tea as I drank nearly as fast as my glass was filled.

"You haven't been here long enough, but you'll soon notice N'Orlins is more than just the people. She's a character herself. She takes bits and pieces of each of us and pulls us apart and puts us back together in a mosaic. See, the thing about N'Orlins is that she's enchanting and evil all at the same time. She will love you one minute then chew you up and spit you out the next, but you always love her because she's majestic."

The goosebumps on my arms verified her words.

"What part of California are you from?"

My response was automatic. "Central Southern. The desert, halfway between Vegas and L.A."

"You like it there?"

I recalled the searing summer heat that hosted murderous wildfires. Dirt yards growing only cactus and tumbleweeds. Short autumn rainstorms that left everything with the scent of freshly washed sage.

"It's beautiful." The homesickness took me by surprise. I cleared my throat. "Antoinette. Is that a family name?"

"The family name's Beaveau. Antoinette Jane is mine," she said. "My daddy read it in a book or something. Had I been a boy I'd probably be Caesar or Napoleon."

"My first name's Penny," I said. "Jo is my middle name, so I go by Josie."

She sipped her sweet tea thoughtfully. "Well, now. Josie is a right fine name. But I think Penny might be it for you."

I shrugged. I hadn't been called Penny in years, but I liked the idea of a new, old name in a new, old place.

"Then Penny it is." She cheered.

"Penny." I lifted my glass.

The lanyard irritated my neck, and I gently scratched away the nuisance.

Toni raised an eyebrow. "Momma Tristan?"

"You know her?"

"A little. What's it for?"

"Something about power. You ever have a mojo bag from her?" If Toni believed in the magic, I could give myself permission to do so, too.

"No," she said. "But plenty have. You name it yet?"

I shook my head.

"Better name it." She pointed with her fork. "It can't do its job if you're not willin' to do yours."

I peeped down my shirt and smirked. "Fred."

Toni giggled and swiped her hair behind her ear. Her bracelets once again caught my attention. "Those are beautiful."

She pulled her hands into her lap and removed them. "Take a look. They're bits of who I was, who I am, and who I hope to be. They're also reminders of others in my life. I keep them close so I never forget. I guess you could say these are my mojo."

The first dangled with a fleur-de-lis, coffee cup, two-story house, Mardi Gras mask and trolley. The second held a different fleur-de-lis, medical cross, a puzzle piece, chef's hat, and ... a monster? I was about to ask when the waitress checked in. I took the opportunity to order a dessert coffee.

When I glimpsed at Toni, she seemed distracted. I returned her bracelets, and she again dropped her hands to her lap to put them back on.

My coffee arrived, with a slice of pie.

"I didn't order this," I said.

"Lagniappe," the waitress said proudly.

"Lan-what?"

"*Lan-yap*," Toni said. "It means a little something extra."

"Oh. Thank you."

The waitress smiled and left.

"So," Toni said. "What do you for a living, Ms. Penny-from-California?"

How much history did I want to share? The pang in my throat wouldn't let me fully smile. "I used to write now and then."

"A writer? Used to?"

I stuffed pie in my mouth as a distraction. "Life kinda got in the way."

She pursed her lips before replying. "Then we better get you back on that train and give you something to write about. Seek no further, honey. Your N'Orlins tour guide is sitting right in front of you."

"Were you born here?"

"Born and bred. Can't think of any better place to live and die. Course, it all depends on how you die." She winked.

She asked more questions than she answered. We talked food, travel, books, and more. Had we only met hours ago, or had I known her my entire life?

Being social had invigorated yet exhausted me. I politely declined her pleas for more sightseeing.

She left me at the hotel, with a promise to return after tomorrow's breakfast.

Two young boys chased each other with loud laughter through the lobby. I pushed against a wall to avoid them, and dropped my keycard.

"Sorry," they both hollered. New Orleanians were sure polite, even when they were rude.

"'Scuse me, ma'am." A man bent to retrieve my card. "I believe this is yours."

I saw the badge before I saw his face. "Detective Jackson. Thank you."

"Off duty. Was in the area. Wanted to check on ya and give you an update on your laptop."

"You found it?" A surge of happiness wrapped me.

"No, I'm sorry. Didn't mean that. But we may have a lead. Checking pawn shops and the like. Report will be ready in a day or so. You make an insurance claim?"

"I hadn't thought about it."

"Might want to." He escorted me to the elevator.

"I'll consider it."

"You'll find the majority of us 'round here to be helpful. Still, it's a big city, easy to get lost in. You need anything, have any questions, call me. I'll keep an eye out for you."

"For my laptop."

"That, too." He winked and walked away. "Have a nice rest of your day."

I hated to think of my laptop like a lost pet or child, out somewhere being abused or neglected. Maybe Joni Mitchell was right. You never know what you've got 'til it's gone.

The longing to write was regurgitating from its hibernation. Subtle but strong. But a familiar habit needed a familiar outlet, and I wasn't ready to learn a new computer.

In a city like this, full of characters, ghosts and food, history, and cemeteries above ground, modern conveniences didn't completely belong. Still, I had to find something.

Shoes clicked on the tile floor as the elevator dinged open, and I knew.

Tomorrow, I'd find an antique typewriter.

CHAPTER FOUR

"LITTLE WARM FOR THE JACKET, ISN'T IT?" TONI paced in the lobby.

"Anything less than seventy degrees and I'm shivering." In a dry heat, maybe. But this humidity made it seem warmer than it really was, and already my arms were clammy.

"It's seventy-three," she said.

It could be ninety and I'd still wear the leather. "California thins the blood."

She smiled and handed me a small bag. "Got you something."

"What's this?" I pulled out a modest jewelry box.

"Open it and find out."

A striking black and silver fleur-de-lis charm dangled from a thick silver bracelet. "Toni, it's gorgeous." I lifted it for closer inspection. "I can't accept this."

"Already did." She started out the door. "It's a start. Fill it up. Tell your stories."

Again with the stories. Maybe New Orleans was less about running away, and more about running to. Maybe it wasn't leaving life behind, but rediscovering it.

She assured me we would sightsee on our way to several antique stores, not taking no for an answer. I wondered if she ever took no for an answer.

Her car was a newer model BMW, sleek but not too eye-popping. In a dark parking lot, the black exterior would blend with the asphalt and shadows. It seemed like a month since I'd been in a vehicle. Sitting, watching the world pass by instead of walking through it, was almost unnatural.

"You don't want to carry an armload of writing supplies a mile or more," Toni said. "Starting with this." She handed me a peacock-covered journal.

"You don't have to spoil me," I said.

"I take care of my friends."

"You hardly know me."

The corners of her eyes crinkled. "I know you. You just ain't recognized it yet."

I crunched a fortune cookie and stuffed the little paper in my pocket without reading it.

At nearly every corner, she had a story to tell. "That's where Old Mrs. Cavanaugh's little Chihuahua had his accident. She called him Bruce, of all things. Said she loved Bruce Willis action flicks. He was down here once doing a film and she flipped. I can think of a million reasons to not name a small dog Bruce, and a million other ways to honor an action hero. But. Wasn't my dog, wasn't my hero. So, Bruce done got run over early one Christmas morning—the dog, not the actor. You should have seen him, all decked out in this little reindeer outfit she bought him. Bless her heart. He didn't like the bells. The more they jingled, the more he tried to outrun them. Ran himself into a tizzy and right out in front of Dodson's cab."

Dodson couldn't possibly be the same cabby who dropped me at Café du Monde days ago, but I couldn't shake the mental picture of his shocked smirk as he ran over the poor yapper. The cabby did say New Orleans was the murder capital of the state, didn't he?

"Mrs. C. never forgave him." Toni continued as if I should know these people she talked about. "Shortly after, she was found in her apartment under the Christmas tree which was decorated with homemade doggie treats and toys. They say she tripped over a bone and didn't have the will to get back up. Thing is, people swear they see that dog reincarnated still running in and out of traffic to this very day."

I tried not to laugh as I imagined an elderly woman resigned to eating doggie treats and using piddle pads under red and green blinking lights until she passed away.

Toni's stories continued. The requisite homeless that every inner city holds. The history of this older building and the future of that empty lot.

"Does it cloud over like this every day?" I peered up.

"This time of year is hit or miss."

She pulled into a parking lot where several hand-painted signs announced we were at a yard sale for the benefit of St. Joseph's Catholic Church and their economic outreach programs. Blankets, tables, and displays overflowed with donated goods throughout half the parking lot and most of the grass.

The church was a beautiful, ghostly building. I fingered the historic bricks.

Two priests walked out one of the large doors. The elderly one approached with a smile. "Would you like to come meet your neighbors?"

A glimpse inside revealed people kneeling, lighting candles, chatting. I took a mental step back and shook my head. I'd be pulled into salvation kicking and screaming later. Right now, I was attracted to everything outside the church.

I retrieved the fortune from my pocket.

There is nothing new under the sun.
Except your perspective.

The heavy air filled with zydeco music and playful children. Barbecues lined the fence and burly men carried on conversations with friends and strangers alike. Families shopped second-hand for their needs.

And then I saw it. Sitting on a long, plastic table. The keys worn from years of use. Nothing else mattered as I took the few long strides to stare at its magic. This was my new, old typewriter. "How much?"

The seller caught my gaze."Momma Tristan!"

She broke into a loud laugh. "The writer," she said. "I tell you, you find it. You still have your mojo bag?"

I pulled lightly at the lanyard.

She laughed again, louder, and patted the typewriter. "Twenty-five dollars."

"Twenty-five?" Toni asked over my shoulder. "Now, Momma Tristan, that ol' thing ain't worth much more than ten."

Momma Tristan ignored her. "Seventeen-fifty now. When what you write sells big, you come back and gimme the other seven-fifty. We got a deal?"

I chuckled. I'd have to write something before I had anything to sell.

"You do it," Momma Tristan said. She stopped her busy work and stared. "Make your own stories." Her finger almost jabbed me as she whispered loudly. "Write them. Find the ending so you can start the beginning." It sounded like a blessing but felt like a curse.

"Deal." I accepted. Was it really this simple? Was Toni my good luck charm?

"Where'd you get the typewriter?" Toni asked.

"I found it in the attic," Momma Tristan said.

"Whose attic?" Toni pushed.

"Mine."

"Really?"

Momma Tristan put her hands on her hips. "Maybe yes. Maybe no. Cudda been a dumpster."

"Where's the ribbon?" Toni fingered the open space.

Why hadn't I thought of that?

Momma Tristan shrugged.

"Do you have a real investment in any of this stuff?" Toni rifled over the table.

"Oh, all right. Take it. It prob'ly don't work, anyway." Her eyes scrunched and she leaned toward me. "But we know it really do."

I wanted to test it right then and there. But she had told me to take the broken-down piece of junk. What if it did work? She might ask me to pay for it. I slapped a ten on the table and picked it up, convinced I was doing her a favor by taking it off her hands. Didn't she offer it to me for free? And I still had to buy a ribbon.

Toni turned to the crowd. "Don't look now, but it's about the get stormy 'round here."

I peeked at the darkening sky then turned to see *him* walking toward us. My pulse fidgeted and I forgot to breathe. I'd never seen him, but my soul had met him before. He made me thirsty, and I wanted to know him. I didn't pay attention to what he was wearing, but I knew he looked good in it. I bet he looked good in anything. His black hair clashed with his piercing blue eyes. There was something hidden there, a forgotten sadness that refused to leave. And then he smiled.

He made me feel the way I felt when I first saw Ted. Memories tumbled into me and I lost my grip on the typewriter.

He caught it before it crashed to the ground. "Safe."

"Thanks." Who cared about the typewriter? Would he be the reason to wear my new black dress? My cheeks heated, and I hoped no one noticed.

Toni did. "I do believe you've upset the status quo again," she said to him, and took my arm. "Boo, I want you to meet my new friend."

He cradled my typewriter against his left hip and offered a handshake. "Nice to meet you."

"Josie," I stammered.

"Penny Jo," Toni said.

"Anyone ever call you PJ?" He winked.

"Not unless they want pencil shavings in their coffee," I said as innocently as I could.

"Well, then. Nice to meet you, Lucky Penny."

Like I hadn't heard that one, either. But hearing it from him was new. Like magical music, or a hoodoo spell.

A drop of rain splatted on my cheek.

He sheltered the typewriter as best he could. "Where'd you park?"

Toni linked her elbows in ours and escorted us to her car. After he set the typewriter in the trunk, he gave her a hug. A very friendly hug.

"Well, it's 'bout time you gave me a proper hello," she teased.

"I'm sorry, darlin', but I'm busy playing hero to your new friend Penny here." He winked again.

"You solo today?" she asked him.

"Mm-hmm. You?"

"You see any ghosts over my shoulder?"

He peered and shook his head.

"Then I'm solo, too," she said. "Proper introductions all around. Penny, this is Rain."

"Ray?" I asked.

"Rain," they both corrected. As if on cue, a flash of lightning preceded a horrendous boom and then the storm fell. We rushed into the car. I sat in the back, an adrenaline-laced fly on the wall as they finished greeting each other.

Toni lifted the damp hair from her neck, and I viewed a garish scar. Jagged, yet smooth and pinkish. Healed over inasmuch such a wound could heal.

A sickening recognition churned in my stomach and throat. I glanced away and breathed through my teeth so I wouldn't vomit.

Rain eyed Toni as if he'd not seen her for weeks. I couldn't tell if they were involved or just flirtatious. Then again, Toni had been nearly flirtatious with me. Was this part of New Orleans-friendly?

"Rain." I joined the conversation. "That's an interesting name."

"Isn't it, though?" Toni said. "It's short for—"

He put a finger to her lips. "Patience, Antoinette. My name, my story. Quit doing that." He turned to me. "My parents—"

"Momma B and Papa Raleigh," she said. "Named after Raleigh-Durham."

"North Carolina?"

Rain nodded. "My family's always loved a good Southern city."

"Nice names," I said.

"Nice people," Toni said. "May they rest in peace."

He glared at her. "My parents were true aristocratic southerners. The kind that go back for a few generations."

"More than a few," Toni interrupted before he covered her mouth with his hand.

"More than a few," he conceded. "Great-Great-Granddaddy was a Rainier, of the Delta Rainiers. His family helped forge most of the land New Orlins is built upon, way before it was New Orlins. He left my great-granddaddy a nice sugar plantation south of the city, and that's where I grew up."

Toni pulled his hand away. "Greyford Manor."

"My momma loved to travel," Rain said. "Always said one of her favorite places was Mt. Vernon, Virginia."

Toni kept his hand away from her face. "And so, when their precious boy was born—"

"Vernon Rainier, at your service." He tipped an imaginary hat. "I outgrew the Vernon part some years ago."

Vernon Rainier. Rain. It fit him. Stormy but refreshing.

"Careful, sugar," Toni warned him. "You'll end up a character in one of her books."

He draped his arm over the back of the seat. "You a writer?"

"No," I said.

She giggled. "What'd you think the typewriter was for? Mouse trapping?"

He gave her a sideways grin. "What's next?"

I shrugged. "I'm good with whatever."

Rain's eyes squinted and he smiled. "Oh, we don't do whatevers down here, Penny. This is New Orlins." He tapped Toni's shoulder. "Something decadent."

She gave an exaggerated sigh and started the car.

The precipitation sounded an emphatic banter on the umbrella above as Rain brought bananas Fosters to our sidewalk table. He pinched the expensive watch on his wrist and checked it before he sat down.

"How do you like the dessert?" he asked.

"Mmm." The warm caramel and rum sauce complimented the cool vanilla ice cream over cooked bananas. The flavors reflected my day—new, enticing, sweet, and bold.

Rain and Toni plotted out the next few days with maybes. Maybe we'd eat crawfish. Maybe I'd listen to real jazz.

Maybe they assumed I didn't have a problem with strangers planning my schedule.

Maybe we'd visit the tomb of Voodoo Queen Marie Laveau.

Maybe I didn't have a problem with any of this.

Everyone knows the diversity New Orleans has to offer. How it gave birth to unique musical and literary flavors. How differing religions blend. How excess lives next door to the homeless. How one of the worst hurricanes in history can't stop this city. Here, life is celebrated, even in death. Here, superstitions flow out of their above-ground cemeteries like steam from a kettle. Yes. I wanted to experience all of this.

Some passersby carried umbrellas, some wore rain jackets or trash bags for protection. A young man strolled by in a yellow T-shirt with a graphic of something between a crazed man and a vicious werewolf.

"What is that?" I asked.

"That's a rougarou." Toni fingered her monster charm. "Folklore says if young children don't behave, the rougarou will attack and kill them."

Intriguing.

"There's another myth," Rain said. "In daylight hours, the afflicted is in human form."

Toni continued. "At night, if he's attacked by another human, he transforms back to a man, tells his name, and the attacker must not tell anyone for a year what happened. If he does, he, too, becomes a rougarou."

My chair grated the pavement as I shifted forward.

Rain sipped his tea. "Some say the curse lasts one hundred and one days. The only way to become fully human again is for a rougarou to bite someone else."

"Sort of a bad pay-it-forward gig, I guess." Did they believe these myths? "Well, you two must have been well-behaved children. Doesn't seem like the rougarou got to either of you."

Toni eyed the sky before scooping the last of her dessert. "We should leave before it gets worse."

CHAPTER FIVE

RAIN SET MY TYPEWRITER ON THE HOTEL ROOM table. "What do you write?"

"I told you, I'm not a writer."

Toni frowned. "Not without something to write with."

"What's that?" he asked.

"Sad story," she said.

He tilted his head. "I haven't heard it."

"My laptop was recently stolen," I said. "NOLA's finest are on it."

"It happened here?" Did he bristle? "Welcome to New Orlins."

"Says everyone," I grimaced.

"Show him your dress." Toni nudged me.

"Oh, no," I muttered.

"Show me." He sat in the easy chair.

Toni crossed the room and he pulled her to the arm of the chair. How friendly were they?

I wasn't ready to play model. What if he didn't like the dress, or me in it? Would it matter? Perhaps my self-worth could withstand a crushing blow from someone I'd met only hours ago. Perhaps he'd be my grand adventure. Perhaps I should kick them out, get drunk, and go to bed. Alone.

"Show me." His plea took my breath away. And my resolve.

I retrieved the dress and held it against me.

He stood. "Dinner tonight. My treat."

Into the storm.

Toni squealed her way to my side. "We need shoes."

"I got this." Rain moved toward the door.

"Red for me. Black for Penny."

He viewed my feet. "Seven?"

"And a half." I twisted my toes, and my mouth.

"I need a dress, too," Toni shouted as he closed the door behind him.

It took forever and just a minute before I looked and felt better than I had in months, perhaps years. Ted should see me now. I wanted him to care that I didn't care what he thought. I wanted him here to show him I could be happy without him.

Toni helped me into my dress, and even with my bare feet, I exuded more elegance than I could have imagined. She made sure my mojo bag was securely hidden. My copper hair glistened in its amplified humid craziness, and I was wearing lipstick. The skirt of the dress danced about my knees as I claimed my new adventure.

The balcony railing begged me to cling to it so I wouldn't float away and explode like fireworks into the cloudy sky.

A knock on the door turned my attentions back to the room. Toni opened it for Rain. He was dressed in a dark suit and white shirt, the top two buttons undone.

I was right. He looked good in anything.

"Whadja get her?" she asked.

He held up a bag from her store and took out a box.

She nudged him. "Good choice. Okay, you two. My turn." She playfully snagged the larger bag and turned toward the bathroom. "Y'all behave without me."

Rain's gaze was inexplicable, mysterious, delicious. There was ten feet between us, and the evening shadows played against the dim lights. I was drawn and frozen at the same time, and wished for clarity. I obviously had the wrong mojo bag.

He whistled low and reached his hand, beckoning me in. There was no ring. Maybe nothing would happen, but I elected to enjoy my momentary fantasy.

I held loosely to his hand as he twirled me once, and led me to sit on the edge of the bed. My lungs may have quit working.

He knelt, unboxed a beautifully simple black shoe, and gently slipped it onto my right foot. The singular embellishment glistened like a diamond. I wriggled my ankle and was surprised at the excitement. I'd forgotten this, too.

"One more, Cinderella." He reached for my left foot.

"Don't mock me." I recoiled and bit my fingernail.

He pulled my hand down, then reached again for the back of my calf. "I'm not mocking. Promise."

I winced as he slid the shoe onto my foot.

"Too tight?"

Red curls flicked as I shook my head. "I cut myself the other day."

He tipped my foot up and suddenly our relationship became medicinal. "That's not good."

Assuming massive pain or blood loss were the signs to watch for, I thought I was healing nicely. There was no delicate way for me to bring my foot up for my own inspection without flashing him. I had to trust his judgment.

He scoped the room. "First aid?"

I pointed to the nightstand drawer.

He returned with the blue and white box. I lifted my foot up awkwardly, but he moved it back to the floor. "Not the foot." He applied a thin bandage to the inside of the shoe and coated it with cream, then ran a delicate touch on my sole, and slipped the shoe back on.

In the desert, I preferred to be barefoot, but could acclimate to the restrictions of flip-flops or soft canvas when necessary.

This wasn't that, and my heart danced at the stir inside me.

As we waited for Toni, Rain took a cup of coffee and people-watched from the balcony.

I did my best to watch anything but him.

I kept focus on my coffee and pile of papers. "Medical stuff."

"You're awfully dressed up for reading medical stuff. You seeing him again?"

"Ted." I didn't want to have this argument. Not again. Not now. I didn't think a nice top and jeans without holes constituted dressing up, but, whatever. I kicked the heels off and let them clatter to the tile floor.

He poured a cup of coffee and stood behind me. "You going out or is he coming here?"

I hoped my silence would stop him. It didn't. "He's married." I could almost hear the sneer as he spoke over my shoulder.

"He's Martin's caregiver, and I'm meeting him at the house."

He sipped noisily, then pointed with his coffee cup. "What is all this?"

My head tipped, accidentally bumped the coffee, and the papers were soon drowning in caffeine.

"Ted!" I raced for the paper towels. He didn't move. "Help me."

"You can't think I did that on purpose."

I ignored him and sopped up as much as I could before tearing off more towels.

"Gypsy."

I thrust the roll at him, snatched a handful of papers, and dangled them before moving to the sink.

"Josie," he said in that bewildered tone of his.

"Oh my—" I dropped the sheets and slammed my hands on the counter's edge. "How does that even matter right now?" I faced him. "You've been jealous since day one. Jealous. Do you even get that, Ted? My uncle—my only family—is dying, and you're jealous." I pivoted toward the window and tried to lay the pages flat on the counter.

It happened all at once: Ted's hand lurched forward and a confusing collision of brown liquid freed itself from the ceramic vessel which smashed into the side cabinet and ricocheted into the window, sending a thousand shards in a helter-skelter attack as they dug into my cheeks and arms and hands and fingers. I heard a long shrill before I realized it was me, which made it only louder and shriller and in the jagged pieces of glass still stuck in the frame, I saw the reflection of him coming

toward me. I grabbed the only thing within reach—
the wretched papers that started it all—and held
them as a barrier he easily circumvented. I couldn't
stop the screaming noise and the more he asked
me to be quiet, the louder I got. Red dots began to
form on the painful spots. He took a damp towel
and tried to clean me, but the red, painful spots
scraped and grew. I screamed as he pleaded. Everything hurt from the inside out so I screamed as
loud as I could to get the demons out and then ...

I blinked. The cool floor was under my sweat-
ing cheek. My breathing was fast and hard. I was
feverish and chilled at the same time, and I needed
to throw up. Ted was sitting next to me, on the
phone, patting my face with the red-stained towel. I
jerked away.

"No. It's okay, she's waking up. Josie. Babe. Are
you okay? Yeah. No, she's not responding. Josie,
don't move. It's okay. Help's on the way. I'm so sorry,
Josie. I'm so sorry."

I couldn't close my eyes. I swallowed and stared
at the splattered baseboard under the cabinet.
What could possibly be next?

CHAPTER SIX

TONI APPEARED IN ALL HER CRIMSON GLORY, her hair in a wispy up-do leaving a few stray curls that hid her scar.

Rain extended his elbows and escorted us proudly down the elevator, through the lobby, and to Toni's car. We drove across town to Restaurant D'Arcy, an exquisite establishment in the French Acadia Hotel that made my dress investment seem almost underpriced. A shimmer of déjà vu crept through me.

He must have called ahead, because the staff greeted him by name and led us to a reserved table in the corner. We were treated like royalty, and I chewed my lip to avoid gaping at the opulence.

The opposing wall held floor-to-ceiling windows that overlooked the sidewalk and grounds, with a glimpse around the corner to the street traffic. Lush greens and string lights wrapped around the interior pillars and crawled up the walls which were papered halfway up then topped with mirrors.

"What do you think?" Rain clasped his hands under his chin.

"I'm speechless," I said. "I can't believe we're not actually outside. What a beautiful atmosphere. And the candles and lights everywhere. It's like a Shakespearean garden."

Toni giggled. "I don't think you're as speechless as you say you are."

A ragged man approached the hostess, who led him to a round table near the entrance where three other scroungy patrons were trying not to shovel food into their mouths too quickly. One dropped his fork and reached a dirty hand to pick it up. The hostess was quicker, and replaced it with a clean fork and a smile.

"What is that?" I asked.

Toni didn't turn. "That's the Premiere Guest Table."

"The owner set it up some years ago," Rain said.

"Are they...?"

"Homeless," she said. "But why should that mean they don't get to eat well now and then?"

The sight mesmerized me. "Every night?"

She took a quick view. "Every night. From five 'til closing. Not more than four at a time. No fighting allowed. No drinking. No smoking. No begging. They come in, give their names, and they eat. They stay for an hour, then the table's cleared for the next four. They're allowed to come in once a month for food and a shower."

"Do they ever trick the system with different names and come more than once a month?" I asked.

Rain lifted his head. "You'd be surprised how respectful they are when they're respected in return."

"And because of that," Toni said, "they require respect of each other, and don't let others take advantage."

The newest attendee made eye contact until I turned away. "Once a month," I muttered.

Rain shifted. "It's a big population. The owner set up the guidelines to provide the opportunity to those who want it."

Toni clicked her fingertips on the table. "Doesn't seem like enough, sometimes. Some come back month after month. Others, we don't see as often."

"We?" I asked. "So, you both come here often?"

"Often enough," Rain said.

I looked around again. Ted had mentioned the restaurant once. It had been another late night with a DVD and two bottles of wine. We'd sat in the dark and talked and drank our way through the movie. He'd seen Restaurant D'Arcy mentioned in some southern style magazine at the market. I didn't remember the Premiere Guest Table being mentioned, but I'd fallen asleep as he'd recounted the article.

Now here I was, reading the menu and trying to recall what Ted had said he'd wanted to try so I could avoid it.

I chuckled as Rain started to order for the group. "What do you usually eat when you go out?" he asked.

"Blackened salmon." I tried to find it on the menu. "It's my favorite."

He pulled the menu from me and handed it to the waiter. "Want to try some New Orlins cuisine instead?"

I never liked when someone else ordered for me, but I had to be near these people. And while I had no reason to believe I'd be kissed before midnight, this evening was about new experiences. After all, this was New Orleans. Anything could happen.

The maître d' poured the wine, and after verifying Rain's satisfaction, left us to enjoy our solitude. We passed conversation with loud whispers and quiet laughter, enjoying the drinks and get-to-know-you questions.

"Oh, Rain," Toni gasped. "The food. Mais yeah."

Our table overflowed with plates of steaming veal lasagna, smooth pasta under seasoned chicken breast and creamy white wine sauce, and the Chef's Special—a hearty steak and red potato hash.

I loved every moment of it. After my second glass of wine, I was loving it even more.

Our conversations carried us through dessert and back to a semi-private hallway between the restaurant doors and hotel lobby. Perhaps a private entrance to a VIP lounge?

Rain gripped his wristwatch between his thumb and forefinger.

"Somewhere you need to be, boo?" Toni asked.

He dropped his hands and pressed his lips into a thin smile. "Not tonight."

Toni put a hand on his arm and whispered. "Everything okay?"

"Mm-hmm." He nodded and followed with an authentic smile. "Promise."

I decided to let my guard down even more and blame it on the alcohol. If I offended anyone, I could later feign memory loss. I learned long ago to not ask a question unless I'm prepared for the answer. Or incapacitated.

I sucked in deep. "Are you two together?"

Rain's eyes tightened and his lips turned down, as if he'd unintentionally hurt someone. Was it me? I felt like an awkward teenager. Perhaps he did, too. Perhaps every adult felt un-adult through most of their life.

Toni protested, her hair bouncing with every movement. "Oh, honey. No. He's married."

A strange *whoosh* stuck in my ears and eyes, and I tried to steady myself against the wall.

"Don't worry." She leaned in and patted his chest. "We're not all debaucherous here. I do know some limits. Despite appearances, we're just very good friends."

"Very good," Rain agreed, but pulled her hand away. "Toni and I dated only briefly in junior high."

"Very briefly." She stepped back. "An entire two-and-a-half weeks."

"How'd you meet?" I didn't care, but needed time to ground myself.

She grinned. "In Mr. LeShaw's second grade class."

"When she sat next to me, took my pencil, and told me we were going to be great friends."

Toni's attractive personality had recently captured me. If she'd always been this way, I could only imagine the effect she'd had on an eight-year-old boy.

"She introduced me to my wife." The sad cloud entered his eyes again.

"In second grade?" The dots refused to connect.

"No." They piped in unison.

"After college." She giggled and kissed his cheek.

"Don't be doing that." Rain wiped it away.

"I forget," she said. "You're wife's mighty jealous."

His eyes met mine. "She's mighty dead."

"Or so he thinks." Toni put a hand on her hip.

"What?" Dizziness attacked with a vengeance, and my hands tingled. He's married? To a dead woman?

Rain turned from Toni, a distant shadow in his somber eyes. Was he sad that he was married? Or that she was dead? "She *is* dead."

"You don't know that," she said.

"I know it." I could barely understand him.

"Don't matter." She spoke to me as she put a hand on his arm. "You ain't got nothing to worry 'bout. She—"

He shifted from her touch. "No." He stepped closer and tucked down to meet my eye. Was he trying too hard to smile? "This is Lucky Penny's night. Let's leave the sad out of it."

"You think Cheryl will mind?" Toni said over his shoulder.

He darted a scowl at her.

My heart fogged my senses. I felt drugged. This was more of that New Orleans voodoo-hoodoo, I was sure of it. How else could it be explained—this unwanted magnetism, this breathless draw to a widowed man I'd met hours ago?

I wanted to know more, and wished I knew less.

I kept Rain's gaze. "Who's Cheryl?"

Toni cocked her head. "His dead wife."

Sweat poured from my hand onto the wall with each loud pump of my heart. My legs were jelly and my thoughts a jumbled mess. This conversation was confusing. Complicated. Was it even a conversation? Or just words mixing themselves up in my head? And me pretending the last few minutes hadn't happened, trying to forget about *her* and wondering—hoping—he was trying to do the same. I didn't even know him.

But I wanted to.

The nonsensical way they acted with each other. The way he looked at me. The way my heart made me look at him. So many blurry lines. So much noise in my head screaming to get out.

I couldn't fault him. With my hands still behind me, I twisted Ted's ring. But it wasn't on *that* finger. It shouldn't confuse anyone. And it certainly shouldn't blindside anyone in the gut.

Mine was just a ring, without a guy. His was no ring. With a wife. A dead wife.

New Orleans has all sorts of ghosts.

Rain's voice called me from the haze. "You like dancing?"

Did he mean a crowded, pulsing nightclub? Or a good, long, solitary sway? I dropped my hands and smiled. "Yeah."

We made our way from Decatur to Frenchmen Street. I'd strolled part of it in daylight hours but as all things are, it was different at night. The combination of false lighting and harmonious dissonance was a wonderful overdose of energy. The autumn-scented breeze fought against the hot congregation. I couldn't get enough of the unbalanced atmosphere.

There were too many people and I was already unstable in these new shoes. When Toni came to my rescue with a steady arm and another drink, I remembered to forget to say no.

I didn't pay attention to how many drinks I'd had, but I knew my name and the names of my companions. I wasn't driving, and the more I drank the less these new shoes bothered me.

Slowly and suddenly, we were crowded and drinking and dancing and in and out of bars and nightclubs and wearing beads and hugging strangers and talking to no one and watching lightning and feeling raindrops and making sense of creeping shadows and crawling spirits and moving and laughing and singing and living—

I spun on the sidewalk and stopped, captured by his gaze. Something inside me wanted more. A familiar but foreign longing for him.

Him. With the dead wife and the black hair and the blue eyes and the flirtatious friend and the money and the clothes and the cologne on his neck and that smoldering grin. And my drink in his hand.

He teased and pulled away from my reach. I took the bait, and took the step. My heel caught on the uneven pavement. My ankle didn't cooperate and there I was, being graceful as never. There the world was, spinning out of control.

Strong arms seized me as I began to tumble. I let myself sway and Rain embraced me tighter. Oh, to be fully conscious for this moment. He set me on a low brick wall and squatted to inspect the blood trickling from under my pinky toe to the pavement. I wriggled and tried to make designs with the splatter.

It didn't work. I tugged a thick strand of hair behind my ear. How to get out of this one? "Can't take me anywhere."

He rose. "Ya think?"

Toni retrieved my shoes and bag as Rain picked me up. It was awkward. It wasn't a scene from a movie or romance novel. But it almost was. If I'd had any control over any of this, we'd be fifteen years younger and I'd be thirty pounds lighter. And not as drunk. It was a perfect moment.

The combination of too much pain and too much alcohol made me swoon more. The ebb and flow of nightlife did nothing to help.

"Keep your head down," he murmured, and I obliged, trying not to see the world move chaotically around us. My arms draped around his shoulders through this roller coaster ride.

There's something about a man when his neck is exposed, something about the scent of musk and the touch of his almost-sweaty, salty skin. His smile. Those eyes.

I laid my head on his shoulder and studied his jaw line and five o'clock shadow. The only part of him I could concentrate on. He pulled his head slightly away from the lips I was trying to brush against him.

Rain and Toni were talking to each other, and at times to or about me, but I didn't listen. I let myself be blissfully rocked to sleep by smooth motions.

The process was slow, painful. Tweezers plucked shards of glass from around my eyes. I tried not to flinch. Bright lights, medical terms, IVs added to my frustrations.

The deputy introduced himself. Christopher Something. "She's almost done." He motioned to the nurse working salve and gauze over my million tiny injuries.

"I have to get back," I said. "He needs me."

"You sure about that?" he asked. "It's a pretty ugly mess back there, and now you're here. I've seen it before. You sure you want to go back?"

"Not to him." I wanted to move. The nurse put a gentle but firm hand on my shoulder. "My uncle. He's sick. I missed an appointment. I have to—"

"Keep your head down," he said again. "We got it. We took the call, and he's fine. Wants you to know it's fine."

"You can move now." The nurse handed me a mirror and stepped back.

I cursed the bandages around my cheeks, scalp, arms. Tiny strips of tape made it difficult to bend or move my fingers. "I'm a wreck."

Deputy Whatshisname held out a card. "Listen. My wife works in social services. She's got resources. It doesn't take a lot to see you're in over your head right now, but it's a temporary situation. Let us help you and your uncle."

Unsure, I pinched the corner of the card.

"Give us a call. Even if it's only to talk. We all need to talk now and then. Or not talk. Anne, she's a great listener."

My head hurt more inside than out. These scratches were only a distraction.

The nurse approached again. "You can get dressed. We'll be discharging you soon."

CHAPTER SEVEN

A VAGUE DREAM OF STAGGERING AND CHANGING clothes and falling into bed. Something had happened. I just couldn't remember.

Invisible marbles of cotton filled my mouth and ninety thousand thistles dug into the sole of my foot. My entire body begged for relief. My toes curled involuntarily. Right. Self-induced sin and salvation.

Please, God. Let me at least still be alive. Anything else, we can chat about after I'm conscious again.

I blinked. The hotel room was familiar, and so was the Strumbellas T-shirt I wore. But nothing else made sense.

"Morning, sunshine." I heard the husky whisper.

My heart choked and I caught my breath in a swear.

The comforter was a stale hiding place filled with incoherent flashbacks. The dancing and shouting. The drinks. His touch. Toni had stuck close by, making sure none of us behaved badly. But what was their definition of badly? And what was mine? I peeked out.

Rain was in the chair, sipping coffee. He put a finger to his lips and pointed.

Toni was asleep on the other side of the bed, wearing my other favorite T-shirt: a heather-gray V-neck with the Beatles' faces on it.

His hair was deliciously sloppy, his feet bare, and his shirt half-open. I savored the image and took the coffee he offered. "You slept in the chair?" I whispered.

He shrugged and reached for another cup on the table.

Emotions crawled over me. Embarrassment. Anger at my own behavior, and guilt at the extravagance. A misuse of everything Martin left me. A misrepresentation of everything I wanted to be.

I'd transplanted myself to New Orleans days ago and done nothing except engage in the pagan rituals of drinking and man-hunting.

And then I smiled. Because I'd had fun. And because he was still here.

Running away never felt so good.

Toni stretched and propped herself up on one elbow. "Gimme that." She reached over me and stole his coffee.

He moved to the counter and started another cup. "Y'all ready for another day?"

I stared at my unused typewriter. I should stay in. I should write and be productive.

But that wasn't going to happen. "Meet me in the lobby in two hours."

Nothing beats a warm, morning-hangover shower. I inhaled the moisture and washed the forgetfulness away. I was on a see-saw, wanting to explore New Orleans with my new friends, and needing time alone. Wanting to go out again, and needing to get my footing.

Did I still know how to be alone, or was their company so intoxicating I didn't want to—or couldn't—let go?

This whirlwind trip suffocated me with a freedom I'd not enjoyed for years. I pushed aside the notion I should be doing something different, something *responsible*.

That wasn't really why I came here. It certainly hadn't been responsible to fly away in the middle of the night. I craved escape from that house, that life. Those memories of Ted. There was nothing responsible in anything I'd done recently. Why pretend to start now?

New Orleans, in the beginning, had been a place to go to. Now it was a place to stay. I wanted to discover more of it. And more of me.

I stepped into the lobby where Rain and Toni waited, refreshed. He was different from last night, subdued even from two hours ago. Troubled? I couldn't tell behind his sunglasses.

Something inside wanted me to reach for him. I stuffed the impulse under my mojo bag. I couldn't imagine after last night he felt the same.

"How's the foot?" He took my arm.

"Secure." Why did I withdraw from his touch?

"Glad to hear it." His empty hand hung in the air for a millisecond.

How strange to silently accept his approval, as though I'd done something worth noting. Sticking on a Band-Aid shouldn't be a big deal. But now it was an Olympic event, and I'd just won the gold medal. I stood a little taller.

The sun ushered Friday in. I hadn't really looked at the

calendar until now. People loomed in from nearly every side. I
hid myself in my jacket. "Sure got crowded."

Rain pointed to a poster. Crescent City Blues and BBQ
Festival. The vibrant photos showed deliciously styled foods
and energized performers in front of jubilant crowds.

"Enticing," I said.

"Great music, great food," Rain said.

Toni glanced between us. Did he nod?

He drove her car across town. I wanted to ask him to slow
or stop at every corner so I could take it all in. But I didn't
because I needed to see what was next. I could always return.
Storefronts weren't going anywhere.

There was so much green. Green grass. Green painted houses. Green beads hanging from green trees and on
green fences.

He pulled up to the Audubon Nature Institute. The earlier awkwardness vanished as I bounced about the earth-scent-
ed air and watched an abundance of wildlife watch me back.
Bears, giraffes, alligators, and so many others captivated my
imagination. Peacocks strutted along the path ahead, fanning
their colorful feathers and calling to their kingdom.

"It's not the L.A. Zoo," Toni said, "but it's ours and we like it."

"I've never been to the L.A. Zoo," I confessed.

"Then it's a good thing you came to N'Orlins."

I tugged at my shirt in the humidity and removed my precious jacket when we stopped for a lemonade.

Rain stayed back as Toni linked her elbow in mine and
led me to the Louisiana Swamp Exhibit where I was immersed
in Cajun culture including a rougarou display. I told myself it
wasn't real, as prickles blended with chills along my spine.

We made our way past more animal enclosures until I stopped in front of the zebras.

"Beautiful, aren't they?" Toni asked.

"I'd love to be one," I said.

She laughed. "How do you mean?"

"They're so empowering. Occam's Razor states, simply, the easiest solution is usually the best. If you hear hoofbeats, think horses, not zebras. But I don't have time to play games. So, I'm gonna call a horse, a horse, and I'm gonna call a zebra, a zebra."

"They're pretty mean, though," Toni said.

"They don't let anyone mess with them." I pointed at the majestic animals. "Life is a blend of black and white. It's a balance of both, and it's personal. Each zebra is striped uniquely. Like human fingerprints or retinas. Every single one is different. So, I want to be a zebra. I'm not saying I always want to stand out in a crowd, but I'm not a fan of playing follow the leader."

"Little chance of that happening." Rain tugged a strand of my hair. How long had he been behind me? Did he notice the blush creeping up my face? He reached over my shoulder with my jacket. "Left this back there."

We continued through the zoo and made our way back to the gift shop. Before we left, I made sure to buy a zebra charm.

Excitement perched inside as the warm sun led us to St. Charles Avenue, and a splendid green and mahogany vessel dinging its way past alluring history.

"What a beautiful trolley." I took a window seat.

"They're not trolleys, they're streetcars." Toni sat next to me.

I scooted further but Rain took the handrail and stood in front of us. "Streetcar," I mulled. Tennessee Williams's Streetcar? I wrapped my jacket against the thrilling shiver and could almost sense the writer's ghost pushing us along the track.

"There is no Desire." Rain caught me in my thoughts.

"What?" My insides started to crumble.

"There is no Desire," he repeated in a matter-of-fact tone. "Desire is a street. The Desire line of streetcars ran through New Orlins until 1948, and car 922 was featured in the movie. But there wasn't one car specifically named Desire. And that line no longer runs." He rubbed under his left collar bone and shifted toward the window.

A man and woman sat a few rows up on the opposite side. The man whispered something as the woman sneered at Rain and whispered back.

Toni eyed them before turning to me. "But there's been chatter of revivin' it. I sure hope they do."

Rain's eyes narrowed. "Point is, there is no Desire here."

He was wrong. There was a lot of desire in New Orleans.

I caught him gripping his watch now and then, as if he'd rather be someplace else. Or maybe he'd lived here long enough to be bored with what I found new and exciting.

A helium balloon bounced its way to the back seats, tugging a small boy and his parents.

"Happy birthday," I told him.

He grinned and hid behind his balloon.

Toni tapped my arm. "When's your birthday?"

"June first," I said. "Yours?"

"Mine's May twenty-third. But yours." She drew out a low breath. "That's the official start of hurricane season."

"And yours?" I tried to get Rain's attention.

"Oh, he doesn't celebrate birthdays."

"At all?"

He concentrated on the outside world like he couldn't—or didn't want to—hear us.

"No. Just his."

His mind was elsewhere. Should I feel guilty about last night? Even Toni shifted uncomfortably. What had happened from the time we separated at the hotel until we met back up?

He'd left to go where? Home? What was there that could change his mood so drastically? Cheryl. *Dead* Cheryl.

Rain pointed out the window. "Coming up is the Romanesque Brown House. It's the largest building on St. Charles." His voice was reminiscent of a bored, requisite tour guide.

"Really?" I falsely enthused.

His manner flowed between angst and appreciation as he and Toni shared the history of buildings and sights we passed. During a tour lull, she stood and whispered something, and he nodded his response.

"He'll be all right." Her hand was once again protective and caring on his arm.

"I know. He's being so—"

"He's being himself, Rain. He can't help it, and you know this. Don't worry. Get through tonight and this weekend. He'll be fine."

What were they saying? Did Rain have a son? With his dead wife? And did he leave him alone? Or was she there with him? I envisioned her ghost with the baby in his crib, thought of a tiny boy babbling back to things unseen.

He brushed her hand away and stared out the window again.

"Rain." She rubbed the back of her neck.

His jaw clenched. That jaw I'd adored in the dark was still strong, but now alienating. Did I want to know this man who could steam so easily? His nostrils flared and relaxed.

"Hey." He pulled her hand from the back of her neck, placed his other hand over the scar, and kissed her forehead. "Hey," he repeated, and got eye level with her. "I'm sorry. You okay?"

Her smile was false. "Mm-hmm."

"Atta girl." He patted her arm.

"Lee Circle." She pointed and sat back down. The statue of Robert E. Lee had been removed amid ongoing civil disputes, but the historic site remained.

The streetcar tour continued, and any remaining discomfort fell aside when we stopped in front of a gated populace of alabaster tombs.

St. Louis Cemetery No. 1. Marie Laveau was entombed here. The air electrified its greeting as we strode through the gates. Rain didn't seem interested, and I wasn't keen on manipulating him, so I moved past and walked with Toni. Every cell in my body was charged with excitement.

"Mystical, isn't it?" Toni asked. There was a deep message in her eyes I couldn't translate.

This was the first moment in New Orleans I'd truly felt something spiritual—dark or otherwise. My mojo bag was all in fun, a way of connecting. But this was different. My sensibility told me it was my imagination. My senses told me it wasn't.

How many of these decaying vaults were waiting to release their contents? I contemplated the engravings on the tiny buildings with their tiny doors, waiting until dark so they could open and let their spirits come out to play ... or get to work.

Goosebumps began to dance, and I pulled my jacket tighter.

How far back did Rain's family go? Was Cheryl on these grounds?

A stillness overtook me as we approached a weathered tomb covered with scratch marks and triple X's, and evidence of vandalism and restoration. Marie's resting spot. If she was indeed resting.

"What are all the X's?" I fingered a few of the markings.

Rain walked closer. He also traced a trio of X's. A lingering, wanting trace. "Long time ago rumors began that even in death Marie could grant wishes. A person needed only to draw three X's, turn around three times, knock on the tomb, and yell out their wish."

"You're kidding."

A young boy bounced over, scratched his mark, made his turns, and shouted. "I want a new basketball." He raced back to his encouraging mother. She patted his back and guided him away.

Should I be amazed people believed in such witchery, or try to believe in it myself?

Rain shook his head. "If the wish is granted, they're to come back here, circle their own X's, and leave a throw for Marie."

"A throw?"

"An offering." Toni pointed. The ground in front of the tomb was covered with flowers, coins, Mardi Gras beads, candles, and other trinkets.

67

I fingered an invisible trio of X's. Should I use a marker? What gift could I leave in return? What would I ask for? What was I doing here?

The City of the Dead continued with its beautiful, decaying structures and diminutive pyramids. The worn fences left rusty debris on the palm of my hand. Toni dusted hers off like a Las Vegas card dealer. So many plaster and plaques on so many vaults announced each person's date of birth and death, but there was no Cheryl Rainier that I could see. There were no Rainiers at all.

Did he cremate her? Was that why he was acting strange—were her ashes haunting him? Was he mad at me because she was mad at him?

We don't talk about ghosts in the desert, much. And we don't talk to them. At least, I don't. It seemed New Orleans had ghosts at every corner, and I was starting to collect one or two of my own.

It was harder to talk with Rain when he strayed behind more often than not. Toni politely shared more touristy information when she could and stayed silent when she couldn't.

I longed for a brass performance of "St. James Infirmary," a reason to celebrate life and death. Not finding it left me unfulfilled but grateful.

We exited the cemetery and Rain stepped to the side. "I have to go."

"Go get 'em," Toni said.

"Thanks." He kissed her cheek without smiling, then turned to me. "See you later?" And he kissed my cheek, too.

What was I supposed to do with that? He'd been distant and distracted all day, and now he left me with a kiss. I didn't want to read anything into it. Maybe he was just New Orleans-polite.

When he disappeared around the corner, I tugged Toni's arm. "What's the story with you two?"

She contemplated a thought then shrugged. "His isn't my story to tell."

I grasped the mojo bag through my shirt, and repeated a childhood prayer for protection. But was it sincere enough to keep the rougarou away?

CHAPTER EIGHT

OUR SWEET TEAS SWEATED CIRCLES ON THE
sidewalk table. I avoided asking about Rain. Toni avoided telling me. That night was still in my mental shadows. How much
of it actually happened? Yesterday hadn't been much clearer.
If she didn't say anything, maybe it was my imagination ... or
nightmare. It was easier to let time pass and to pretend I didn't
know all the things I knew.

"Come on." She stood and finished her drink.

"Where?"

"Trust me." She knew I would.

I finished my tea in a gulp. "Where's your car?"

We stepped onto a city bus and it groaned into traffic.
"Where I last left it, I hope. This is easier."

With the dash of New Orleans characters, the ride became
its own adventure. A young couple played with each other's
wedding bands and kissed each other's fingers and faces. An
elderly woman clutched an overstuffed bag and slept with her
head against the window as the bus became her bed.

A wobbly man leaned in far too close for comfort and
breathed his liquor on me. I turned away but he persisted.
"Pretty," he repeated.

"Thank you," I replied three times then gave up.

"Where y'all from?" A young man leaned our direction. He was dressed too slick to be taken seriously, and his smile was full of bleached arrogance.

"You first," Toni said with a playful smile.

"Why, I'm from right here." He tried to drawl. "Right over on Washington Avenue."

"Tremé," she said with enthusiasm.

"That's right, darlin'." He kneeled on the seats in front of us, hooked his elbows over the back and laced his fingers as he faced us. "Now what brings you to my city? You need a tour guide? You got questions? I'm your man."

I needed roach spray and a disinfectant shower after he spanned us up and down, speaking each word slowly and forcefully. "Yes, ma'ams. I. Am. Your. Man."

"Well, I do have one question." Toni blinked coyly.

"What's that?" He leaned closer and I coughed from his aftershave.

"Well." She moved forward with a bashful smile. "I'm just wondering ..."

"Yes?"

"I feel a little foolish." She winked at me. "Am I blushin'?"

"Now don't be shy, honey. What is it you wanna ask me?"

"Okay." She sat up. "Well. I was wondering. Where did you get your accent, the five-and-dime?" She stood. "C'mon, Penny. This is our stop."

The man sat still in his embarrassment as Toni and I stepped to the exit.

"And another thing." She turned back with a glare. "Washington Avenue's in the Garden District. Not Tremé, you wannabe. I'm betting you can't even afford to breathe the air. Don't try to fool us, mister. N'Orlins is as authentic as you can get. And you, well, you are not. It's time for you to ride this bus right out of town, don't you think?"

The newlyweds laughed as the young man slunk further into obscurity.

"Welcome to New Or-leens." Toni smiled.

An assortment of aromas and familiar music greeted us on our approach to Lafayette Square. "The BBQ Festival?" I inhaled the air filled with energy and aromas. "Why isn't Rain with us?" I couldn't help myself. Anything good I was to experience should include him.

"Come on." She nudged with enthusiasm. "We about to pass a good time."

Swarms of people danced and clapped along with their favorite bands. Children with sticky hands presented crafts and treats to their parents. Souvenir hawkers were everywhere.

The variety of restaurant booths emitted a mix of pungent, sweet, and salivating aromas. "Here. Try this." She paid for a basket and stuffed a small fried something into my mouth. It was warm, juicy and tender. Chicken? The spices were strong yet smooth.

"Good?" she asked.

I swallowed. "It's real good." I took another piece and dunked it in a thick sauce.

"It's alligator."

I winced, mid-bite. "Alligator."

"Like it?"

I answered by swallowing and took another bite.

Booth after booth attracted lines of people. I trusted Toni's judgment for which ones to try or pass. We beelined through the crowds to the booth at the end.

Restaurant D'Arcy. I recognized the name. This was where we had eaten. This was where I went without Ted. My short New Orleans history was giving me a personal connection to the festival, and my wounded foot tapped to the beat.

At least twelve people waited for food, but Toni circumvented the crowd and peered into the corner of the booth. "Service," she yelled loud enough to get the attention of several workers inside as well as nearby patrons.

A teen manning a fry station turned. "Yo, Momma. You bringin' the heat today. Looking go-oo-ood."

Toni cocked her head. "Ain't your momma, Cedric. Ain't never gonna be."

"Cedric." A man in a black T-shirt pivoted from his commercial-sized griddle. "Watch yourself."

"Sorry, Chef Ben." The boy dropped his head. "Sorry, Toni. What can I get you ladies?"

Toni leaned in. "Where's Chef? No offense, Ben."

"None taken, Toni." He served the next in line and motioned over his shoulder.

From behind the booth, a familiar voice sounded. "Patience, Antoinette." Rain came around the corner, wearing a white Chef's jacket and carrying a filled plastic basket. His smile was big and authentic. "How are you, Lucky Penny?"

At least I didn't stumble or fall. "You? This?"

"Me. This."

Toni pulled him closer to me. "Isn't it great?"

"You're the chef?"

73

He winked at Toni. "Something like that. Here." Knowing the shrimp and wine sauce came from his kitchen made it impossible for an honest critique. Which did I like better—the food, or the fact we were talking?

"Sorry about yesterday." His voice was tender, personal. "Lot on my mind. Hope you can forgive my rudeness."

I ignored the itch to ask about his son. Or his dead wife.

He led us behind the booth, and we sat in lawn chairs, amply supplied with food and spirits.

I wanted to taste everything he had to offer.

"How is it?" Toni asked.

"I could get used to this," I confessed. "Tell me everything."

Toni started. "We told you about his plantation."

Rain took it from there. "Full disclosure. My parents and grandparents, coming from old money, had certain expectations. They were eager for me to keep the family business going. Down here, tours, rooms, and alcohol are where the new money's at. We didn't keep the plantation open to the public, but we did entertain now and again. And it's history. So, with their blessings, after high school, I spent a few years in Europe to learn the hotel and restaurant business. I've always had a knack for food. When I came back home, it took a few years, but I bought my own."

"You bought a restaurant?" I reached for another shrimp.

"And hotel."

I tried to swallow gracefully.

Toni grinned. "And for the most part, we're all exceptionally glad you did."

Rain leaned back. "Why, thank you, darlin'."

"Anytime, sugar." She returned his smile. "He can run

the entire establishment, but he's best in the kitchen. Least, that's my opinion."

Rain stood and lifted his eyes toward the sky. "Hang on. I'm about ready to get out of this steam bath."

I left Toni at the booth and walked into the crowd, turning in a slow circle.

"Ms. Embers." Detective Jackson approached, chewing his toothpick.

"Hello, detective. Working?"

"Call me Douglas. Event Security." He turned and pointed to the label on the back of his shirt, then faced me again and extended his hand. "You enjoying your stay?"

"Yeah. Not quite what I expected."

"N'Awlins never is." His eyes darted as he tugged my hand closer. "Listen. I told you I'd watch out for you. And I don't mean to intrude."

"What is it?" My heart murmured and I withdrew my hand.

"You trust me?"

"Yeah," I half-lied. "What's are you talking about?"

"I'm talking 'bout the company you been keeping."

Maybe New Orleans was helpful and friendly, but years in the desert made me suspicious. I stepped back and wrapped an arm around my waist.

A rambunctious group of teens rushed past and knocked me off balance. Douglas hollered at them as he caught my arm.

"Thanks."

"This place," he said. "It does something to people. It's the kinda place where good and bad mix a lot more than what you're probably used to. Some folk, they come here and don't got no one to keep an eye out for them or help them process the environment. A lot of good and evil in everyday life 'round here. People can get mixed up in all that voodoo." He scanned the area. "N'Awlins is a good place. But things ain't always good. And they ain't always what they seem."

I followed his gaze.

Rain's face turned bitter when he saw my companion. He'd taken off his chef's jacket, revealing a black T-shirt, muscles and a cleaver tattoo on his upper left arm. His fists were tight, and he took long, hard strides in my direction. Our eyes met for less than a second. It thrilled, excited, and frightened me. Someone was in danger. But who?

Douglas tapped the toothpick on the back of his hand. "Just because someone's nice to you don't mean they're good for you. I can't tell you what to do, but please, watch out. Meantime, you need anything, you got my number. And I got yours."

Rain put his electric hand on my shoulder.

A few people stopped and gawked. Two pointed and whispered. New Orleans sure likes a good scene.

Douglas straightened and bit his toothpick. "Vernon." He sneered and motioned for me to call him, then stepped into the crowd.

Toni crept next to Rain. His eyes narrowed, and his lips tightened. "What did he want?"

I kept my focus on Douglas. "He said to be careful."

"Of what?" Toni's voice cracked. Her face was mottled and spotted with perspiration. She rubbed the back of her neck with one hand and reached for Rain with the other.

"Of the company I keep."

Rain seethed. "Of course, he'd say that."

"You know him?" I asked.

"Yeah, we know him."

Toni squeezed his hand as her eyes danced around things unseen.

Rain's voice was a low growl. "I swear I'll kill him."

Was Douglas's warning true?

Toni moved into Rain's line of vision. "Rain!" She removed him from his trance.

He gritted his teeth. "Don't worry about him."

Worry wasn't on my mind before two minutes ago. But now it was. The problem was, I didn't know what, or who, I should worry about. And it wasn't going away any time soon.

Rain stood like a warrior, one arm shielding Toni and the other fingering under his collarbone. Was this hatred for Douglas, or protection for her? Maybe both.

It wouldn't be a bad thing to build my guard up a little. Maybe there was a mojo bag for this. "Who is he to you?" I asked.

Toni opened her mouth, but Rain spoke first. "He's nobody. He's my cousin."

CHAPTER NINE

GETTING AWAY FROM THE FESTIVAL, FROM THE crowds, was fine with me. Rain asked permission to drive Toni's car as he'd left his at the restaurant, then asked her to sit in the back.

We drove for miles in silent reverence through what remained after Katrina. This was a bewitching place. It wasn't in the history or cemeteries. It was in the people. They held a bond much deeper than anything physical, much deeper than anything a storm could dislodge. They were rooted here by far more than their residence. Condemned buildings were shelters for so many. It was an extreme mix of hopelessness and love, and the tragic beauty of it all overwhelmed me.

Shame tangled in me. Shame that I'd wanted to run away from my past. Shame that I had. Shame at the thought my life back in California was worth running away from, when so many would have wanted to run to it, or not run away at all.

New Orleans is made up of people who endure.

The landscape changed from structured to natural, with tinges of brown and orange among evergreen, and the road turned to a well-driven dirt path edged by murky waters.

"Rain." Toni caught his eye in the rear-view mirror. "You know I don't like the bayou."

He parked near a dock. The dark churning unsettled something inside me. He pointed to a flat-bottomed boat near a line of marshy trees. "I know you don't like a lot of things, but I also know you'll do this because Penny hasn't seen the bayou yet."

"Maybe she doesn't want to. Not everybody likes things the way you do, Rain."

He got out of the car. "We're already here, C'mon. This won't hurt. Promise."

I stood and eyed him over the roof.

He bent down and called to her through the open door. "Toni."

She exaggerated her exit from the car, and after a moment we were on the simple vessel. Rain stood at the back and used a pole to push us through the waters.

Our excursion was a gentle pace, and I considered the phrase "Big Easy." There was so much to New Orleans. I'd been here almost a week and barely scratched the surface. It was easy to get lost in the culture and big surroundings. It was also easy to take a break from the commotions. Was this why people didn't always use their return ticket home?

Rain's silence was comfortable, and Toni hummed a jazzy tune. I leaned back and enjoyed the shared solitude, taking in the strange sounds and unusual sights.

A pungent odor, putrid and intriguing, lingered in my nostrils. The orange of the tall Cypress and Tupelo trees was a stunning contrast to the green lily pads, and the water jungle had no end. The songs of bullfrogs and birds completed the sensory overload. Strangely, the humidity was less intrusive here on the water. It was as if it recognized its presence beneath us and was no longer striving for our attentions.

"Why don't you like the bayou?" I asked Toni.

She shrugged. "I guess I'm over it."

How could a person get tired of this colorful experience? Someone else might wonder how I could get tired of the sage desert and blue skies.

"You want to know about Douglas." It wasn't a question. She fingered the back of her neck. "He's not just Rain's cousin."

I waited with intentional stillness.

"It was a few years after high school. A lifetime ago." Her eyes focused on nothing over my shoulder, as though the movie of her memories wanted narration. "It happened when Rain was in Europe. I wasn't in love with him."

"Douglas?" I asked.

"Rain. Never was. But I missed having someone to go around with. We'd been best friends so long. My daddy got sick, and Momma moved him out to Arizona for dry air. I had no one else to talk to, really. No one I could trust."

Rain made a guttural sound. When he refocused on the bayou, his jaw was set tight. This was undoubtedly a conversation he'd heard before, and never liked.

Those feelings were familiar to me—abandonment and loneliness. The need to be heard, to be valued. I understood the desire to fill emptiness with anything. My thumb stroked the ring on my finger.

"Douglas knew Rain was gone, so he started coming over to check on me. About the same time, I had a secret admirer getting out of hand. Douglas was fresh out of the police academy, knew some guys. Said they'd take care of it for me. Keep me safe."

Surprise took me as I thought of Toni needing to lean on someone for strength.

"They'd come over a few times a week, make sure things were good. A few weeks go by, the situation settles, but only briefly. It got worse. We go for coffee one afternoon while his crew puts in a new security system. Douglas, he was Rain's family. He was familiar. And after a few more coffee dates, he was more."

Rain stoically pushed us through the waters as Toni pulled more memories from the unseen fog, "We fell in love." She shrugged. "But after a while ..."

"I get it," I said. "He was the one who got away."

"No." Her blue eyes flashed. "You don't get it. I was the one who got away from him. It didn't end well, but here we are."

I shifted onto my elbows and let my bare feet slip over the edge to dance in the cool green bayou.

Toni smiled at Rain. "Family, you know?"

I did know. I missed Uncle Martin, and even Ted, with all our problems. I missed having problems I knew how to handle. I hoped New Orleans would have problems I could actually solve. Or, just maybe, no problems at all.

"Move!" Rain hollered with a cursed urgency.

My elbows slipped and feet splashed as, in a chaotic rush, Toni pulled me to the middle of the boat. We panted as Rain stood over us with an oar, yelling profanities, and angrily hacked the bayou.

An immense, ugly-green beast hissed and grunted as it slid away.

Rain roared and hacked once more, raised the oar behind his neck and hung his wrists over it. "Gator. Big one."

Trembling, I tried not to focus on the fact my leg was almost stomach stew. Retribution for the festival snack? Maybe I could consider becoming a vegan, for a different sort of self-preservation.

"You okay?" He sat down and secured the oar.

"Yeah, darlin'." Toni gasped. "We're fine."

"Stupid thing to do." Rain glared at me. "Sticking your foot in the bayou."

CHAPTER TEN

RESIDUAL NAUSEA FROM YESTERDAY'S NEAR-
alligator attack was still causing a bit of instability, but the
current excitement overrode it.

Rain had driven Toni's car off the main road, but not
before asking me to close my eyes. The car slowed and I heard
gravel crunch under the tires, then felt the transition to a flat
foundation. My heart accelerated. The smooth, slow motion
and echo of the engine told me we were in a large garage.

After the car stopped, Toni guided me out to where a
warm breeze greeted us with the tingling scent of fresh-cut
grass and songs of distant birds.

"Ready?" I could almost hear Rain's smile.

"Yup." I chewed my lip in anticipation.

"Okay." Toni removed her hand from my eyes.

I squinted from the sun and peered out. Mature trees and
half-hidden fences lined the expansive property. The gravel
drive eased its way past the four-car garage, which nearly dis-
sected the property between the road and the house—a separa-
tion of civilization and retreat.

"So, you do own a vehicle," I teased.

"More than one." Rain laughed as I viewed the deep blue Cadillac Escalade and blood red Rolls Royce Ghost. A well-used motorcycle leaned toward the wall.

He led us around the corner of the garage.

It was a breathtaking sight—a three-story estate from generations ago. Protruding from the grand yellow structure with rich red shutters were two layers of stately white columns supporting the wrap-around balcony and attic. The first and second story railings were a beautifully intricate design. Each window and door invited a grand view.

The drive path narrowed to a walking strip that cut through the manicured lawn.

"What is that tree in the middle of the yard?" It was taller than the house yet dwarfed by the size of the lawn. Little red pods hung between smooth, glossy leaves.

"That's his magnolia," Toni said. "It's 'bout a hundred years old now."

Two colorful peacocks walked on the mulch under the tree as a white one strutted in the distance.

"So not the desert." I took photos with my cell phone.

Birds flew from the grass to the trees to the buildings and beyond. Ancient willows draped their long fingers to the ground and gave a breezy welcome. A trio of leaves played across the gently sloping path.

The most grass I'd seen during the past week's adventures was at the Blues and BBQ Festival, weak and flat from so much foot traffic. This massive, healthy expanse now before me was more than I'd enjoyed in decades.

The fresh-mown odor invited me to take it in deeply. What a glorious sanctuary.

Rain picked up a peacock feather and extended it to me. It could have been a brick of gold. "Welcome to Greyford."

The wrap-around verandah invited company, with rockers and chairs gathered intermittently. Colorful pots of petunias and foxglove spotted the porch with new life, and hollyhocks mixed with decorative cabbage on the ground.

"Do you get much company out here?" I fingered a stalk of Queen Anne's Lace near the banister.

"The folks used to. The yard and house would be full of company. Haven't had people here for quite a while, really."

The doors opened to a marbled entry. I lifted the peacock feather to my mouth in breathless joy, and glided past a closet door and down the three short steps into the foyer.

The oval interior was more than twice the size of Uncle Martin's living room. Crown molding edged the high, vaulted ceiling. Cream- and sky blue-striped wallpaper led down to intricately carved chair rails and wainscoting.

My inner writer immediately noticed the lavish, yellow floral upholstered sitting chairs and short table tucked into a windowed reading nook to the right, before double doors were open to a large room with a stone fireplace and long table.

I continued to peruse the foyer where doors led straight ahead, to the left, and to the right. A wrought-iron railing curled with the staircase along the left, leading to the second story landing and more doors. Under the curve of the stairs, a majestic mahogany Grandfather clock stood sentry behind an antique desk and cushioned chair.

Sheer blue curtains whispered a subtle welcome dance from each window.

"Is that a door?" I motioned behind the reading corner.

"It's a jib window." He strolled over, raised the pane and opened two panels underneath. "Most of the windows in the house are. They were designed so people could easily step in and out without going through the main door."

Books, antique décor, framed photos, and a few plants decorated the built-in bookshelf that stretched from the floor to the second story landing. In front of them was a baby grand piano.

Toni spoke in hushed tones. "Kinda leaves you speechless, doesn't it?"

This was history, gorgeous and compelling. His history. I was lost in the richness of it all. Gilded accents, hardwood floors, portraits of long-ago people.

What it must be like to be so deeply rooted, to still call "home" the place your ancestors knew. To be tethered through generations to something so lovely.

Without warning, the closet door slammed open, and in the shadows stood a man, pointing at me with a trowel. "Who's she?"

Rain slid between me and the man as Toni spoke. "Hey, Lou."

He glanced over Rain's shoulder. "Hey, Toni." He pointed again. "Who is she?"

"This is Penny," Rain said.

He appeared older than Rain, yet somehow childlike. He wore jeans and a Teenage Mutant Ninja Turtles T-shirt, and spoke with an innocent tone. He tapped his fingers against his thighs. "Penny."

"Josie," I said.

"Penny Josie." He continued tapping. "I'm Lou. I live up there. That's my room." He raised his trowel toward the landing then back at Rain. "Why is she here?"

Rain raised his hands slightly. "She's a friend."

"A friend?" Lou kept his eyes on me. "Is she your girlfriend?"

Rain shook his head. "She's a friend, Lou. Can't do anything about her gender."

Lou stared at him long and quiet before turning back to me. "A new friend?"

"Yes," Rain said.

"Okay, new friend Penny Josie. You're pretty." He shrugged back into the closet, still tapping his thighs. He left the door open and sunlight seeped through the large window facing the verandah. It wasn't a closet, but a small room, perhaps at one time a guard or welcome station. Shelves held various garden pots, framed floral artwork, and outdoor tools.

I turned my head slowly. "Who's that?"

"That's Lou," Toni replied. "That's his brother."

Rain clapped his hands. "Ready for the tour?"

Lou poked his head out of his room. "Don't go without me."

My fingers played along the bird fountain as our quartet moved outside. A peacock shrieked, and Rain chortled at my startled reaction.

"Stop!" I admonished him with a casual backhand.

He blocked my slap and leaned into me, then slid his hand into mine.

It had been too long since someone—anyone—had reached for me. I turned away so he couldn't see my delighted shock. He gave my hand a light squeeze, and I squeezed back.

We continued around the corner on lush grass. It was

rejuvenating, the living thickness trying to tickle my ankles with each step.

The scent of wet dirt welcomed me as baskets peeked from alternate rows of leafy green produce and harvest-colored vegetables. Various pots of growing herbs and leaves populated benches in a doll-sized greenhouse.

"What a huge garden. Do you take care of it yourself?"

"We live alone, if that's what you're asking," Rain said. "There's a weekly crew that takes care of the property, and security. We like our solitude. As for the garden, Lou does most of the work. He's good with dirt. Aren't you, bud?"

"I like the dirt. I like the garden."

We passed a yard table and chairs, a shallow bird feeder, and another fountain filled with rainwater. Rain plucked out a yellow leaf floating on the bottom basin and played with it as we strolled.

Farther into the tree-strewn distance was another gated structure, obscured by weeping willow tendrils and a vine-covered gate. Toni set a hesitant hand on my arm. "That's not a workhouse."

I peered, suddenly aware of the alabaster exterior.

"That's okay." Rain dropped my hand. "She can see it."

Toni stayed with Lou as Rain and I approached the weathered, ebony fence. It was like most I'd seen around New Orleans, worn and more decorative than protective.

The tarnished knob sagged, and I stroked it with no intention to turn it. Seventeen nameplates were fastened near the sealed door. Some were faded, others were easier to read. Rain shared the stories he knew. His paternal great-grandparents, a few distant relatives, both his parents.

I'd not considered he could be an adult orphan, and a companion sorrow tugged in my throat until I cleared it.

How different the older names were from today. Meredith. Augustin. Pierce. Cheryl.

I stopped. "Is that ...?"

"My wife?" A guarded expression crossed his face.

"I thought ... Toni said she wasn't dead."

"She's dead." He stroked the nameplate.

"You don't know that," Toni called.

"Yes. I do." Rain growled over his shoulder.

"No. You don't." She hissed and led Lou back to the garden.

"I don't understand," I said.

He didn't meet my gaze. "It's just a plaque." He rubbed his chest. "They never found the—her—body."

"Then ...?" I watched him caress her name, and was torn between reaching for or running from him.

"I just know."

My legs weakened, and I fought the swoon. His hand fell lightly around my waist. I steadied and inched away from him. Oh, how I wished he wasn't touching me as I met her.

There it was, written in brass: Her full date of birth, a dash, and a year with no month or day attached to it. She had been thirty-two years old. And then, the words. In Memoriam: Cheryl D'Arcy Rainier.

D'Arcy. The restaurant—he named it after her? The food turned sour in my memory, and I hated Ted even more for introducing me through the magazine. I wanted to go back in time and rip it into shreds, burn the store down, stop the printing presses.

Rain wore a pain unspoken, with familiarity.

She was here because she was family. And I was the vacationing outsider. My dreams had just been sucker-punched.

He pulled the gate behind him as we left.

Twilight seeped through the trees. I'd always imagined plantations as dark and swampy, like the bayou. But this was lush and green.

The end of the yard reached ahead, with a faded path jutting into more trees. Crumbling wooden shacks peeked from their hiding spots among them. I was both drawn to and repulsed by the realization of what they were.

Dizziness overtook me, a combination of too much knowledge and too much fatigue. Too much haunting. I squared my feet like a pitcher ready to throw against the intruding ghostly screams.

"It's called Pushmo' Ghetto," Rain said.

"Why?" My voice surprised me.

"It's what the slaves called it. It's where they lived. When all this was an active plantation, the masters used to tell the slaves to do more, push more, work more. Always more."

I dropped my head, ashamed of my freedom, ashamed I'd abused it with running away.

"I'm not proud of it," he said. "But it wasn't all bad."

I snorted and shook my head, unable to agree with him.

"It wasn't a crime to own slaves. They weren't abused."

I shifted away from him.

"I know the arguments," Rain continued. "They were uneducated. Forced to work every day."

"Beaten and put down." I hissed.

"Not by my family. They lived back there. They sang, talked, ate, gave birth and grew up. They lived and died with their families. With my family. They were fed, clothed, cared for. If they turned on themselves, it wasn't brought on by us."

"You mean, they killed each other? And you did nothing to stop it?"

First, the dead wife. Now, the murderous slaves.

His hand clenched. "Not me. My ancestors. This may come as a shock to you, darlin', but we can't all go back in time to save the world. Slave owners followed a different justice, Penny." I loved and hated that he spoke my name aloud. "My family treated them fairly according to the time. And when a few got out of hand, their logic was it was better for them to take each other out before the mentality infected the rest of them."

"Infected? Like a bug or disease? They were people, Rain."

He sighed heavily, the weight of generational errors in his soul. "I can't change what my great-great-granddaddy thought or did. I can't make amends to the dead. But I can acknowledge it. And try to make the future a better place for the rest." He stepped into my eyesight. "It's history, Penny. I can't pretend it didn't happen. But it's history. Promise." He was seeking absolution for family sins.

No words in my throat, I kept nodding.

The trees creaked lightly, a voice to the nature around us. What ghost stories was the wind telling as it blew from the ghetto to the mausoleum? What spirits were still in bondage to this world, and which ones refused to leave? The environment was so different than either the desert I ran away from, or the city I ran to.

Rain softened and put a gentle hand on my arm. "About Lou."

"He has autism?"

"High functioning," he said. "He sometimes can't connect with others as well as he'd like. It frustrates him. He has his structure, his schedule."

"Does he have a caretaker?"

"No. He does all right on his own during the day." Rain's attention shifted to Lou in the distance. "I try to be here as much as possible at night and when I'm not at the hotel. Take him with me, sometimes. He likes that."

"So, during the day you take care of the hotel and restaurant, and all other times you take care of Lou and Toni."

His lip pulsed up. "Toni pretty much takes care of herself."

"Who takes care of you?"

"You applying for the job?" He looked away too soon. "Having a disability gives Lou a disadvantage, but it doesn't define him. At least, it shouldn't."

I caught his line of vision. "He's your family. No explanation necessary."

"Family always needs an explanation." Rain stuffed his hands into his pockets.

CHAPTER ELEVEN

SHADOWS AND MEMORIES CLENCHED AROUND me. Rain reached for my hand with a polarizing touch. We strode in quiet tension back to the garden and greeted Lou as he stood up.

"Rain." He pointed to the basket Toni held. "It's a good harvest tonight."

"That's great, bud. Is this what's for dinner?"

Lou snatched the basket from Toni and shoved it at me. "Do you want to make dinner with my garden?"

Rain winked. "Show us what you got, Lucky Penny."

"Cooking in a restaurant owner's home kitchen?" I dramatically lifted my hands to my cheeks. "That's not intimidating at all."

Toni whooped. "C'mon. We'll all help."

French doors opened from the verandah into a kitchen straight out of an issue of *Southern Home* magazine. Modern influences did not distract from its charming heritage. The top-quality pots and pans hung above the marble-topped island. Appliances stood between rustic cabinets, painted antique white. A porcelain apron sink divided the countertops beneath the large window that peered onto the verandah and back lawn. Two ovens were stacked into the opposite wall, and a stainless-steel refrigerator completed the row.

"Can I help?" Lou asked mechanically.

"Why don't y'all wash the vegetables in that sink there. Toni, can you get me a cutting board and knife?"

Rain whistled. "Listen to Penny saying y'all."

Being in a kitchen, wherever it was, always felt like home. Cooking with friends always felt like family.

The Great Room table held a feast of ratatouille, ravioli, and salad. The ambiance was from a different era.

"You actually live here."

"For the fourth time, yes," Rain exaggerated.

The corner wet bar was made of intricately sculpted wood panels. Six Winchester rifles hung above the mantel. To the right of the rifles was a framed Confederate uniform and flag. To the left, a large oil painting of a gray-haired man in a dark suit.

"Great-Great-Granddaddy." Rain draped his arm over the back of his chair.

"So, you're the fourth generation?"

"More like the sixth, but it gets complicated saying that many greats."

"A rifle for each generation, then," I said.

"The first rifle belonged to him after the war. There's a Winchester up there for the first boy in each generation since 1866."

"What about the younger boys? Didn't they get a rifle?"

"We all got Winchesters. The rest are around here some-where. In the attic, I think."

"You think?"

"Don't much need to know. I'm not big on guns." He picked up a glass pitcher and filled our water glasses.

The dishes and silverware were of fine quality. The open jib windows glimpsed onto the front and side lawns as the eve-ning breeze encouraged the pale blue curtains to reach toward us. Late shadows crept along the foyer and toward the stairs.

"How did it get its name? Aren't manors and plantations different?"

"Smart girl," he said. I may have sat a little straighter. "They're similar in structure, the way they were designed archi-tecturally and as land operations. Great-Great-Granddaddy was Charleston Greyford Rainier. He didn't much care to be called Charleston."

"Seems no one in this family likes their first names," Toni teased. "It's a southern thing."

Lou leaned in. "I have two first names, and I like them both. Like you, Penny Josie. I like being Louis. I was named after Louisville, Kentucky, wasn't I, Rain?"

"Tell her why." Rain rested his chin on his clasped hands.

Lou sat straight. His eyes turned up in remembrance. "Because when I was born, it didn't take any time at all and Daddy called me his race horse."

I smiled. "And the Kentucky Derby is held in Louisville. So, he named you Louis."

Lou's eyes widened. "Did someone tell you the story?"

"No." I chuckled. "I guessed."

"You're a good guesser. Isn't she, Rain?"

"That she is, bud."

"I like being Louis, and I like being Lou."

"Of course, you do," Toni acknowledged. "You're unique."

"I'm not con—con—Toni?"

"Contagious." Toni spoke automatically and continued eating.

Rain and Toni didn't react as Lou sat proudly.

"Tell me about this place," I asked.

Rain dropped his arm to the table. "Greyford Manor. Great-Great-Grandmomma liked calling it a manor. Said when she spoke it out loud, it was more intimate than a plantation."

"But it is a plantation," I said.

"The entire property is the plantation. This, the Big House, is the Manor. We call it Greyford."

Toni reached for the other pitcher, and Lou grunted. "Sweet tea is bad, Toni. You know that."

Rain's jaw tightened. "Lou."

He hung his head. "I'm wrong. It's not bad. And I didn't make it."

Toni poured a glass and took a sip. "See, Lou? You don't have to drink it, but it's not bad."

"Secret tea is. I don't drink secret tea."

"What's secret tea?" I asked.

Rain's eyes shifted in my direction. "Something Cheryl used to make. To help her, uh, feel better."

"I don't make tea anymore." Lou rocked. "I don't make it, and I don't drink it."

He stared and tapped on the table. He was a chaotic version of Rain, a bit on edge. He had similar eyes, but they danced differently in his taut face. "Penny Josie."

I wanted to ask about him. Toni gave me a silent "no."

"What was that?" Lou asked.

"What was what?" She raised her eyebrows.

Rain set his glass down and put his hands on the table. "Don't do that." Lou pointed at her.

"Can we not do this, Lou?" Rain asked. "Not now."

"Lou," Toni started. "Tell Penny about—"

The plates and glasses jerked as he slammed his fists on the table. "I'm not a rougarou!"

I instinctively scooted my chair away.

"Lou." Rain sighed.

Lou made eye contact with me. "I'm sorry."

"It's okay." I blotted the table with my napkin.

He muttered a chant. "Lou, Lou, the rougarou."

The Manor cast its yellow light in square patches on the ground. Toni sat in a rocking chair behind me as I leaned against the verandah steps. Melancholy piano jazz wisped through the open doors. There was almost nothing more beautiful than this moment.

Tranquility attached itself to me. I tugged off the jacket and breathed it in, deeply. Again. The jazz was replaced with soft stereo music, and I sensed Rain's presence as he sat in a chair against the house.

Lou squatted at the flower bed and talked to his plants.

"What are those blue flowers?" I asked.

"Chicory."

"For coffee?"

"It can be dried and ground," he answered. "Rain uses it. He uses a lot of my herbs. I grow them, and he cooks them. I grow oregano and chives, and parsley, too."

I pointed. "I've eaten Queen Anne's Lace before."

"That's not Queen Anne's Lace," he said. "That's water hemlock."

"Hemlock?" I laughed. "Tell me he doesn't cook that."

"He doesn't. He knows. I take care of plants. Rain takes care of people."

Rain's chair creaked. "And you do a great job, bud."

"Why do you grow it?" I asked.

"To protect people from the rougarou. People are afraid of it. But they shouldn't be. The rougarou doesn't eat the pretty people. Unless they deserve it. Only the ugly ones. Maybe they're ugly because they deserve it. Do you think I'm ugly?"

I wasn't sure how to react and since no one else did, I ignored him.

My focus shifted to the finely manicured grounds. I imagined Greyford as it used to be, full of life and enjoyment. "There must have been quite a few characters here once. You ever think of opening it up to the public again, but different? Maybe a bed-and-breakfast?"

Rain sipped his drink. "Got the hotel and restaurant for that. This is my haven. But my parents and grandparents did use to have the best parties here."

Toni nodded. "We'd sit at the top of the stairs and watch all the people come and go."

"It must have been extraordinary."

"I remember the parties," Lou said. "They were fun."

Rain smiled. "They were great parties."

Toni leaned toward him. "Let's have one."

"One what?" His eyes squinted.

"One party. C'mon. One."

"Toni." Should she already know the answer?

"New people." She pointed at me.

"We don't do parties here," he said.

"Why not?" I asked.

"We just don't."

Lou rocked subtly. "We do parties here. We do my birthday here every February."

"That's different, bud. I like celebrating you."

Lou pointed to Toni. "And we do her birthday here every June."

Rain set his glass down. "We don't do other parties here."

"We don't do your birthday."

"Bud."

Toni slid to the edge of her chair. "How 'bout a small gathering?"

"The four of us?" Rain asked.

"Unless you wouldn't mind it being a bit bigger."

"How much bigger?"

Her eyes brightened and she put her chin in her hands. Excitement drove her words. "A costume party. Like they used to do."

"A party." Lou smiled. "Like we used to."

Toni stepped behind Rain and wrapped her arms around him. "Remember the parties, Rain?"

"I remember," he said without enthusiasm.

"We'll celebrate like we used to." She spread one arm in front of him.

"When is this party supposed to take place?" Rain's blue eyes captured me.

Before I could respond, Toni already had the answer. "October thirty-first."

"Toni." He growled.

"Halloween," she whispered loudly. "The third best reason to have a party in New Orleans."

"What are the other two?" I asked.

"Mardi Gras and hurricanes," she said.

"Halloween." Rain tried to turn toward her.

She hugged him tighter. "Yes."

"Toni ..." He tapped her arm.

"It won't be that," she said.

He pulled away. "You want to put together a grand party in two weeks."

"That's the beauty of it." She returned to her rocker. "We don't have to put it together. We can let others do the work."

"Others," he said.

"I can help," Lou said. "I like to help with parties."

"The kids could do it," Toni said.

"Kids?" Did I want to ask this question? Did I want the answer?

Toni's excitement bubbled over. "He didn't tell you? Rain teaches a cooking class for at-risk teens every week at the restaurant. It's part of Rainfall."

"Rainfall?" So much I didn't know.

Rain waved his hand. "Just a small thing."

"Small?" Toni said. "Honey, please. The Rainfall Now Foundation is his charitable organization. He teaches kids how to cook, spends time helping the community. He's been helping to rebuild after Katrina. Let me tell you. He's a real hero 'round here."

"Toni." He shifted.

"No." I studied him. "He didn't tell me."

He leaned back. "You want the kids to put together a party in two weeks."

"The menu." I caught the excitement. "We can decorate. Or at least order party supplies."

Toni paced the verandah, her eyes glistening with things unseen. "Imagine it, Rain." She winked at him. "My gramma's been wanting a visit."

He rolled his eyes and rested his arms on the chair.

Lou clapped. "I know what that means."

Rain picked up his glass. "You don't know what that means."

"Yes, I do." Lou laughed and mimicked Rain's posture. "It means you're gonna say yes. Everyone says yes to Gramma."

Rain held his glass to his lips before taking a long, slow sip. "What do you think, Penny?"

Did he really value my input? I blinked. "I think—"

Toni scooted to my side. "She thinks it's the best idea you've had. It's a great way to give her a real welcome to New Orleans, and for the kids to show their skills to the families."

I waved for attention. "I would love an authentic New Orleans party. And, I think, if you don't give me one, I'll have to seek it out. Just sayin'."

Rain smirked and clasped his hands behind his neck. "I don't have a choice, do I?"

"No." I leaned my elbows on the verandah and gave him a flirty pout.

Lou mimicked my wave. "Please, Rain?"

"You want this, too."

I peered around the verandah and imagined hanging lights, carved pumpkins, echoing music and laughter. Ghosts celebrating in extravagant antebellum costumes, flowing across the lawns and drinking champagne from fine crystal.

Rain shrugged. "I'm not planning it."

Toni hugged him wildly. "Oh, it's going to be great. You'll see. Just like it used to be."

"Yeah." His eyes met mine. "Just like it used to be."

Lou gaped in happiness. "I have to sleep now. I have to dream." He turned in the doorway. "Rain? Will I have to sit at the top of the stairs?"

Solar lights illuminated the path through the front lawn and flickered along the fences like lightning bugs. Ivy clung to the rear of the garage, camouflaging it back to a bygone era as the peacocks called from a distance.

Real fireflies flitted about as birds sang the world to sleep. I admired the fireflies for not needing light but making their own.

I want to be a firefly—to bring so much light into the world for no other reason than it's what I was born to do. They know no other way to exist than to just be themselves.

I half-expected ghosts to wander in from the shadows, and was half-disappointed when they didn't.

There was no need for words in this moment. I'd come so far from where I was, who I was. A year ago, a month ago. Last week. The past few days had been bittersweet. Full of excitement and adventure, ideas, strength, and mishaps. And now here I was sitting on a porch drinking a Sazerac. Completely ordinary. Except it wasn't.

I'd be going back soon. Back to the desert with its black widows, searing heat, and homeless tumbleweeds. The dichotomy was no longer cute. What did it matter? Having answers for here was going to do me no good once I returned there.

The breeze would have been comforting if it was the dry air I was used to. But this air was thick with dampness and getting thicker. My chest heaved with the weight of it.

"You okay?" Toni asked quietly.

I chugged the last of my drink and held the empty glass back toward her. "Another, please."

CHAPTER TWELVE

"WHAT WAS IN THAT SAZER ... SAZ ...?" I SAT ON
the edge of a bed and tried to set the world back on its axis.
My eyes still shut, my body wobbled to an unheard song.

"It's not the drink." Rain's voice carried a tone of concern.

A foreign drum pounded loudly in my head and my foot
burned with a strange fire. I lay with a moan, and opened
my eyes.

Toni and Rain spoke in hushed tones as their shadows
towered around me.

He cleared his throat. "Hey."

"I hurt," I whispered.

"Bet you do."

"What happened?"

"You put your foot in the bayou," he said with a touch of
condemnation.

"Your open wound," Toni said. "You got an infection. You
need to rest. You got a fever, but you'll be okay."

"I'm going home." I swung one leg to the floor before energy left me. But I couldn't stay here, not where his dead wife
used to be. I wanted my own clean sheets and coffee pot.

She put a gentle hand on my shoulder and turned to Rain. "What do you want to do?"

"You're not thinking clear." He pointed at me. "You can't go home."

"Rain!" She hissed.

He paced to the door and back. "I don't want her in Cheryl's room."

"Why can't she remain here for now?"

"No," I agreed with him. "I'm not staying here in Cheryl's room." I tried to stand once more. Their voices blurred as the shadows played.

"Good," Rain said. "This isn't her room. It's mine." He nudged my shoulder with his finger, and I allowed myself to fall back onto the bed.

Separate rooms. How very *Gone with the Wind.*

"Not staying here, neither." I draped an arm over my eyes. "Help me up."

Toni opened the door. "I'll make tea." She smiled encouragingly before leaving.

I rolled slowly back and forth on the bed.

Reality collided with whatever was affecting me, and I fought for sanity. I tried to peer out the windows, certain we were still in Rain's boat or Toni's car. Towering bayou buildings dodged the moon, and stars screamed a rapid path through the slit in the balcony doors. I was terrified of each ripple the water sounded, of each branch the wind bent. The road whirred under the boat, offering an occasional double-thump as we drifted over train tracks and under floating traffic lights. Clouds transformed into monstrous hands and trees turned into terrible spears.

The storm intensified. We hydroplaned over evergreen Tupelo until the tires settled on churning bayou waters. Tree limbs lit on fire and flew at us with determined strength. Lightning illuminated ghastly shadows. We were going to die in this wretched tin can bayou buggy and it was all my fault. That stupid alligator. That stupid broken mug. That stupid, stupid lightning strike.

Another bolt of lightning peeled the roof off the room. I cried out to no avail. From a distance, the jazz wail of "St. James Infirmary" beckoned my body to float out of the open ceiling and down onto the waiting hands of pallbearers.

Screaming thoughts joined the chaos. *I'm not dead. I'm not dead!* But I couldn't speak. Panic welled and pushed on my chest until I had nothing to exhale.

I tried to claw my carriers' hands, to remove myself from the procession. *No! No! This can't be happening!* In the stormy darkness they carried me, draped in sheer, blue window fabric. Past the garden. Past the mausoleum. Into the woods. Into Pushmo' Ghetto. Slaves mobbed and buzzed out of their shanties to participate in the commotion. Hard raindrops splashed on my fevered body, and I shivered as it evaporated in a steamy mist.

The slaves joined their hands on me. Hands on my arms, legs, head, body. Hands everywhere. Hundreds of hands until there was nothing left of me and I was suffocating under their fleshy ghosts.

They pulled me from the funeral procession and stood me upright. *Please. Someone, help me!*

A blur of people walked from the House, dressed in black. *Focus!* Rain. Lou. Ted. Toni. Anne and Chris. They stepped in unison. Stopped in unison. And started again. Step. Stop. Step. Stop.

Another lightning strike illuminated the deathly slave faces, their sallow eyes and skin-and-bone bodies.

Uncle Martin emerged from the shadows, his burial suit now too big for him. He tossed a large silver coin from one hand to the other and back. He held it out to me, but I couldn't move, couldn't reach him. A hand reached from behind him and took the coin. Martin searched his empty hand and pulled a smaller coin from his pocket. Again, he tossed it. Again, he offered it. Again, someone else took it. A third coin. A third toss. A third disappearance. And anguish in his lifeless eyes.

The slaves grouped tighter and I could see nothing else. I tried to call out, but sorrow drowned me. Rain broke through the mass and reached for me.

"Rain! Help me!" But my shrieks were the sound of peacocks screaming under the magnolia tree.

"No help." The voice was familiar, but I couldn't turn my head to see.

"No help," she cried again. The slaves parted as she came into view.

"Momma Tristan." Oh, such relief. She would help!

"No help. You learn to help yourself."

She took a step back. "No help."

Another step. "No help."

She backed into Toni and took a cup from her hand, poured its contents onto the ground, then let the cup smash as lightning struck its daggers all around us.

Lou viewed me with wild, child eyes. Toni screamed and held tightly to him as Douglas appeared from behind her.

Douglas extended a hand toward me. "I can help you. I can protect you."

"Stop!" Toni screamed. She reached an arm to stop him, but he strode ever closer to me.

"Be careful of the rougarou," he said.

"Rain!" She kept anguished eye contact with me but could do nothing else.

Lou began to hunch and growl as his eyes glowed red.

I shrieked again. My painful, misunderstood, peacock shriek.

Douglas struggled a step in my direction. "Let me help you. You can trust me."

Rain put his hands on my shoulders. The warmth felt good on my cold body. It felt like life, and I drank it in a heavy gasp of gratitude.

He brought his face next to my ear. "I love you," he whispered.

I tried to see him, but he was too close. My head wouldn't turn. My body was immobile. I felt the steam of tears rise off my cheeks as my vision blurred.

"I love you," he said again.

I couldn't respond.

"I love you," the slaves wailed and circled around me in strange unison.

I want to wake up now.

"I love you," Rain said again, and his hands were pushing my shoulders, pushing me back.

"I love you." The slaves continued their morbid song and dance.

The ghetto transformed to the front of the mausoleum. My back was against the door with nowhere to go. Still he pushed me, hard.

"Rain," I whispered, and his eyes met mine.

But they weren't his eyes. They weren't eyes at all. They were nothing, an animalistic blackness I couldn't turn away from.

"Rain!" I hollered. "Stop this! Please. Momma Tristan!" He wasn't himself. None of them were. They were all stifled, watching a devastating event, unable to participate, unable to turn away. I was their disaster movie, their unavoidable train wreck. We were all bound by a dark spell.

Rain looked at me with a strange trance on his face, all the while pushing me back. He released one hand to grip the drooping brass knob, and with ease, the door opened and he pushed me into the tiny room, toward an open vault in the corner.

Douglas reached out a hand before he evaporated in the dark fog. They all did. Leaving only me. And Rain. And this dark, dark place.

The room was now an enclosed cemetery and he was pushing me down, down, down into the mire.

"I love you," he repeated. "I love you, Cheryl."

Her tombstone loomed over me, her carved-out name leering its victory. Horror surged its terrible flickers through every nerve. He was burying me in *her* grave!

"No!" I fought, as the tiniest motion came back to my fingers. "No! I'm not Cheryl."

No one heard me. I was muddied up to my waist. My wrists torqued, my fingers clawed.

Momma Tristan stood in the open door. In her hand, a ripped mojo bag faded from red to purple to black.

"Help me," I begged.

Her head dropped with compassion. "You learn to help yourself," she said softly, and clapped the dust of the disintegrated pouch to the ground in front of me.

Douglas's concern echoed from behind her. "Be careful of the rougarou."

Rain towered over me, his foot pushing on my shoulder, pushing me down.

"No," I whispered.

"I'm so sorry." His tears scorched my face.

"Rain." I gave a final gasp. "I'm not Cheryl."

He turned away.

I closed my eyes and prepared to swallow the mud.

His voice broke, a jumbled call out of the foreboding terror. "What did you say?"

My hands gripped the sheets. My toes curled, uncurled, and curled again. I opened my eyes.

He leaned forward from an overstuffed chair. "What did you say?"

"Rain." I swallowed and tried to inch away from his presence. "What?" I scanned the room, not trusting its normalcy.

"You have a fever. You were dreaming. Nightmare."

Trees outside creaked lightly. The anticipated thunder didn't come. The soft reality was a relief from the storm I'd just awakened from.

I stared at the ceiling and exhaled, hard. "What happened to Cheryl?"

"What?" He sat back.

"How did she die? Your wife."

His eyes shifted past the window toward the hidden mausoleum. "I don't know."

I counted four beats. "Then how do you know she's dead?"

"I know."

"How?" I persisted, and coughed.

He handed me a glass of water. "She wouldn't leave. Not like that. She wouldn't up and disappear."

I sipped and handed the glass back. "She loved you."

His laugh was sad. There was that distant, painful gaze in his eyes again. "Yeah," he said. But did he believe it?

"Where's Toni?" I asked.

"Making medicinal tea for you."

"I'm not thirsty." I licked my lips.

"It's medicine, and you'll drink it."

Did he say Momma Tristan? My heartbeat doubled and the sweat on my hands increased. I reached to make sure my mojo bag was still around my neck. Or should I have ripped it off?

He put the back of his hand on my forehead. "What do you remember?"

"Of what?"

"Your dream. As you woke up, you said you weren't ... what?"

His hand was still on my forehead. "I don't know," I lied.

CHAPTER THIRTEEN

THE VERANDAH KEPT ME COMPANY AS MY BODY slowly regained its strength.

Crutches leaned against the railing where Rain had brought them down before he left for the restaurant. As if I wasn't awkward enough already. But my foot was still tender, and I welcomed his attention.

A tap came from the window behind me.

Lou was in his potting room. He waved at me, unsmiling, with his trowel. I waved back. It was hard to tell if he wanted me at Greyford.

The sound of tires on gravel echoed past the garage. A beige sedan drove up the path until it was feet away from the verandah. Detective Chase gave me a cursory wave from behind the wheel.

Lou tapped again, more powerful.

I reached for a crutch and stood to greet Douglas as he opened the passenger door. "Did you find my laptop?"

"Still working on a few leads."

I knew what Rain and Toni thought about him, and now Lou was nervous. But Douglas was nice to me, helpful.

I couldn't figure out the Jekyll-and-Hyde dynamics of this pseudo-family. Still, the dream ...

There was a lingering discomfort in the air. "What are you doing here?" I asked.

"I'd heard you was out here. Heard you was hurt."

"I thought only doctors made house calls," I said. "How'd you know I was here?"

He climbed the steps. "Believe it or not, there's people who appreciate me being a detective."

"Confidential informants?" I chuckled. "For me?"

"Well, now." He chewed his toothpick. "I wouldn't say you." He scanned the property. "I come by to see if you need any help or anything." He was saying all the right words to make me trust him, but something felt wrong.

"I'm fine. You didn't have to come out here for that. For me."

"Ms. Embers. Penny, if I may?" He cleared his throat and paused for the approval I didn't give. "I know 'round here I'm not the most welcome fella. Sometimes people have a distaste for others. The question you have to ask yourself is, why?"

I shifted my weight. "What are you talking about?"

"You said they told you 'bout his wife."

"You know they did. So?"

He took his toothpick and pointed toward the screen door. "If she's dead, why they still looking for her?"

The crutch shivered, and I held it with both hands for balance. I wanted to ask what he meant, but the words stuck in my stomach. I felt the skin tighten around my eyes, felt my nostrils flare.

He pulled a paper from his shirt pocket, unfolded it like a treasure, and handed it to me.

I didn't want to let go of the crutch, but I had to reach for the paper. It was the billboard woman. The same face that welcomed me to New Orleans. Probably the same phone number.

I regarded Douglas, and he tipped his head toward the paper. I continued reading. *Cheryl D'Arcy Rainier. Missing.* My eyes wouldn't see the rest.

"What if she ain't dead?" he asked. "What if she's still out there, waiting for someone to help her?"

"I don't understand," I whispered, surprised I could talk at all.

"Neither do I."

"What are you doing here?" Toni hissed as the screen door banged. I heard Lou's tapping behind her.

"Well, hey there, honey." Douglas grinned. "That any way to greet me?"

"Get off this property. You're trespassing, and I've already called Rain. He's on his way." If she was lying, she was good at it. Her voice unwavering, she couldn't have been any more intimidating if she'd pulled one of the Winchesters off the wall.

"Now why'd you go and do that?" Douglas asked, sickly sweet and edging closer to her. She blocked him from Lou and he reached to take both her hands in one of his. "Still charmin' as ever, Ms. Beaveau."

She was frozen in place. Did she stop breathing? Her eyes glazed over, as if sleeping or in a trance. He took his other hand and shifted the bracelets. I saw what he saw—scars on each wrist. Different from the scar on her neck, but just as painful. "Aw, honey," he said. "I wish—"

She yanked her hands back. "You best get out of here before Rain shows up."

114

"I come by to check on our friend here. Wanted to make sure she weren't getting any worse. We both know some unsavory happenings are known to occur 'round here."

Toni fumed. "She's doing fine. We're all doing fine, without you."

My head spun. I needed to sit but my knees were locked.

Douglas pointed again at the flyer in my hand. "Makes you wonder, don't it? If they think she's dead, why keep asking if anyone's seen her?"

"Toni." I nodded in her direction with immediate guilt. "She doesn't think Cheryl's dead."

Her eyes narrowed. "I don't know anything about those flyers."

Douglas cocked his head with a patronizing grin. "She ain't the one paying for them."

Toni growled as I clutched my mojo bag. "I'm not gonna tell you again. Get off this property."

Detective Chase stood at the car door. "Jackson. We gotta go."

Lou began to hum, a frantic noise with no melody.

"What are you gonna do?" Douglas asked. "Call the cops?" He took a step closer. When he spoke to me, he seemed harmless. Informative. Caring. This rancor was his personal fight with Toni and Rain, and I was smack in the middle of it. "What about you, Lou? You gonna call the cops?"

Toni shifted forward. "You leave him alone."

I steadied the crutch and leaned forward. "What's this about, Douglas?"

He motioned toward Lou. "He knows. Don't you, Lou?"

Lou's tapping was violent, his humming like an engine. "No. No. No."

"Nothing to worry about. It's between me and Lou." Douglas backed down each step slowly. He raised his hands and shook his head. "No rougarous here, Lou. Okay? No cops. Right?"

"No rougarous," Lou repeated. "No cops."

"Atta boy." He pointed at the herbs and flowers. "Keep up the good work. I'm sure I can trust y'all to tell Vernon I'm sorry I missed him. Ms. Embers. I mean, Penny. Ms. Beaveau." He opened the car door. "You got my number."

Detective Chase gave a sympathetic nod as he started the engine and drove away.

I collapsed into the rocker as Toni's white knuckles gripped the verandah railing.

Her eyes pierced the vehicle until it was out of view and she turned to me. Her mouth had an odd shape, and her bracelets jerked a trembling tune.

For a place that prided itself on leaving the past in the past, there was obvious animosity. Terror, even. Whose side was I on? Knowing him less didn't make him the devil. Being friends with them didn't make any of us saints.

A dark SUV skidded sideways past the garage and the driver took the steps two at a time. My heart lurched when I realized it was him, first in fear and then in relief. And then in fear again.

"He was here," Toni cried. "He was right here!"

"It's okay." He pulled her tight, his body a shield from the road. "You're okay."

She tightened her arms against her chest.

116

"Hey," he whispered, and lowered his head to meet her eye-to-eye. "You're okay."

"Mm-hmm."

"You talk to Chase?"

She stepped back. "It's Douglas. You know he'd be on his side. They're always on his side."

His thumbs massaged under her bracelets.

They jangled awkwardly. Her self-made mojo spell hadn't stopped this trouble.

Or maybe it had. Maybe, without Toni, it would have been a whole lot worse.

Or maybe, because of her, it was.

He tucked her head under his chin and spoke to me. "You okay?"

There again was that violently protective behavior. The same I'd seen at the Blues & BBQ Festival. I didn't care what Douglas said. I jerked my head. "Yes."

"Where's Lou?" He ushered us inside.

"Upstairs?" Toni suggested.

"I'll check." I dropped my crutch and stumbled up the staircase. Whatever emotional fatigue I'd had moments ago was replaced with an urgency to make sure Lou was okay, and to make sense of these strange happenings.

"Lou," I shouted. "Where are you?"

I scoured Rain's room and bathroom. I peered out the balcony door at the magnolia tree, but there was no magic there. No Lou. No salvation to this story.

I went to the first guest room. Empty. Bathroom and balcony, both empty.

Lou's room. The dark curtains were drawn. I pulled them

open and searched the back yard. His beloved garden was visible to the right, but he wasn't there. A staccato glance at the trees, gates, ghetto, told me he wasn't anywhere.

A familiar whimper turned me. Red tennis shoes stuck out from under a large antique desk against a wall opposite the bed. "He's here," I called out, and took a step. "Hey, Lou."

He was rocking, holding his arms, tapping his fingers violently against his biceps and humming loudly. I wanted to hold this man-child, to comfort him. My heart shattered for the walls around him.

Rain bounded into the room, followed by Toni. He fell to his knees. "Lou. Bud. You okay?"

"No rougarous," he cried.

"Yeah. No rougarous." He held Lou's hands on his arms. "Come on, bud. No rougarous."

"No cops." Lou pulled away.

"No cops, either." Rain's hands held nothing, inches from the brother he couldn't reach.

"You promise?" He was a little boy, trying to stay out of trouble.

Rain stood, pulling Lou with him, and hugged him as a father would a scared child. "Promise brother. I promise."

Lou pushed him and stared at the floor. "No rougarous. No cops."

Toni put her hand on my arm. Since Douglas warned me about her at the festival, she'd often appeared unsure, afraid. Was this her normal? What happened to the strong, independent owner of Fleur de Fanci? Maybe she'd tried to be all things to all people, and it was catching up to her. Didn't matter. She was my friend. I put my hand on hers, glad to have the opportunity to give back some of the courage she'd previously instilled in me.

The walls were clean, off-white. The sparse furniture was necessary. A dramatic, four-poster bed with dark green coverings protruded from the wall. Matching drapes covered the windows and jib. The wall above the desk was covered with drawings and magazine clippings about the Teenage Mutant Ninja Turtles.

Rain's whispers assured Lou, and his hums grew softer.

One section of the wall had been outlined with green tape. Within its confines were magazine articles and crude colorings on the rougarou. *Be Careful Who (or What) You Talk To.* Distorted heads with glowing red eyes. *Myth or Monster: The New Orleans Rougarou.* Hands with claws. *Children, Behave.* It was mesmerizing, entrancing. And frightening.

Rain's focus shifted to the wall. "Where did these come from?"

He reached for a page as Lou whimpered. "Rain. Don't."

Rain paused, his hand in mid-air. "Lou? We talked about this. I thought you were done with the rougarou."

Lou stopped tapping his thighs and stared at his collage. "We talked. You said I was done. But I'm not. The rougarou is back and we have to protect ourselves."

I leaned to whisper to Toni, but she held up a finger. I wanted to leave, to stop this allowed eavesdropping, but something kept me from moving.

Rain lowered his hand and spoke softly. "What makes you think it's here, bud? How do we protect ourselves?"

"I just know." Lou said matter-of-factly and pointed at the wall. "We have to learn more about it so we can stop it. Information is power. This is information."

"Where did these come from?"

"I drew them."

"Not all of them." Rain gently pulled a clipping down.

"Put it back," Lou begged. "Put it back, Rain. It's not yours!"

"Shouldn't be yours, either." Rain's eyes moved from the clipping to his brother. "I think we need to put these in a different spot, Lou. For safe keeping."

Lou hummed as his eyes tightened. "It's not yours." He watched as Rain slowly pulled the clippings and drawings from the wall.

"What about the Ninja Turtles?" Rain asked. "Can't they protect us?"

"Ninja Turtles aren't real."

The walls of the Great Room echoed our stilled breaths.

"I'll have to get more security," Rain said to no one.

Lou pulled his chair into a corner and bent over. He covered his ears and rocked. "I can keep a secret. There are no rougarous here." He repeated it over and over.

"I don't understand," I said.

Rain gripped his watch without paying attention to it. "Nothing to understand. Get your stuff together. No one's staying here 'til it's safer."

"Safer from what? Douglas was—"

"You know nothing." He growled and turned to Toni. "I don't want you at your apartment, either. Not for a while."

"I can't—" Toni began.

"Stop arguing," he yelled. "I'm already in two places at once with the Acadia. I can't skip out on these kids today, and

I won't be worrying about you being somewhere else, alone. I'm not doing this again." He stormed out with his cell phone at his ear.

The dark mood permeated the sunny day. Rain's strength was venomous, dangerous. Was this the anger Douglas told me about, the violence he warned me against?

Lou followed Toni as she paced, laughing each time she turned to him with a funny face.

What was I doing here? I didn't know, couldn't think. My first world had turned upside down, and this one was going more than sideways.

Rain returned with determination on his face. "I have to get back to the Acadia. Everyone to the Escalade."

I took two steps into the foyer.

"I'm not being locked up in a room," Toni challenged.

"D'Arcy won't be open for dinner for a few hours. You can stay there."

Did the name sour in his mouth like it did it my ear?

Lou clapped. "I like the restaurant."

"What about the lunch crowd?" she said with disdain.

"Toni." His teeth were clenched. "I'll close it down if I have to. Let's go."

"I put my hand in front of him. "It's ... He came here for me. I should go back to the hotel."

"It's not that simple," Rain said.

"Then what? And don't tell me nothing."

Toni reached for the back of her neck.

Rain's eyes skirted to her and back to me, his voice low. "Okay. I'll tell you everything. Later. Right now, can we please get to the hotel?"

He was standing too close and not close enough. I wanted to hold him and have him hold me. I wanted to go home and stay here. I wanted to find out why I shouldn't trust him, and prove Douglas wrong. I wanted to be the one to change Rain, and I wanted him to stay like this forever.

"Okay." My voice escaped in a squeaky whisper.

CHAPTER FOURTEEN

WHICH WAS THE WORSE TORMENT—STAYING AT a place that might not be safe, or going to a safe place Rain created for his might-now-be-dead wife?

With vigilant determination, he drove the Escalade into the busy city, in and out of traffic as he made calls on his phone. I tried not to listen to words like "protect" and "threat" and "not again." The digital road signs warned of construction and impending storms. I searched for Cheryl's billboard but didn't see it. Maybe I didn't look hard enough. Maybe I didn't want to.

"How did I not notice this last time?" The world outside captivated me. "We're in the Garden District."

"Yeah," Toni said.

"Not what I expected." Silver and colored concrete buildings and lush florals flew in and out of blurry view.

"I don't imagine any of this is what you expected."

Silence took over. How much was Toni trying to ignore things, and how much was her not wanting to talk about it?

A young valet attendant greeted us, but Rain waved her off and signaled to an intimidating security guard. Rain was tall and fit, but the guard easily had two inches and twenty pounds on him.

Toni, Lou, and I clustered as Rain and the guard murmured to each other before the guard took control of the SUV.

"This way." Rain hustled through the doors. We had little choice but to follow. He deposited us in the empty dining room and went to the kitchen.

Our own private bastille.

I handed Lou my notebook and pen. Keeping his head and humming low, he busied himself over the pages.

I stared over my coffee at the mirrored reflections, their empty offerings expanding our isolation.

"The rougarou." He pointed to his drawing. It was an ugly creature—a hairy man-body under the head of a wolf. Large teeth and sharp claws. Dark eyes. The amateurish lines added a grotesque beauty to the design.

He flipped to another sketch. Two adults with another rougarou and a stick-figure princess, all holding hands. "That's Rain and Toni. And you're the princess."

"And you?" I asked.

"I'm in disguise. I'm not really a rougarou." He shook his head. "I could never hurt children."

I recalled the chant he muttered after upsetting our dinner in the Great Room, remembered Douglas tormenting him with the suggestion earlier this morning. How early in life had kids started teasing him, knowing he couldn't defend himself, knowing he didn't know they were mocking him? Or did he?

"The rougarou isn't bad," he said.

"He seems pretty bad to me," I confessed.

"He makes you behave. He leaves you alone if you're good. Or pretty. I'm good so he leaves me alone. You and Toni are pretty so he'll leave you alone." He sat straight.

"Don't you think you're pretty?" Toni asked.

He blushed and dropped his head. "Toni. Men aren't pretty. I'm a man. I'm older than Rain." He faced me. "Did you know that? I'm his big brother."

"I did know that."

"But I'm not really bigger. I'm older. When I'm big, I'm in disguise. I protect him from the rougarou. He doesn't need it, though. He's good. Like me. I'm good. The rougarou leaves me alone."

"Good for you, Lou." I couldn't keep Rain's darker explanation of the beast out of my mind.

Rain pushed a silver cart through the kitchen doors. "Compliments of Chef Rain."

"Kinda makes your mouth water," Toni said.

"I forget how grumpy I get when I don't eat," I replied.

Lou pointed. "You must not have eaten today."

We burst with laughter, a hysterical stress release.

"Try some maque choux. It's a Cajun corn recipe." Rain spooned the colorful food onto my plate.

"What are you eating, Lou?" I admired his large sandwich.

"Moofa—muffa—mu ... Toni?"

"Muffaletta. It's like an Italian olive salad on bread."

"Italian?" I questioned. "I thought New Orleans was mostly French."

"Mostly," Rain said. "French, Cajun, and Creole. But not only. You'd be surprised at the influx of cultures we have down here. We even get the occasional Californian."

"Hey," Lou said through a mouthful. "You're from California."

"I am." The food didn't sit well in my stomach. My foot was sore, my body weak, and my nerves shot. Eating from a menu prepared for Rain's dead wife might be the way they did things here in New Orleans, but it wasn't my idea of a good time. What innocent voodoo-hoodoo could I find to counteract this darkness? I took another bite and gave myself permission to enjoy it.

"You're okay in the kitchen," I told Rain.

"Thanks," he chuckled. "I bet you're an okay writer."

I dusted off a forgotten memory. "I used to dream of opening a writer's café."

"I'd be a bartender," Toni said. She was right. We would be great friends. Or worst enemies.

"I'd be normal." Lou shrugged. My heart ached. I wanted to hug him, protect him from the world. But it was too late. He already knew he was different from the others, and they'd already let him know it wasn't okay. "Or a rougarou."

"What?" Rain chuckled.

"Children. Yum." He slurped imaginary bones before spitting them out.

Rain pushed open the doors to the cooking classroom. More than a dozen youth clustered in the back with snacks and loud conversation. I recognized two from the BBQ Festival.

"Meet the Kitchen Krewe," Rain said.

"Mmm." Cedric swaggered up. "Fresh meat for the cooking class."

"Watch yourself." Rain pulled on his chef's jacket and walked to the front. "Everyone in place. Let's go."

"What are we doing today, Chef?" A slight girl raised her hand with the question, which was greeted with mumbles from the other students as they took their spots.

"First, I want to introduce you to a good friend of mine." Rain pointed his knife.

All eyes on me. Not awkward at all. I gave a shy wave to the group.

"Yo," Cedric's partner hollered. "Yo, yo, yo. What's yo name, gorgeous?"

The room unsettled with bits of laughter and gasps.

"Her name is Penny. And you'll show her the respect you show me and each other. Or you're out. Get me?"

The kids calmed and Cedric gave me a smile. "Props, Money Girl—I mean, Penny. Don't mean no harm." He elbowed his friend. "Teeg, man."

"Yo. What he said." He extended his hand, "I'm Teegan. Call me Teeg."

"Nice to meet you." I shook his hand, which turned into shaking everyone's hands, until I circled back to the front of the room.

Rain slipped an apron over my head and tied it behind me. "I'm helping you?" I asked.

"You said you wanted to be a chef."

"Something like that." I took my place next to him.

He considered his students like they were his flesh and blood. "Who's first?"

They jostled each other as some raised hands and others called out.

"They're pretty enthusiastic," I whispered.

Rain kept his focus on the class. "They worked hard to get into the program. Work hard to stay. They take a lot of pride in it. A lot of them didn't think they could contribute to society."

Cedric got rowdy. "We was unfunctional, wasn't we, Chef?"

"Some of you were."

Teegan nudged Cedric. "But we been re-hah-bill-uh-tated, ain't we?"

"You got that right, brother."

The room erupted with catcalls and cheers.

"All right." Rain raised his hands. "Settle down. Back to it. Who's first? And not Cedric or Teeg. Y'all shown off enough already."

"Busted," a younger, brash girl called out as the students reacted.

Slight Girl raised her hand again.

"Veronica." Rain acknowledged her. "Whatcha got?"

She pursed her lips and stuffed her hands into her pockets. "Well, after the last class, I went home an' axed my momma for some grocery money and she thought I was really trying to score with it, so I axed her to come with me instead. She let me take twenty-seven dollars from her money, and I showed her how to shop for three days including snacks for the twins."

Rain led the class in applause. "That's great, Ronna. So, tell us. What was your favorite part?"

She pulled her hands out of her pockets and swayed a little dance as her face brightened. "Well, my favorite foods part was showing the twins how to pack better lunches and they's helping me make snacks and my momma axed me to plan the next shopping trip." She tipped her head for a moment. When she faced Rain, a few tears fought for her cheeks. "But the best-best part was my momma trusting me to make groceries alone last Saturday. I used some coupons and come home with extra stuff and we made homemade ice cream together, me, momma, and the twins."

"Baby girl." Cedric and Teegan clapped the loudest.

She fidgeted but held her head up with a proud smile.

"Yeah!" Rain walked to her. "Way to do it, Ronna."

She wiped her face as she let him hug her. "Thank you, Chef."

Rain scrunched down with his hands still on her shoulders. "You did this. Don't you forget it."

"No, sir." She promised. "I won't ever."

"Atta girl. All right." He came back to his station. "Let's get started. We're doing something a little different today. I'm taking a risk on trusting you guys and gals with this."

A low buzz of excitement started to build.

"Oh, I know," Teegan shouted. "We fixing them little, uh, upper-a-teefs."

"Man." Cedric shoved him. "You so dumb. You mean aperitifs."

"What's them?" someone asked.

Cedric threw out his hands. "Don't you know nothing? Those are them little cocktail drinks they serve at parties and weddings and stuff."

"You're not making drinks," Rain said.

"Chef!" Brash Girl called out. "You getting married and having a party? Can I be a bridesmaid?"

I'd not seen Rain blush before. "No, Georgina." He choked on his laugh. "No. I'm not ... we're not ... no. No wedding."

Cedric jumped and waved wildly. "Then you mind if I ask her?" He raced to the front of Rain's station, tied a strand of chive into a circle, and dropped to one knee. "Ms. Penny, would you do me the honor?"

Rain gave a downward wave and turned his back on the room as Toni and Lou entered with a serving cart loaded with pumpkins and gourds.

"What'd we miss?" Toni asked.

Lou pushed himself into a corner as the noise increased. Ronna wriggled a tiny hello, and he reciprocated.

Rain caught his eye. "Okay. Last time. Settle down or we're done."

The room quieted. Toni pushed the cart around and placed a pumpkin and gourd in front of each student. As they manhandled their new possessions, Rain paced the center aisle.

"Something fun's about to happen in New Orlins, yes?" he asked. "Got some Halloween action going on soon?"

Their agreement came in hushed tones.

"Almost time to wrap up the classes before the holidays."

Everyone moaned, including Toni as she made her way next to me.

Ronna raised her hand again. "Will we come back after?"

Rain surveyed the room. "Well, I don't know. You wanna come back after the holidays?"

Cheers, claps, and stomps answered him.

"You think you can stay out of trouble for the season?"

"Yes." The same reaction, amplified.

"No!" Toni hollered and bumped me.

Rain swigged his water bottle and pointed at her. "Hush, Antoinette." He focused on the students again. "So, here's the deal. If you can stay out of trouble—and I mean really stay away from it—y'all are welcome back in January. But if any of you gets into it—with cops, school, parents, anyone—then you're out. Period. You get me?"

"We feel ya," Teegan confirmed.

"All right, good. 'Cause I like having you in the class." He playfully grabbed Cedric and Teegan by the back of their necks. "And I think your folks probably appreciate you being off the streets for a few hours."

"Man." Cedric shrugged him off. "My momma said you the best thing ever happen to our family. My daddy didn't get drunk til *after* dinner last night."

Teegan shoved him. "Shut up, man. He serious. Yo, yo, Chef. I'm staying outta trouble, like you say." He raised his hand like a Boy Scout. "I. Promise."

The other students mimicked the salute.

I leaned toward Toni. "He's really good with these kids."

She tipped her head in admiration. "He's been doing it for almost eight years now. Seen some of them get into college. It's been good for everyone."

"I need," Rain continued, "to celebrate y'all. So. We're having a party."

"What?" "A party?" "So cool!"

The students romped and danced.

Lou clapped his hands over his ears. Ronna shuffled over to him and covered her ears as well. "You guys." She shouted back to the room. "Stop."

Cedric and Teegan led the crowd into calm. "Yo, man. Sorry, brother. Sorry, Lou."

"Okay." Lou kept his ears covered.

Rain raised a finger to his lips and stretched out his other hand. "Now, don't go crazy. Because if you do, it's off. But if y'all behave, you'll be catering the Halloween party at Greyford Manor."

I anticipated another ridiculous outburst. Instead, the class took on a hushed air of importance.

"And all your immediate families are invited."

The room exploded. Lou howled. Ronna put her hands over his ears and yelled again at the class.

"Gumbo ya-ya," Toni said.

"What?" I asked.

She circled her hands in the air and shouted. "All the noise!"

Rain swigged his water patiently. "Two things. Extra class tomorrow and next week for those who can make it. And, you're gonna be responsible from start to finish. Set up to tear down. Ninety percent of the menu, but it all has to be approved, and supervised, by us." I was surprised—pleased— he included me. "We'll help and guide, but this is your success. You earned it." He pressed his hands low in the air. "Who's in?"

The Krewe had just won the lottery.

"Chef Rain?" Ronna almost whispered. How could this girl, so outspoken for Lou, be so unsure of herself? "How will we all get there? We get rides here and the bus, but the bus don't go that far. My momma don't drive, and Georgina don't even have a car."

"That's a problem." Rain pretended to think. "I suppose, if y'all can get here for class, you can get here that day, too. Then there might be a charter bus waiting for you and your families."

Wide mouths and shining eyes greeted us with unspoken amazement and thanks.

"All right." He clapped. "Let's carve pumpkins."

Tension returned in the lobby as Rain arranged rooms for us at the concierge desk.

Because that's where it was. In the sitting area. On the wall. Above two racks of newspapers, magazines, and travel brochures. Black and white behind glass. Like a treasure.

Have You Seen Me?

I stopped so quickly Toni knocked into me.

Rain took four large strides toward us. "Let's go."

"No." I stared at the poster. Bile filled my throat. "I want answers."

The scent of him confused my anger. "Please," he whispered, as his breath came out his nose in tiny puffs.

I met his stare. My arm stayed low as my finger pointed emphatically at her face. "I. Want. Answers."

His eyes shifted briefly to the poster then back to me. I saw strength and sorrow, and although I wanted to comfort him, hold his cheek, hug his body, I couldn't move.

Staff and patrons mingled on their way in and out of the lobby, slowing to catch a glimpse of the reserved man face-to-face with the fiery redheaded woman.

I, too, began to breathe in short bursts, and raised my voice to compensate for his quietness. "Either she's dead, or she's not. If not, why is there a plaque on your mausoleum?"

"I told you, it's—"

My hand rushed up. "If she is dead, why are there signs all over for her? And if you love her so much, why aren't there any photos of her at the Manor? And if you don't love her—"

It wasn't possible for him to come closer without touching me, but he did. "Keep your voice down. I'll explain everything."

I backed up. Lou chewed his lip, patted his thighs, rocked from the waist up. Toni whispered to him as he blinked and nodded, blinked and nodded.

"Then explain it, Rain." I lifted my palms and spread my arms. "You've been saying you will, but I haven't heard anything yet. Why do people step away and whisper when you're around? Why does your own cousin tell me to stay away from you? Why—"

"Stop!" It was worse than any growl I'd heard from him. It was threatening, traumatic. It was the end of his rope.

A woman gasped and rushed outside. The counter phone echoed a garish ring. Lou's humming intensified.

"Rain," Toni said softly. "Let's go."

His body relaxed. His face didn't. He jerked his head toward the elevator. "Let's go."

I dropped my arms. "Answers first."

He glared a hundred fiery icicles into me before escaping around the corner.

CHAPTER FIFTEEN

ANGER PROPELLED ME OUTSIDE AND INTO THE fresh scent of concrete and traffic. I made it through two and a half miles of I-don't-care walking, five missed calls, and three inquiring texts.

What was this mojo bag for, anyway? Power? Awesome. Let's take some power and do something instead of waiting for something to happen.

A hefty payment bought me ten days in a Petite Room at the French Market Inn. I didn't want to go back to California, and I wasn't ready to stay with Toni or Rain. But this was my getaway. It was worth the expense to make my own decisions, my own new memories. This was how I should have started New Orleans. It only took me two weeks to figure out how to be my own person again. Two weeks, and three years.

Otis Redding brought life to my playlist. I bought a coffee and chocolate chip muffin from PJ's Coffee—because more caffeine is always helpful when adrenaline is high—and traipsed up to my room. The music, the food, the atmosphere, all conspired to keep me in the Crescent City, and my resolve shifted from finding direction to finding a solution.

Uncle Martin always told me, "Forget the end. Take it to the beginning." He would remind me what I originally wanted, needed. And we'd work backwards until we could identify where it went sideways.

I shut the ghostly conversation from my mind but the gut-hunger for something more lingered. Or the idea I was still doing something wrong.

Make new memories. Turn it around. Take it to the beginning. A confident glee gripped me as I scurried downstairs to hail a cab. I had left most of my stuff at Greyford Manor, and I was on a mission to reclaim it.

I talked my way past Rain's new security by showing him photos on my phone: Toni and me, Lou and his trowel, a few candids of Rain in the kitchen or drinking coffee. I pointed through the window. "That's my jacket on the sofa."

I told the guard I knew why he was hired today, and when he finally let me into the Manor, I kept to myself that I also knew why he'd be fired tomorrow.

My typewriter greeted me from the desk. I shuffled to the piano and tickled a few keys. The House welcomed and alienated me. The second story landing was lit with dusk. As I reached the top of the stairs, a beautifully wretched idea came to me.

I slipped into the dress, and then the shoes. I recalled Rain's soft touch when he first put them on my feet. My new jacket admonished me for deserting my new friends.

I texted Toni to let her know I was okay, because I didn't want her to worry. But I didn't say I was going out, because I didn't want her to worry.

I grasped a set of keys from the side table and walked to the garage. The remote lit up the Ghost. Sweet. I'd driven nice cars before, but never a Rolls. Rain had said he didn't drive it often. Well, driving keeps the engine in tune, right? The lights beamed from their deep red frame.

It was pure oxygen and the exhilaration was more than expected. It fed me and begged for more. I had to keep going. It wasn't stealing if I had access to the keys, right? What was Rain going to do? Call the cops? An ironic satisfaction brought clarity as I started the quiet engine and programmed the GPS.

I left the Ghost with the valet at the French Acadia, and walked away, trying hard to not do a sultry victory dance.

The sun retreated behind the brick horizon and clouds huddled over Frenchmen Street. Forget what anyone else wanted from me. I was a sinner ready to embrace my sins.

New Orleans once again glistened in the electric autumn evening. It was always the best moment of the day, when natural lighting collided with neon, and that wonderful, exciting energy pulsed like a Tesla coil through my blood.

I scooped a go-cup and drank my way to my destination.

Was every night in New Orleans like this? A happy, galvanizing mess? Did it matter I didn't know what day it was? As so many others throbbed their way to louder locations, I chose a vaguely familiar, more intimate, piano bar.

The first Hurricane mellowed me a bit. The roar in my head flew off, and I hummed along with some jazz tune I wasn't sure I actually knew. Most of the booths and tables were empty. A woman indecently nuzzled her male companion a few tables away, and in the corner, a man appeared far more lonely than I thought anyone could. When he mouthed a distorted "hello," I turned away.

My cell phone screen was blank. How could everyone ignore me like this? Why was I sitting here? Alone? In a bar?

The rain splat hard against the window and I didn't have an umbrella. I wasn't keen on walking in these shoes much longer, or paying for a cab. I had to stay put and wait it out.

The fortune cookie crumbled onto the table as I freed the paper.

You learn more when you listen than when you speak.

I shrugged it off and ordered another Hurricane. I didn't get dressed up to the nines to have a pity party. There was no way I was going back to whatever, nor let all this go to waste.

After my third Hurricane, the familiar rumblings started to emerge from their hiding spot deep within me.

I picked up my phone and fumbled a call.

"Hello?" He answered. Of course, he answered.

What did I say? Nothing.

"Babe, is it you?" *He called me babe.*

"Hi." I stammered, then steadied myself with another gulp of liquor.

"You okay?"

"The good news is I don't have a chip to lose."

"What are you talking about? Where are you?"

"I think ... I made a mistake." I tried to read the nonexistent tea leaves in the bottom of my glass, and motioned to the bartender-waiter-all-purpose-guy for another. He promptly obliged.

"What do you mean?" I wasn't ready for the concern in his voice.

"Can you come get me?" The words surprised me. I'd wanted to be solo tonight. Just not by myself. Would he know this was more voodoo-hoodoo magic in my drink? I peered into the foggy juice and almost tipped the glass as I groped for my mojo lanyard.

"Babe," he said again. It comforted me, even if I doubted the sincerity. "What's going on?"

"It's storming and my foot hurts and I think I may have had too much to drink again and I can't hear the piano anymore." I tried to focus. "And I miss you."

I counted to six before he answered. "I miss you, too."

"So, you'll come get me?" This couldn't be the moment the wall broke and I started crying again. I bit my pinky finger.

"Where are you?" I heard him rustling, heard keys jingling.

"I'm at that piano place near Frenchmen."

His noise stopped. "You're *where?*"

I took another sip of the Hurricane. "I'm in New Orleans, Ted."

Time passed in a swirling, dizzy blur. The only clear sound was the piano, although I couldn't understand the music. I tried to watch the player, or peer out the window, but they tumbled together and confused me. The bartender waved and I weakly raised two fingers before closing my eyes.

My neck hurt, but I wouldn't be a drunk with her head on the table. Tipping back against the booth didn't help, either. I sat perfectly still. Thankfully the drinks muffled the world so I didn't have to concentrate on anything except my own breathing. But what if I stopped? Ted once told me it was impossible for the body to die like that. I didn't believe him. I didn't believe a lot of things he told me.

My eyes fluttered as I heard a scrape on the table.

"Drink this." I heard Rain mutter as he slid next to me.

I smelled the vicious coffee and scooched away from him, pushing the coffee with my finger. Not only because I didn't want it, but because I didn't want to give him the satisfaction.

"What are you doing here?" I slurred through half-closed eyes.

"What did you think would happen when you drove away with my car?"

"And you came all the way here to rescue it. Thought you had other things to care about."

"I got security set, if that's what you're worried about."

I turned, seething. "Of all the things on my mind right now, Rain, trust me. Your security isn't one of them. How did you find me?"

He waved his cell phone. "GPS tracker. You have any idea how many bars I walked into tonight looking for you?"

"You have any idea how much I don't care?" I reached for the remains of my Hurricane.

He pulled it away and shoved the coffee closer. "You're not a pretty drunk. Drink it."

An expletive left my mouth before I had a chance to gather my wits.

"Back at ya," he said with venom.

I pulled my hands into the leathered sleeves and wrapped them around the mug. If I could lift it without shaking, if I could sip it without gagging ... And if I stared at the coffee, I didn't have to look at him.

Rain put two Ibuprofen and a water bottle on the table. "Take these."

I resentfully complied. I hated that he knew how to take care of me, and I hated that I let him. I especially hated both in this particular situation.

We sat while I drank my coffee and water. Him. Me. Us. Together. But not together. I was glad he was here. But I hated it. I hated him for seeing me like this, and for not walking away so I could hate him more.

"Knock it off." His voice was rough.

"What?" I stared away from him.

"This victim dance. Always ready for a fight, aren't you? You think you know everything. You know nothing. Nothing. You come down here, you hear things, you get drunk—again. You got a problem, Penny, but it ain't the drink. That's just the symptom. Trust me."

"Trust you?" I spit. "I trust no one. People are always wanting something, always taking. I'm tired of the fight, but who else is gonna fight for me? I've always had to fight. If I don't, who will?"

He draped his arm on the top of the booth. "We got our own messes to take care of here. You can't keep distracting us from things that really matter. You act like you ain't got no ghosts in your closet and you're not responsible when they show up. Newsflash, boo. You do, and you are."

How dare he attack me with the truth? "I can't—"

He continued. "If you're so fire-bent on getting out of here, I'll drive you to the airport myself tomorrow. What do I care? But right now, it's late. I'm tired. It's been a hard day. So, if you don't mind, we're going home—"

"Home is California." I interrupted with a hiss. "Take me *there*."

"Get up." He stood. "I'm not closing down a bar. I don't do this crap anymore."

Anger and embarrassment, apologies and forgetting stalled in my mouth. I gaped at him with no words.

"No," he said. "Get up."

"I ... can't." Not because I was still that drunk, but because being this close to him made me that dizzy.

He scooped me in his arms, picked up my backpack, and started walking.

"Put me down." I struggled against him, which made him hold me tighter. A delightful consequence. I would get drunk and fight him every night for this.

"So you can get hurt again? Cut your foot or hit your head? Dammit, Penny. When are you gonna stop?"

I silently loosened my grip.

He propped me against the side of his SUV and opened the passenger side. The rain beat a gentle nonsense rhythm all around us. "Get in."

"I don't wanna." I let the raindrops fall into my eyes and mouth.

"Probably toxic," he said.

I closed my mouth and glared.

"You want a coffee?" he asked, softer.

I ignored him with a slow blink and caught more rain on my tongue.

"What do you want, Penny?"

"Not to talk to you." I fell into the seat and let him adjust my legs properly.

I wanted to let go but I couldn't. I'd wanted to make new memories but instead, I'd gotten drunk. Again.

But he'd come to my rescue. Again.

He was right. I had a problem.

"I wanna ask you something," I garbled. "Did ya love her? Did she love fighting you to make you prove it?"

He answered by tightening my seatbelt.

I hated that he sought me after I abandoned them—him— at her restaurant.

"Did ya kill her?" I leaned toward his delicious ear. I wanted to hiss it at him, let him know I hated him for being so believable. Hated that he stayed with her memory. Hated the entire world for throwing us together into this chaos of a city with no direction on how to fight our way out of the emotional jungle and its melancholic tendrils that kept roping us down to the pits.

I hated myself more for being incapacitated. I needed another drink to settle down and find my strength. I was a little broken and wanted him to know it. I wanted him to tell me he was going to save me. Save us. I wanted him to mean it. I wanted to fight him every inch of the way as I let him win. Did Cheryl fight? Did he fight her back? Did they ever win?

He pushed my door closed with both hands and pounded the hood as he walked around.

I waited for him to buckle up and start the engine. "Bet she ran away and left you. Bet she hated you, too."

I fought the rhythm of the windshield wipers, but it was no use. The last thing I remembered was wanting Rain as he sighed my name.

The storm was a teaser and by the time we drove past the security guarding the plantation entrance, the rain had dwindled to a refreshing mist. Still, Rain parked close to the verandah.

"Wait here." He took the keys and went inside. What was I gonna do? Hotwire the SUV?

I drained a bottle of water and started another before I glimpsed his shadow returning.

His hand held a mug of coffee. His face held a mix of concern, anger, and compassion.

"Rain." I lowered my head. I was in no condition for a serious conversation, but I was incapable of waiting.

He put one arm on the open door and the other on the SUV roof. Oh, how inviting those arms could be, even in his reserved stance. I wanted to escape completely into him.

"Can we start over?" I sipped, then held the coffee to my pounding head.

"I don't know ..."

I gulped to stop the dry tears.

"I've never been a fan of starting over."

Figured. I gave a sad chuckle and bit my lip.

"Hey." He set my mug on the roof and pulled me to him. His arms were strong, warm, safe. His finger hooked my chin and nudged me to meet his eyes. "I don't want to start over, because I don't want a repeat. We're both imperfect, Penny. But we can both be better. I don't know how long you're staying in New Orlins, but how about instead of starting over, we take a different path and—"

I couldn't help myself. I had to shut him up so he could kiss me. So, I kissed him first. A quiet, beautiful kiss.

His hands wrapped the back of my neck and drew me closer.

My mouth watered with each tender, passionate kiss. He smelled of garlic and musk, and his skin was salty. Fireflies danced in the distance as I turned to catch my breath.

"Momma Tristan?" He fingered the lanyard.

"Mm-hmm."

"How's it working for you?" He laughed.

What was it for? Money, clarity, success? "Pretty good."

"Penny," he said between kisses. "Full disclosure. I have to tell you something." He started to unbutton his shirt.

I shifted. "What kind of disclosure is this?"

"Something I want you to see."

"Sure." I bit my fingernail.

He opened his shirt and pointed to a tattoo scripted over a scar above his heart.

Cher

There it was. He was branded with her name and XXX below it. The same circled triple-X I'd seen him trace on Marie Laveau's tomb. First her restaurant, now her mark. Cheryl was definitely haunting him. She was never going away. And he wanted me to accept that.

I turned away, glad for the drink still in my veins. "No."

"Penny, wait. Closer."

I shook my head. I was nobody's second choice.

"Please." His eyes were full of pleading, and I would do anything in my control to stop the hurt. I nudged the shirt aside.

Char
XXX-II

145

"Cheryl was six months pregnant when ..." He stepped back. "Her name was Charlotte."

Charlotte. Char.

I swallowed hard and gazed up.

His eyes were red and his voice a whisper. "She was two days old. The day Cheryl vanished I knew something was wrong. Toni knew it, too, in that way she does. She told me to get home. I left the restaurant early. When I walked in the door, it was quiet, like nothing I'd ever experienced. I went upstairs, and it was ... strange."

I leaned against the side of the SUV and tugged his arm. He resisted, so I sat in the seat as he gripped the door.

"No one was here," he continued. "Something bad must've happened. I went searching for her. Called for help. She was an adult, so the cops wouldn't do anything. Except Douglas."

"Because he's family," I offered.

Rain's cheek tightened at the word. "Anyway. Lou was saying she left but I didn't believe that. Something about the way he was saying it. And then I got the call."

He needed a break, a distraction. He sipped my coffee and banged the mug back onto the SUV. After he licked his lips, he puffed out a hard breath. "Douglas found her."

"I don't understand. Did she leave again? Is that—"

His eyes were full of confusion, then painful understanding. "No. No, not Cheryl. We never ... never found Cheryl. It was Char. Douglas found Charlotte. She was so little, and I wasn't there when ..." He cleared his throat. "I met her at the hospital. Douglas, and now the cops, finally took me seriously." His voice drifted into the night. "But they never found Cheryl."

"What do you think happened?" I whispered my unwanted question.

He shook his head. "I don't know. I honestly don't know. There've been so many theories and rumors. Some say there's no way a mom could run away from her baby. Others, well, they think I killed her."

"But you didn't ... Did you?" The words tumbled before I could stop them.

He rubbed his tattoo in anguish.

I saw it again. Triple X's. Marie Laveau. Was he so desperate for his family he prayed to whatever god he thought would hear him? Or did he not pray because it was no use? What could I say? I understood him, and wished I didn't.

Suddenly sober, I put my arms around him and let him caress my back. This was deeper than any kiss or drunken rescue. He was letting me in.

We stood entwined against the Escalade. His wet cheek was on my neck, his chest rose and fell. I brought my hands to his face. I wanted to kiss it all away, wanted to whisper in his ear it would all be okay. And I wanted it to be true.

I wanted to believe everything—and everyone—was good. That there was less evil in the world, and the evil that was here would be clearly seen for what it was. I wanted it all to be black and white.

But New Orleans is a colorful town.

CHAPTER SIXTEEN

RAIN HANDED ME A GLASS OF WATER AND joined me on the sofa in the Great Room. "Better?"

I stifled a yawn, gulped the water, and nodded.

He dropped his arm around my shoulders, brought me close, and fingered the ring on my hand. "I told you mine, you tell me yours."

I tucked my hand under my left arm. "Nothing to tell."

He kissed my temple. "Tell me."

I squirmed but he didn't let go, so I leaned into him.

"Tell me," he whispered again.

I blinked, slow. "Ted. We were engaged a few years ago."

He waited but I said nothing more. "That's it?"

"I don't want to talk about it, is all."

"Now, hold on. Why'd you separate? Why'd you keep the ring?"

I yawned and snuggled deep into the safety of him, where I didn't have to look him in the eye. "You ask a lot of questions."

"It ain't as simple as you were engaged and now you're not."

"You talk different when you're tired."

"Still retain that Southern charm my momma instilled, I hope."

I kissed his neck. "Yes."

"You're not gonna tell me more?" He gave me a light squeeze.

"Rain." I sat up. He already knew more than I wanted him to. I didn't want him peeking inside my soul. I needed to bury it, leave it behind, like so much else in my life. But he also deserved a better response. "The long and short of it is, we were oil and vinegar."

"Food reference," he said. "I can get behind that."

"Ted was great, at first. But things started to fall apart when I couldn't pay as much attention to him as I used to."

"Why was that?"

I stared into the empty fireplace. "My uncle. He was sick and needed me more."

"I'm sorry." Rain withdrew his arm from the back of the sofa. "And the ring?"

I rubbed it. "Nothing, really. To be honest, I didn't want him to have the satisfaction of controlling everything, even this. I guess I figured if I kept it, it was a reminder that some-where, someone once loved me. And that I was strong enough to let go when he no longer did."

He brought his lips to my ear. "And you don't think you could want, or deserve, love again?"

I peered at him. "Can we please change the subject?"

"Okay." He kissed the top of my head. "When you're ready." He kicked off his shoes and stretched out.

I nestled between him and the back of the sofa. I wanted to put my hand under my cheek for comfort, but the tatt was there. She was alive on his heart, and I couldn't disturb their bond. Such a tiny thing, such a little life. "Rain?"

"Mm."

"Can I ask you something?"

He lifted his head. "Full disclosure."

I ran my fingers over his shirt.

"Hey." He stilled my hand.

"Tell me about the scar."

He sat up and ran a hand through his hair. "Darlin', that's a long story I don't mind telling. But you mind if I make myself a drink first?"

I pushed myself up. "That kind of talk?"

He walked behind the wet bar and clinked into a clean glass. "Want one?"

"You're kidding, right?" I didn't understand him, didn't understand New Orleans.

"Yeah." He took his glass and paced. "Thing is ..." He cleared his throat and his free hand kept clenching and releasing. He made a full lap around the table, took a long swallow and set the drink down.

"Rain?"

He unbuttoned his shirt again and walked toward me.

I was on my feet before I made the choice to stand.

"This." He rubbed the scar as his face sought the ceiling.

I tried not to absorb the tangible darkness.

When he turned back to me, there was a tear on his cheek. A different pain in his eyes than earlier, a hurt mixed with bewilderment and anger ... and regret.

He slid his fingers down my arms until we were holding hands. "I want you to know."

We could have been dancing, he stood so close. I could smell the liquor on his warm breath.

"You heard stuff," he said softly to the ghosts behind me, and let go.

"Yup."

We weren't looking at each other. Weren't holding each other. We were as close as two people could be, and a universe apart.

He held up a finger and retrieved two drinks.

"One better be for me, 'cause I know you ain't making one for her." Toni stood in the doorway, rubbing the back of her neck. "No offense, hon, but we all seen your liquor tends to control you instead of the other way around."

"Toni." Rain set another glass on the bar.

"Water," I said.

He obliged as Toni walked over to me.

We sat on the sofa and watched him ramble a haphazard pattern about the room.

"You telling her everything?" Toni kept her gaze on the floor.

Rain continued as if he hadn't heard her. He finished his drink in two gulps and wiped his mouth. "I didn't know. For the longest time, I was blind. I'd trusted her. I'd warned her about him. I saw what he did to Toni." He sat in the easy chair.

"Him?" I asked. "Who?"

"Douglas." Toni peered at Rain and the corner of her mouth twitched.

"When I went to Europe, he saw a chance and made moves on her." He pointed to her glass. "You gonna drink that?"

She let him take it, and his Adam's apple chugged three

times. "Thought she knew better." He gritted his teeth and pointed at her. "You did know better."

"Hey," she answered.

"Sorry, but sometimes y'all are dense as the bayou. She'd just lost her gramma and her folks had already moved out of state."

"Wait." I turned. "Your grandma's dead? You're always talking about her visiting."

"Sure enough," she said.

Rain tipped his head. "This is New Orlins, Penny. We mix a little bit of everything down here, including the living with the dead."

I plucked my lanyard and wondered how much deeper I could get. "So?"

"Douglas swooped in and they got married."

"Married?" I hid my gasp in a fake swallow. "You told me he was an ex-boyfriend."

"I said ex," he said. "You said boyfriend. I didn't correct. Anyway, that's when I knew things were bad. Toni's always the strong one."

"Not always, Rain," she said.

His eyes squinted. "Mostly."

Knowledge has a funny tug when you don't want to recognize it. "Why didn't you two ever ...?"

Toni chuckled as Rain spoke. "She's never been more than a friend to me. A sister, really. Always good with Lou. My folks loved her. But we never had that kind of connection. I need someone who needs to be taken care of. Not all the time, and not fully. But enough. That was never her. Not on a regular basis, anyway. She's her own self, and I love her for it. But we were never in love."

He refilled the drinks.

"He ain't my type," Toni said.

What was her type? What was his? And between Rain, Ted, and any other guy, whose type was I?

She took her glass as he stood over us, his shirt still unbuttoned.

He caught me eyeing the scar and tattoo, and sat back in the chair. "The short of it is, Toni's roommate during and after college was Cheryl. Even after the marriage to Douglas."

Toni leaned back. "He said we needed the rent money."

Rain gave her a sideways glance. "I came back from Europe and they'd already married. Said she tried to call me first but couldn't reach me. Cheryl was a little clingy with them and Toni asked me to be a buffer. So, we start hanging together, the four of us. We fell in love. At least, I did. That's when Douglas started saying things like he'd picked the wrong woman."

Toni stroked her wrists. "So, he started picking on me."

"And then Cheryl starts saying she's afraid of him, too. She saw what his temper was. Saw what he was capable of. But that didn't stop her from living there." Rain's grip tightened around his glass. "Said she had nowhere to go. I figure, since we were in love, she shouldn't have to put up with that. So, I marry her, bring her here to get away from him, and plan to move Toni out, too.

"One night, Cheryl and I are on a date. She tells me they been having an affair, she and Douglas. Said she'd lost the baby I thought was mine. What do you do with that? She asked forgiveness, said she wanted a second chance."

I hid my reaction with a gulp.

He continued. "We're going through this mess, and the phone rings. Toni's crying, screaming. We hear Douglas going crazy in the background. Hitting, smashing things. We race over and it's some big catfight. Blood everywhere, and Toni behind a locked door. Douglas is screaming about cops on the way and not to touch anything. It was all kinds of ugly."

Toni sniffed. "Cheryl told me the baby was my husband's. They'd been together longer than he'd been with me. Worst was, we got together under false pretenses."

"What do you mean?"

She lowered her head and mumbled.

"What?" I leaned closer.

Foul words forced Rain to the edge of his seat. "Douglas was her stalker."

The glass sounded a dull thud as Toni set it on the side table. "Douglas was beside himself, telling me he did it so he could be my hero with Rain out of the country. Said he was playing, immature. But I knew. It was sick. I couldn't live with him anymore, and I'd called Rain."

I wanted to ask how she knew, why she stayed, how she hid it from everyone for so long. Ted's ring screamed at me to keep my mouth shut. I wasn't ready to tell them details of my story. It wouldn't be fair to ask for hers. I could fill in most of the blanks myself.

She snorted. "I don't know how bad it has to be … Anyway, it was finally over. Douglas was furious. Earlier that night,

I'd asked Cheryl to keep Rain out of it. Douglas had threatened him before—"

"Threatened?" I jerked my head. "How?"

He waved me off. "Doesn't matter. Wasn't a real threat. Tell her the rest."

Toni played with her bracelets. "We both said stuff. I told him I wanted a divorce, and he went ape. Like real, BS wicked ape. He worked me over pretty good and he wasn't going to stop this time. Four years and it was getting worse. So, I took the knife, locked myself in the bathroom, and called Rain to say goodbye." She hugged herself and kept her head down. "I needed it all to end." She lifted her head, a sad understanding on both their faces.

He leaned back.

"It ain't something I'm proud of." She faced me. "It ain't something I share much, but it's me. Good or bad."

I tried not to move, not to blink. I didn't want to interrupt or shift focus.

She continued. "When Rain and Cheryl showed up, they were holding hands and Douglas went crazy again. Went after Rain. Kept saying it was his fault." She carefully touched the back of her neck. "Rain had broken the bathroom door in and was trying to get me out when Douglas swung another knife. They went at it, all right. Cheryl got in the middle of it, too. Got knocked around pretty good. Ended up with some scars of their own. I went to the hospital, Rain went to jail."

Rain buttoned his shirt. "Arrested for assault and battery. 701'd after two months."

"What's that?" I asked.

Toni shrugged, continued. "Louisiana law. If an inmate"—
Rain winced at the word—"hasn't been formally charged within two months, he's released."

"You're kidding."

Toni shook her head. "I wish. There was some evidence,
Douglas said. Rain's prints and my blood were on the knife,
Cheryl had some bruises, and that's how Douglas worked it.
But it wasn't enough to stick. I think he didn't want anyone
else to investigate too deep."

"So, you're what? Exonerated?"

"Not quite," Toni said.

Rain's eyes pierced the shadows behind me. "It's more
like in the moment. I was never officially charged, so it's not
like double jeopardy. They can refile with new evidence at any
time within the statute of limitations."

"And how long is that?" I asked.

"Not too long," he said. "We're past that now. But
Douglas ..."

"He'd still use that information against you."

Toni stared at nothing. "He'd certainly try."

Why didn't I let him pour me a stronger drink? "But
weren't Douglas's prints on the knife, too?"

Rain relaxed. "He had the advantage of living there. His
prints were everywhere. Would have been suspicious if they
weren't. Well, Toni and Douglas divorced. Cheryl and I stayed
married. After a year or so, we find out we we're pregnant
again, and I know this one's mine. I wanted to put the good
on top."

"What's that?"

Toni smiled. "What Momma B always used to say. If something goes wrong, you gotta work it 'til it's better and put some good on top."

Rain rested the back of his head on the chair and channeled his memories. "No one cares about the cake 'til they see the frosting. And no one cares 'bout your hard life 'til you make it something worth paying attention to."

They quoted together. "Mud pies always start with mud. You gotta put the good on top."

Rain laughed. "Didn't matter what. Life, to Momma, was meant to share the happy."

"I would like to have known her," I said.

"She would have loved you," Toni said. "I bet she does." She took a fast swallow and stood.

"You leaving?" Rain asked her.

"You want me to stay?" She looked coyly at the both of us.

"Good night, Antoinette." He waved her away.

"Good night, you two." She grinned and closed the doors behind her.

Rain gripped the arms of his chair. I saw his chest rise and fall with determination. I was sleepy, but not too sleepy for this.

I walked over, pulled him up against me, and welcomed his lips to mine.

"BEWARE OF MEN BRINGING
CHOCOLATES AND WINE."

Christopher's words lingered as Anne served dinner.

She chuckled. "Chris is always saying you can't trust a guy who only brings you chocolates and wine. You gotta wait for the one who helps take out the trash."

"I've never brought you chocolates or wine, have I, hon?" He smiled as she sat down.

"And I've given you plenty of trash to take out."

"Yes, you have." He leaned in for a kiss. "And I love you for it."

Ted and I considered each other awkwardly.

"How's that pot roast?" Chris pointed with his fork.

"It's fine, Deputy—uh, Chris," Ted said.

"Good." Chris set his fork down and clasped his hands. "Now. How are those meetings going?"

CHAPTER SEVENTEEN

HOW MANY MEETINGS WOULD MAKE UP FOR last night? The morning fog required copious amounts of strong coffee. Preferably in an IV bag.

And how many times would I wake to find him sleeping sentry in the chair? My throat tightened with delight. I rose to a stealth-stance and headed toward the doors.

"Hey." He ran a hand through that blessed dark hair. "Sleep good?"

"Yeah." I awkwardly smoothed my clothes. He still looked fine. I was pretty sure I didn't.

His throat cleared. "Coffee?"

"Chicory, please."

"Like you live here."

I stopped. "Uhh. What?"

"In New Orlins, Penny." He chuckled. "You're drinking chicory like you already live in New Orlins."

"Right." I smirked in embarrassed hope, and followed him to the kitchen.

"I'd like to borrow the car," I said over my cup.

Toni stared as Lou slurped his grits.

Rain raised an eyebrow. "Well, now. That didn't work out too well last time, did it?"

I bit my lip. Maybe not, but the end result was pretty decent. "I have to pick up a few things."

"Party things?" Lou leaned in with excitement.

"I can take you." I could always count on Toni.

Rain's eyes glistened. "Why don't we all go?"

Humidity dragged itself from the earth into the sun.

Lou laughed and pulled Toni to sit in the back of the SUV. Rain kept my hand in his as much as possible. It was wonderfully awkward.

"Where to first?" Toni asked.

"Food." Lou clapped.

I chuckled. "We just ate an hour ago. Are you hungry already?"

"Party food," he said. "Shrimp gumbo."

Toni glanced up. "I'll make sure Chef adds it to the menu."

"It's added," Rain said.

He drove us into parts of New Orleans I'd already experienced, but it was somehow new, different, with him. The familiar excitement crawled up my spine and bristled my neck. I wanted to be alone with him as soon as possible if for no other reason than to not have to think about anything or anyone else. I needed to be away from him so I could think straight again.

The Hotel Acadia loomed its familiarity around us.

Lou bounced and slapped his hands together. "Can I show her the colors?"

"Of course, bud. Lead on." Rain took us through two hallways and tapped a code on a keypad.

Double doors clicked open, and Lou raced in. Linens filled the floor-to-ceiling shelves. From bright reds to pale yellows to deep purples to everything in between, the expansive walls held a fabric rainbow of tablecloths and napkins and chair covers.

"Is this your favorite?" He asked at every shade. Stacks and rows of folded tables extended into the room. "I like the round ones. Covered in blue." He motioned to the turquoise cloths. "They wave like the ocean."

I imagined him as a child, hiding under the tablecloths during summer parties where the blue would sweep him away from the crowds to peaceful respite. Was he the reason the Manor curtains were blue?

Rain stepped back. "I'm headed to the kitchen. Come with me?"

I peered back at Toni and Lou. Neither moved.

He cleared his throat. "Penny?"

I kept pace as he led me past freezers and storage shelves, through prep stations, stopping occasionally to sample foods or say hello.

"Ben," he called as we entered a small office.

The chef from the festival booth came over and shook my hand. "Hey, Toni's friend. Penny, right? Nice to see ya again. You still enjoying New Orlins?"

"I am." My heart cheered. Rain and Toni weren't the only people in New Orleans who knew me.

Rain took a notepad and scribbled. "We're having a party. Time for you to do your thing."

Ben straightened with pride. "You got it, boss."

"Bring the family."

"Thanks," he said with appreciation. "Listen, Penny. He gives you any trouble, I know where he keeps the arsenic."

"No help." Rain shoved the paper at him and turned to me. "Come on." He tilted his head. "Let's get some coffee." He led me to an intimate patio café where we sat at an ordinary table, drinking ordinary coffee, on an ordinary day.

"So." He smiled. "Let's get to know each other."

"Okay. Tell me about the restaurant."

"What do you want to know?"

"Well." I sipped. "You said you own the whole place, but you're most comfortable in the kitchen. Why?"

"It's all about the food." He leaned back with confidence. "It's always all about the food."

"Tell me."

He straightened, his eyes bright and his hands animated. "When I'm not managing or being the boss, but when I'm creating in the kitchen, it's ethereal. I get to take these tangible objects and see how they go together. I get to make something for someone else's pleasure. You've heard of the New Orlins trinity, right?"

"I think so," I said, enjoying the fact that he didn't really hear me.

"It's a standard down here. A mix of onion, bell pepper, and celery. It's the start of a lot of great food. And it is a little holy. I'm not trying to be sacrilegious, boo, but there's nothing like pairing flavors and aromas, designing these one-of-a-kind dishes that others enjoy." He reached for my hand. "There's just nothing like it."

Could I understand his depth of emotion, participate in his joy? These were his. Being invited to the fringes was enough. For now.

My heart trembled. There was no way I was going to wipe my sweaty hand. That would mean letting him go, and I wasn't about to do that.

Coffee on his breath and his hand in mine. He gave a slight tug and leaned forward.

A whisper of air escaped me and I tilted my head in his direction.

Before either of us could react, the empty chairs scraped and Toni and Lou sat down.

The approaching thunderstorm was trying its best to usher in an early evening.

Toni and I headed to the party supply store. Halloween was a good two weeks away, but New Orleans was already in full spook-mode. It wasn't just decorated for Halloween, it was alive with it. Street lamps glowed orange as they dangled monsters, and witches towered over Jack-o-Lanterns with their menacing grins. Black gauze draped above windows while real spiders and roaches made themselves comfortable in the cotton webs spread through shrubs and fences. Grotesque voodoo dolls hung from fences and doorways, and windows were framed with beads and black cloth as sidewalk soothsayers casted chants and spells.

Toni surveyed the clouds. "Rough one coming in."

I peered up before ducking into the store. We strolled through the first few aisles and I loaded our cart with foam pumpkins and fake leaves.

"Penny, girl. I know you're not from N'Orlins, but down here we kinda celebrate a little bigger than what you've got going on in this cart. You're all set for autumn, but we're planning a Halloween party. Here. Follow me." She pulled the cart down two aisles. I followed and found myself in the midst of all types of costumes from the innocent to the not-so-innocent. "Get into character, girl. It's time to reinvent yourself. Who do you want to be?"

I reached for a long cape.

"You like hiding," she said. It wasn't a question. And it wasn't wrong. "You know, sometimes, not hiding can be the best way of not being noticed."

I grimaced and put the cape back. "You sound like one of my fortune cookies."

She placed a colorful turban on her head and waved her hands. "Oh, yes. I see it now. You will soon have the adventure of a lifetime."

"Give me that." I pulled the turban from her head, inspected it, and put it back on the shelf.

She sighed loudly. "Honey. You're gonna have to let loose. If you want to be alone, you're in the wrong city. If you weren't gonna be a part of the party, you should have said so. Now come on." She rummaged through a few costume pieces. "How 'bout an elf?"

"Do I seem like an elf?"

"You do have that happy-magic going on."

"With devil horns?" I picked up a headband.

We pushed and swayed articles around the racks, pulling out whatever caught our eyes. Candy makers, sultry barmaids, dark angels, and childlike demons all grouped together. It seemed there was no distinguishing between what should be good and what wasn't.

What would Rain think if I showed up in one of the not-so-innocent costumes? Could I pull off a maid-witch? I shook my head and put the outfit back.

A horrific boom shuddered the building and the lights flickered, went out, and returned. A child in the next aisle gave a cry, and a group of young men hollered their appreciation for Mother Nature's display.

"That was something." Good thing I wasn't holding another coffee mug.

"Close to home, for sure," Toni said.

I considered the costumes again. "I have time, don't I? To make a decision?"

"Sure. But you don't want to be stuck with what's left after the best is taken. Besides, sometimes the best decisions are the ones you go with right away, without thinking. Right?"

Her phone rang before I could answer. "This is Toni. Hey, Lou. Yup. Yup, okay. Lou, listen. I need—Rain. Hey, what's— Okay. Yeah, I'll be right there." She hung up and turned to me. "Lou's reacting with the storm and Rain needs to be in the kitchen for a bit. I'm gonna head back to the Acadia."

"What about all this party stuff? I mean, we're already here."

She pulled out her keys and some cash from her bag. "I'm trusting you."

"Are you sure?"

"Yeah," she said slowly. She took a few strides then turned back. "Penny. From here to the restaurant, okay?"

I grinned. "Yes, ma'am."

Enthusiasm gripped me and I continued through the

costumes until I pieced together a blend of cheetah and witchy Cleopatra, reminiscent of a favorite *Twilight Zone* episode.

Getting into the spirit felt daring and a little dark. I liked it. The cart quickly overflowed with ghostly soundtracks, bloody Jack-o-Lanterns, zombie scarecrows. I topped it off with skeleton head bowls and several oversized ravens.

I started toward the checkout and spied the storm through the windows. It was low, heavy. Strong and noisy.

The doors slid open and a familiar face greeted me. "Ms. Embers." Douglas brushed the rain from his sleeves and left his partner at the door. "What are you doing out in this weather?"

My eyes darted about as my hands slipped from the cart. "Detective."

He squinted as he walked up. "Douglas. You okay?"

"Yeah." My heart raced.

He considered me for a moment. "I know what this is." He shook his head. "They told you, didn't they? They told you some story about me, told you I was bad business."

My tongue swelled with the doubts I couldn't speak.

He nodded slowly. "These things they say I done. You really believe I could do them?"

"I—"

"They tell you I'm some bad monster, and you think there's not one hint of evidence other cops could use against me? Answer me one more question, please. What exactly is it they say to you I done that makes you so uncomfortable you can't speak to me in public?"

I glimpsed my new costume. I should have picked the zebra. "They said you were Toni's stalker." How did I not notice how dark his eyes were before this?

He raised his eyebrows and stepped back. "They told you what? I heard some chat before, but this is a new one."

"They were pretty convincing."

"So was Ted Bundy when he first chatted up those girls."

"I doubt Rain's a serial killer."

"But you believe I'm a stalker. C'mon, Penny. What can I do to convince you? I'm not the bad guy. You believe I could do all that, and still be a cop?"

"You don't have any evidence against Rain, but you still want me to think he's a bad guy."

His jaw tightened. "Fair point. But you don't know all that I know."

Fair point. And no proof. Who should I believe, when I didn't know what I believed?

"I'm still on your side, Penny. Don't you forget that."

Was I being unfair, condemning him without facts? Maybe he deserved a second chance. Maybe we all did. I smiled weakly.

He picked up a raven and quoted Edgar Allan Poe before putting it back in my cart. "Getting ready for Halloween?"

"Yup."

Realization slowly crossed his face. "At the Manor? I'm not sure Lou would do too well with a bunch of people playing dress up and making noise. He likes his quiet routine."

"He's excited about it. I'm sure he'll do fine. I have to go."

He followed me to the register and greeted the clerk. "Y'all having any trouble in here?"

"No, sir." She smiled. "But I can cause some if you want to come back later."

Douglas grinned and pointed his toothpick at her. "You keep yourself in line, Abigail. I'm not wanting to be out in this weather any longer than I have to."

"You gonna rescue me later if I drown? Gimme some of that mouth to mouth?"

He grabbed an iced Starbucks from the mini fridge. "Not tonight."

Abigail frowned. "You're no fun anymore, Douglas."

"I'm still plenty o' fun, Abby. Just not with you."

She giggled and started to ring up my items.

His partner strode over, talking into his phone. He motioned to Douglas. "We gotta go."

Abigail shouted as he walked away. "You owe me for that drink."

He winked and waved as he stepped outside. "Find me later."

She turned back to me. "You know Douglas? I mean, you know him well?"

"A little. You?"

Her face flushed. "Naw. I mean, sort of. He helped me out once or twice. Ever since, he checks on me."

"Yeah," I acknowledged. "He's like that."

"Sure is one nice guy. Such a shame what happened to his family."

"What happened?" A queasiness tightened my stomach as I unloaded the rest of the cart.

"Douglas would move mountains to do the right thing, even if no one saw it. He don't care about glory. He's a cop because he believes in making the world a better place. It was years ago. He was kinda new on the force. He got a call for domestic violence." Her eyes darted as she leaned in. Her voice was low, softer. "Turns out it was his cousin and his wife. They been having some marital difficulties, if you know what I mean. According to Douglas, his cousin was arrested at least once before for battery and I don't know what all else. He won't tell me details. But I know that cousin o' his thinks he's all that, beating up on his woman and such."

Every hair on my body sparked to life with each word of this familiar story. "Who ...?"

She handed me the receipt. "I don't remember the cousin's name. I think it had something to do with a President or something. Jefferson? George, maybe. I do remember the wife's name. Cheryl. Always remembered 'cause it reminds me of Cher. You know, the singer? She was beautiful. Douglas shown me her picture once. Such a shame. Wish I could remember the name of the cousin."

"Vernon," I mumbled.

"Yeah, that's it," she said with surprise. "Douglas always felt bad, not being able to help. Even his wife took Cheryl's side, and they weren't that close. You never met a better cop than Douglas. But that cousin of his. Trying to use his money to get hisself off. You know, buying off the cops and judge and all."

I couldn't hear anything else she said. I took my bags and stumbled outside. My ears roared as lightning flashed above the buildings. I couldn't hear the thunder. *Rain.* I turned my face up, letting my eyes blur with each hard drop. *Make it stop.*

CHAPTER EIGHTEEN

HOW DO YOU BOTH TRUST AND NOT TRUST people—the same people—at the same time?

Everyone made perfect sense, which is why none of this made sense.

I left Toni's car with the valet and asked for her at the front desk.

Lost in my thoughts, I jumped when Rain tapped my back.

"I'm sorry." He laughed and tried to pull me into an embrace. "What is it?"

"I saw Douglas."

"Douglas." He gently gripped my shoulders. "Are you okay? Did he hurt you?"

I let him lead me through the familiar hallways, tiny spikes of energy pulsing through me. "I'm fine, I'm okay." But I wasn't. I stopped walking, and started crying. A silent, help-less flood formed by three years of tears.

He reached for me again.

"No." I stumbled back with a jerk. "I'm sorry. I can't do this."

He swallowed and paced. "I understand. And I'm sorry."

"You're sorry? For what?"

He put a hand on the wall and leaned away from me. "You're a smart girl. You have it in you to make up your own mind, and I should let you instead of pressure you. You should hear all sides. Maybe my dislike for my cousin colors how I wanted you to feel about him. I don't discount he's been good for the community. But I know how he's treated the women in my life—"

"Am I in your life, Rain?"

He dropped his arm and stepped close, his voice low. "Do you want to be?"

I couldn't answer. His lips were already on mine.

"No." I lightly pushed.

"No?" A confused hurt flew behind his eyes.

"Not, no. Just ... I need a minute. I need ..." I needed someone outside the situation to tell me what to do. I needed a clear mind. I needed—

"What do you need?" he asked through another kiss.

I tipped my head out of his way. Wine would have been good right about now.

"Food?" He stuffed his hands in his jacket pockets and grinned. "Chef Special tonight. Blackened Salmon."

"Food." Because I'd always made really bad decisions on an empty stomach.

As we walked into Restaurant D'Arcy, he released my hand. His haunting continued to torment me.

Toni and Lou sat across from each other at our table. Our table. What a nice thought.

Rain sat with his back to the wall, which left the only available seat across from him. An undistracted view. I couldn't hold his hand, but I could watch him all I wanted.

I hated being in her restaurant, but I loved being with him. And I had to admit the food made it worthwhile.

"It's dark." Lou jabbed toward the large windows.

"Hey. Trade." Toni stood.

"Musical chairs?" Rain grinned.

"It's still dark." Lou took her seat.

"Yeah, but now you can't see it as much."

He pointed to the large mirrors. "Douglas says even if you can't see it, that doesn't mean it's not there."

I peeked in the mirror. The reflection gave a false sense of immensity to the dining room clamoring with patrons and staff, and the windows with their night view of the city.

Rain met my gaze through the mirror. We were smaller there, less significant.

I excused myself to go to the ladies' room.

Toni offered to join me.

"Not necessary," I fake-smiled, needing the solitude.

She followed me anyway.

The opulent environment distracted me from my irritation. The overhead music was softly playing Sinatra's "Witchcraft." Of course. It couldn't be "My Way" or "All the Way" or any way at all. I rolled my eyes and washed my hands with scented soap that, on any other day, I would have appreciated more.

Toni waited patiently as I stalled for time.

My mojo bag hung heavy around my neck. I checked my lipstick, my teeth, my hair. There was no avoiding it. She wasn't going to leave me alone to figure things out.

She caught my arm as I strolled past. "He's trying."

"He—what?"

"Sugar, he's not good at the trust thing, either. But he's trying. Give him the chance to meet you on his terms. He wouldn't let you stay if he thought ..." Her voice trailed as her eyes dimmed. "He's a patient man. He's asking you to be the same."

"We're getting there," I told her, neglecting to mention she and Lou interrupted our coffee kiss earlier.

"He told me you saw Douglas. I'm sorry I left you."

"Not your fault," I said.

"We good, then?"

My phone buzzed with an incoming text. *Where are you?*

I shrugged away from her. "We're good. We're all good."

She eyed the screen. "Who's Ted?"

Lou's humming was low but noticeable. Toni smirked. "Take the seat across from Rain," she told him. "No windows, no mirrors."

"Just my brother," he said and bounced over, leaving me no choice but to sit next to Rain. I glared at her over my wine glass.

"Order something good?" she asked.

"You know I did." Rain rested his arm on the table between us.

It wasn't fair. He knew I wanted to slow down, to think. He wasn't making this easy. I didn't want to choose sides based on emotions.

Maybe it was time to step back from this New Orleans magic and remember who I was, who I wanted to be without them. I took a quick sip then slid the glass in front of Rain and picked up my water goblet. Tonight, I was going to think things through, and do things differently. Without missing a beat, he casually moved the wine to the other side of his plate.

But his hand was still there. What was I supposed to do with that? Could a person like someone, without knowing everything about them? How deep was too deep? How deep wasn't deep enough?

I put my arm on the table next to his and pretended not to notice the pull between us.

The appetizers and salads arrived. I was glad to have a reason not to talk. It was hard keeping myself in the conversation without rehearsing some later-when-I-get-you-alone speech.

Lou prattled on about his color choices for the party, and Toni expanded on the details.

Rain encouraged them to continue.

I realized he had two fingers on my hand and was puzzled at when and how it happened. It was a comfortable, natural feeling. Until I realized he was touching me, and it became an uncomfortable, natural feeling. I wanted more than his two fingers. I withdrew my hand to my lap.

He glanced at me and curled his hand, all while still talking to Lou.

Our main course was served as promised.

"Blackened salmon. I remembered." Rain smiled.

"Cheryl didn't like fish," Lou said.

Toni shushed him.

"What? She didn't," he replied.

"No, she didn't." Rain leaned back.

Toni shifted toward Lou. "Douglas hates green beans."

"I love green beans. Do you, Penny Josie?"

"I do," I said. "Am I the only one here who hasn't been married?"

"Penny Josie, I've never been married. But I'm not marrying you."

Rain and Toni chuckled.

"And why not, may I ask?" I feigned indignation.

"Who would take care of Rain if I took you away from him?"

My cheeks blushed a three-alarm fire.

Rain gripped his watch and tried not to laugh. His shaking torso gave him away.

Dinner was exquisite and excruciating. It went too fast and lasted too long.

"Dessert?" Lou clapped.

Rain winked. "Dessert?"

"Yes, please." Lou leaned with enthusiasm.

Rain stood. "Well, this could take a few minutes. If y'all will excuse me."

Toni and Lou entertained themselves with knock-knock jokes, while I enjoyed the distraction of not being near Rain. I planned all the messages I wasn't going to send to Ted.

Lightning flashed a conversation in the distance, and the thunder agreed.

Rain soon returned with four small cups. "Rainfall Dessert."

I took a spoonful of the creamy, yellow-white mixture and tasted a new kind of wonderful. My eyes involuntarily closed. "What is this heaven?"

I heard his approval and opened my eyes.

"You like it? It's a seasonal favorite. Vanilla gelato with roasted apple and crushed pralines, topped with homemade toffee crumbs. Pretty decadent."

"Pretty delicious!"

Toni moved forward. "Isn't it? He donates profits from the dessert to the community."

Rain was bewitching me through the food, and I experienced the voodoo in my second spoonful.

"How would you change it?" He set his chin on his fist and pointed with his spoon.

I took another slow bite. "Add a light weave of maple syrup."

"Done." He smiled. It was a different smile than I'd seen before. It was the smile of making someone else smile.

I wanted to savor every moment, every taste. I also needed the evening to finish. I needed us to get back to Greyford Manor as soon as possible.

"Lou." I tried to distract myself between bites. "Why do you like the color blue so much?"

"The rougarous don't come out in the daylight. And they don't swim."

Rain's posture lifted almost unnoticeably.

"The rougarous," I repeated.

Toni reached for her water. "Why else do you like blue?"

He smiled. "It sounds like Lou."

Rain relaxed. "That it does, bud."

A ridiculous white flash filled the windows and reflected off the mirrors, followed by a tremendous thunder as the rain assaulted the outside. The dining room buzzed with low chatter.

Lou clapped his hands to his ears and began his rocking hum.

"We done here?" Rain stood and took one last sip of wine.

CHAPTER NINETEEN

I REALLY SHOULD HAVE TAKEN MY STRUMBEL-las T-shirt with me everywhere.

We were back at the Manor, but this time, I'd left my belongings at the French Market Inn. I didn't care anymore. He was here, asking me to stay. A T-shirt was insignificant in comparison.

Toni and I started upstairs. There had to be something, somewhere, in this house I could sleep in.

The doorbell rang as we reached the landing and peered down.

Rain hollered up. "You expecting someone?"

Douglas entered and nudged him aside.

Toni and I hustled down.

Douglas tipped his head. "Penny. Hon."

Toni shifted behind Rain and put a trembling hand on his shoulder. He fisted one hand and covered hers with the other.

I wavered in my own space away from each of them.

Douglas eyed me. "Penny, I believe this is yours."

"My laptop?" I started forward but came to a quick halt as a man walked through the door. He was blond, tall, with a healthy tan and a grin a girl could drown in.

"Hi, babe."

I gasped. "Ted?"

Rain's arms fell to his side. "Well, Penny. Looks like your baggage is here."

Ted scooped me into a fierce hug. "Gypsy. What happened? When you called the other night from that bar, I didn't know what to think except—"

"You called him?" Rain blinked.

I broke free as best I could, but Ted kept a strong arm around my shoulder. "Rain, Toni. This is Ted."

Rain hesitated before extending his hand.

"Nice to meet you," Ted said.

Lou took a step back. "Who's he?"

"I'm the fiancé."

"Ex-fiancé," I said to Rain.

Lou paced away, hummed, and pointed. "No. No. He's not good here. I can tell. He doesn't belong."

Douglas stepped forward. "A guy willing to fly cross country for ya must be a keeper."

"What are you doing here?" I withdrew toward Rain.

"You called him, don't you remember?" Rain crossed his arms, and I stopped.

"I ... don't." I gulped.

Rain clenched his teeth. "You remember anything about that night?"

The wounds oozed through my heart and soul.

Ted laughed his deep, familiar laugh. "That's my Gypsy Firecracker." He smoothed the hair behind my ears. I used to find him adorable. "You called from our piano bar we always talked about, asked me to come get you." He squinted. "You really don't remember, do you?"

Rain's eyebrows raised. "'Our' bar? Thought your coming to New Orlins was spontaneous, not a planned thing."

"It was. I mean, it wasn't." I was caged, on exhibit in front of everyone, and there was no way to hide. If they would stop throwing facts at me, I could figure all this out.

Ted shifted. "Aw, c'mon now. We always talked about coming to New Orleans for our honeymoon."

I pulled him toward the Great Room. "We need to talk. Now."

Douglas smirked and raised his shoulders.

"You can leave now." Rain steamed.

Douglas pointed at Ted. "I'm his ride. Can't leave 'til he leaves."

I raised a hand to Rain. "Ten minutes. Please."

"I'll put on the coffee." Rain headed to the kitchen.

Ted stalled. "Babe, slow down. Let me see you."

I closed us into the Great Room, and he held me at arm's length. "Dang, girl. What happened to you?"

"Happened?" I stood back and cocked my head. "What the—? How are you even here?"

"You're a little unkempt, Gypsy." He reached for my hair again.

I almost melted. Seeing him made me dizzy. But not the same dizzy Rain made me. This was a convoluted, upside-down-spinning-crazy-roller-coaster dizzy.

I had thrown away so much of him when he left. I'd buried him under necessity and forward movement and forgot the good parts of who he was. For two years I'd relished the animosity I'd fostered when thinking of him. For two years I'd let Chris and Anne take care of me when I couldn't take

179

care of myself, and I'd faked enough sense of strength to pretend none of it happened or none of it mattered. But now he was here, resurrecting himself into my heart and bringing it back with him. And I was too exhausted to find room for any hatred.

I shouldn't have called him. I didn't mean to. But isn't that how we stayed together for so long to begin with?

Anne would have left him out with the trash.

He always had a way of keeping me off balance. Havoc grew its spidery legs and tingled through my body. I wasn't ready to let him in again but here he was, anyway. Why had we split?

I escaped his reach, picked up the glass Rain left last night, and drank two sips of melted ice mixed with warm liquor residue.

"Josie. Why are you being like this? You called, said you missed me and were in trouble. You asked me to come rescue you."

I snorted. Ted was never the rescuing type.

"I get it," he said. "Same old Josie. You can reach out, but I can't reach back, right? You still think everyone's trying to tell you what you're doing is wrong, and you're determined to prove them wrong. To prove *me* wrong." He pointed to my hand.

"What?" I waved emphatically.

"Still wearing the ring."

"Wrong hand, genius."

"Babe. You're still wearing it."

I pulled the ring off and threw it at the sofa. "Now I'm not. And I don't need you to rescue me."

"From what I hear, and by the looks of it, you do." His eyes squinted and his lips tightened.

"You evaluate my life in one shot, Theodore?"

"Life? This isn't your life, Josie. You're a visitor here. And not having that great a time, either. I heard all about it from that detective."

"Douglas?" My eyes widened. "He's not exactly impartial."

"I hope not." Ted took a delicate step toward me. "Babe. Seriously. He told me enough. Sounds like he's been doing a good job watching over you. Sounds like you're not watching out for yourself, as usual."

I growled a guttural girl-scream. "I'm trying to figure things out. I didn't mean to call you. I'm sorry. But I'm not in any danger. I can take care of myself. I wish everyone would let me—"

"But you did call, Gypsy. You did. You called me. And I'm here. Okay? What do you know about these people? That guy out there has a record for domestic violence."

"It's a misunderstanding."

"I don't know how you misunderstand putting your fist in your wife's face. Twice."

Of course, he wouldn't. Ted's tricks were more subtle than that. "Is that what Douglas told you? How did you find me, anyway?"

He waited for me to make eye contact. "I called Chris."

Oh, great. "What did he say?"

"Well, first, that you need to call and check in. Anne's a little upset you didn't make it to Sunday dinner last week."

The ring glistened as Ted plucked it from the sofa and sat down. "After you called, I couldn't reach you back. I asked Chris for help. All he would tell me was that he knew you were here. I figured if you were in trouble, I should come.

Turns out he knew through his connections. The police out here know who you are, babe. What's that all about?"

I turned from his get-out-of-jail-free smile. "Stop calling me that."

"Okay." He put the ring on his pinky and lifted his hand. "Josie. What do you want from me?"

"I want nothing from you. I don't hear from you for two years—"

"That was *your* choice. I reached out to you."

"You gave me an ultimatum."

"And you made your choice."

My aerobic anger took me in laps around the long table. "How? Tell me what I should have done differently."

He leaned back and pursed his lips. "You should have held on, seen us through the rough patch."

Rough patch. I stroked my arm as the memory of a thousand tiny daggers surfaced. "No."

"I guess I didn't realize it was that easy for you to let me go. Well, whatever helps you sleep at night. Unless." He jerked his head toward the foyer. "Is he helping you sleep at night?"

"You can go—" I reached for the door knob.

He sprang up. "I'm sorry. That was unnecessary."

"Yeah, it was."

He crept like a cat about to pounce, and tucked his head lower. "I'm sorry, ba—Josie. You said you were at our piano bar, so I called. The guy remembered you. Said some other guy came and carried you off. I thought you were in real trouble. I got on the next plane—"

"Three days later."

"Well, it took some calls to find you, doll." His anger was rising through his muscles.

"You could have given me the benefit of the doubt."

"Gypsy. Are you serious right now? You call me out of the blue to say you're in trouble, and you're here, and I should ignore that because, oh, I'm sorry, I'm supposed to know you weren't serious? No. I figured if you were here, in our place, I should be, too. I haven't stopped thinking about you. Not since the call. Not in two years." With each word he'd brought himself closer until he was holding me again. He smelled of cigar and Axe cologne.

"I'm not in trouble. Someone stole my laptop. I filed a report. Douglas has been checking up on me. That's how the cops know who I am."

"You sure?"

"Yes, Ted. I'm sure I don't have my laptop, and I'm sure I haven't been hospitalized or arrested."

"Whoa." He let me go. "Let's back the train up, okay? Start over? Hi, how are you? Ted Jameson. I'm trying to find my girl. You seen her?"

My involuntary laughter angered me.

"There you are." He reached for a hug.

I turned. "Not your girl anymore, Ted."

"Been a while, huh?" We sat at the table. "Josie, I messed up. I wasn't there for you when Martin died. Or before. It wasn't enough, seeing you at the funeral. But after you called, I thought, what did my little Gypsy Firecracker go and get herself into now? When Chris and Anne couldn't reach you, I was sick. I had to come find you. And the closer I got, the more I realized, I don't want to let you go again."

His little Gypsy Firecracker. I'd not been that for quite a while. I missed belonging to someone. But there was someone else I wanted to belong to now.

"This can't work," I said.

"Why not?"

I headed to the door. "It's been too long. I've changed."

"Changed?" His lip turned. "Babe—I'm sorry. I know you don't like that. But seriously. Babe. If you've changed, if you didn't want me here in New Orleans with you, why did you go to that bar, get drunk, and call me instead of whoever it is you're living with now?"

"We're not living together. I'm staying at the French Market Inn." My independent indulgence should have wounded him, shown him I could do things on my own.

"You haven't been there in days."

"Privacy Act. No way you really know that."

He smirked. "And that confirms it."

"Just go, Ted." I gave him a dismissal wave and went to find Rain. Ted was five paces behind me as I entered the kitchen. The familiar smell of chicory tried to comfort me.

Rain faced the coffee pot. I stood as close as I could without acknowledging him. He poured me a cup and carried it to the island where Toni and Lou were sitting. Nothing like a big group for a private discussion.

Douglas stood by the sink, an interesting sneer on his face. He extended his arms behind him to grip the edge of the counters. "Used to have some good times round here, didn't we, Vernon?"

Rain scowled and circled in front of Toni's line of vision. "You're not welcome here, Douglas. Not now, not ever."

Douglas picked up his coffee. "That any way to talk to family? Besides, I'm only here to make sure Ted sees that Penny's all right. She did call him to rescue her, after all."

Rain's jaw tightened. Toni placed a shaking hand on his arm as his neck tensed.

I set my cup down and turned to Douglas. "You need to leave. And you need to take him with you."

Ted placed his focus on me. "I misinterpreted Josie's call. Let me say this." He took the ring off his pinky and held it up. "Josie, I'm not perfect. But I still love you. I've always loved you. You know it's true. We've been through it all. But I'm not sorry for my mistakes, because learning from them, growing through them, has made me better. And you agree with me." He waved a finger at Douglas. "Let's go."

"Sure thing." Douglas swigged his coffee and let the cup clank into the sink.

"One more thing." Ted took my left hand. "I'm gonna stay around for a while. If you'd like to get together, if you'd like us to do New Orleans like we'd planned, call me. I miss my Gypsy." He slipped the ring on my finger, kissed my cheek, and walked out.

Douglas chuckled as he followed.

I stretched my fingers and inspected the ring. I'd missed it on this hand. Did that somehow mean I missed Ted?

Lou pointed. "You got a ring."

"What are you gonna do, sugar?" Toni whispered.

I dropped my hand and caught Rain holding his coffee with a death grip. When I fingered the ring, he glanced at me and left the room.

The door slammed.

I longed for melancholy jazz but all I heard was silence.

The darkness of New Orleans both pushed and pulled at my soul, leaving questions and answering nothing.

I ripped the red mojo bag from my neck and tossed it away. It hadn't worked after all. Whatever it was I thought I wanted, it had been far longer than the required week and I was still unfulfilled.

Toni gazed at me with sad understanding. "I know you're not gonna run away again. But I also know you can't be here right now." She tipped her head toward Lou. "I can't leave." She slid her keys to me. "Go take care of you. But be careful."

CHAPTER TWENTY

BUILDINGS REFLECTED THE NIGHT AS SIDE-walks brought me back along a known path. I stopped in front of Bits & Bones. I slipped Ted's ring—my ring—onto my right ring finger. It didn't belong there anymore, but it sure didn't belong on the left one.

Almost against my will, I pulled the door open and entered. I weaved a slow wind among the dark stacks and found Momma Tristan arranging skeleton heads on the bottom shelf of aisle four.

"Hello." I cleared my throat. "Wasn't sure you'd still be open."

She eyed me with an intense smile. "Hello, writer. How are you?" She stood and waved to the air. "Welcome, welcome. The spirits are never closed. You find it yet?"

"It?"

"What you look for. Has the ending come to you yet? Have you started your beginning?" She motioned for me to follow her to the front.

I shook my head. How could I tell her I'd given up believing in something I didn't really believe in, in the first place?

She walked behind the counter, pulled out an orange mojo bag and quickly began to fill it. "Orange embraces change, clears a path, gives direction."

"Thanks." I wanted to protest, but like the first time, I was captivated and unable to move. Instead, an eagerness formed in my stomach and pushed its way to my wallet as I bought not only the mojo bag and lanyard, but a multi-layered candle in a tall glass jar. I needed something more to believe in, and this seemed harmless, yet hopeful, enough to start.

"Stronger together." She fisted the mojo bag into my hand. "Remember what you already know."

She wasn't very good at this spell thing. I had no one to be stronger together with.

"It's okay," she said with her wisdom. "Spending time alone brings you back to your people. You must remember who is true to you. The ones who put forth the most effort to be with you will not always be the ones you see first. You must let yourself know what you know, and feel what you feel."

I bit my lip and wondered what she knew about my life, about me, that I didn't.

"When you are ready, you put on your mojo. You see it come back to you."

The light rain escorted me back to my hotel. The room was confining, a reminder of the freedom I'd had—and not had—at the Manor.

Strong coffee brewed as I showered. I grabbed a cup, climbed on top the comforter, and dumped out Momma Tristan's bag.

The candle was inviting, peaceful on the nightstand. How much did I pay for the lighter she'd thought to add to my purchase?

I cursed myself for allowing the melancholy in. I cursed myself more for drinking coffee instead of liquor.

The TV news announced proper conditions for a new tropical storm in the Atlantic, as the candle caught air and flickered to a steady glow.

I opened my notebook and let the pen flow in abstract patterns. Crude planes, raindrops, IV's. Cemetery vaults and triple X's. Everything blended and nothing was defined.

New Orleans hadn't been the line of demarcation I'd hoped for.

My soul glinted and I pulled the new mojo lanyard over my head. Sinatra always said orange was the happiest color.

My pen carried over pages as my thoughts distracted me from the task.

I closed the book, slid it under the pillow, and slipped myself under the sheets. The candle flickered violently when I turned out the light. It had burned through half the black layer and was still going strong. I pushed it to the center of the table and let it hypnotize me into a haze.

The Mississippi River was in the air and even though it was late and a few blocks away, I thought I heard the Natchez Steamboat jazzing its way along. The notes were a slight echo and sometimes lost in the wind, if they were there at all.

The remote clicked the TV off, and the tangible dark was almost too much. The music emanating through my head-phones didn't soothe anything. The candle danced its flame in time with my thoughts. I leaned up and stared, wanting—needing—something amazing to happen.

I took a lukewarm gulp from the coffee mug as Otis Red-ding began to tell me, "A Change is Gonna Come." Familiar four-letter words came out of my mouth as I turned on the light and retrieved my notebook.

A breeze waved the curtains but did nothing to assuage the air. I sighed, pulled the T-shirt away from my skin, and drank the last of the coffee while remembering my first night at Greyford Manor.

There had to be something more to letting go, something deeper than doodling. I sketched Marie Laveau's tomb, a terrible sketch hidden under layers of colored XXX's. The artistry took over. I etched again over each set of X's, letting my prayers and desires come forth with each one. "If I should die before I wake ..."

There was no wanted poster above the overflowing brochure kiosk. I picked up every bit of reading material I could get my hands on and stuffed them into my backpack, then blindly selected one like a game of paper roulette, grabbed a coffee from PJ's, and headed out.

The weather was warmer, sunnier. My enhanced mood had to be due to more than the natural Vitamin D. Purging into my notebook must have done its magic. I was less confused, less intimidated. I was just Josie, enjoying a coffee, doing Josie things.

The New Orleans Glassworks window displays were full of intricate, colored sculptures. The doors led me to a master craftsman creating detailed work with nothing more than his torch and tweezers. The fluid design captivated me as he heated, rotated, plucked, and continued to manipulate the fluid glass into a multi-colored cornucopia.

I immediately signed up to blow my own glass. My instructor handed me and two other enthusiasts blowpipes and helped us design our crafts. She showed us how to gather molten glass and move it to the marver where I tried to roll mine into shape. The back-and-forth process took several tries, and twice I found myself with a jumbled mess of nothingness. Still no expert, I was semi-proud when my third attempt gave me something that wasn't so easy to shatter in the process. A pout crept up when the instructor locked our creations away to cool overnight. I shrugged and waved goodbye to the uniquely formed orange tumbler.

The next brochure led me to the Crescent City Farmers Market. Vibrant aromas fought for my attention and the multitude of flavors strained to attract my taste buds. Vendors populated overflowing stands and tables with produce of all kinds. A longing for Lou's garden tried to shadow my moment.

Roasted pecans, dried fruits, and more beckoned me to continue. After visiting more vendors than I could count, I stopped near the exit and purchased two clusters of blue, pink, and white forget-me-nots to lighten my soul.

I couldn't escape the intrusion of modern buildings, so I took advantage and sauntered into Tiffany & Co. I touched the perfumes like they were diamonds, spritzed one into the air and walked quickly but gently under it. The light fragrance lingered on my skin and cooled my senses.

I grinned when the clerk offered to gift wrap my crown charm.

"No." I secured it on my bracelet, between the dangling typewriter and alligator. "But I'll take the bag anyway."

It was mid-afternoon. Too late to start another adventure, too early to turn in.

I didn't recognize my hunger until I detoured past Johnny's Po-Boys on the way back to the Inn. A sampling of shrimp and grits and a half sandwich filled my mouth and stomach.

I missed homemade foods and being in the kitchen. I missed my chef.

I wanted to know he missed me, too. I wanted to know if I returned to the desert, if there was a wildfire or an earthquake, that I'd be on his speed-dial before the emergency announcements ended. I wanted to know he breathed my name because he didn't know how to not breathe it.

Momma Tristan was wrong. I didn't want to feel everything I felt and know everything I knew.

I sipped the air from the bottom of the coffee cup.

CHAPTER TWENTY-ONE

"SURPRISED I DIDN'T HEAR FROM YOU FOR A FEW days." Ted scanned the building as I parked Toni's car. "Applebee's?"

"I figured you'd like the food." I lied. I really didn't care where we ate as long as it wasn't any of the places I'd been with Toni and Rain, or any of the places I wanted to go. Ted belonged to his own memories, not the ones I wanted to make without him.

We sat in a side booth and studied the menus.

"You still clean up nice." His chin plopped into his hand. "Why were you limping earlier?"

"It's nothing. There was a storm and I got startled, broke a mug."

"Barefoot as usual?"

"Of course."

"And you stepped in it and cut yourself, right? History repeating itself?"

Ted always thought he knew more about me than he did. "Don't worry about it. It's not your history. And you're not my storm."

"Whatever you say, Gypsy."

I wish time had been cruel to him. "What do you want?"

"You." He winked and ordered two mixed drinks.

"Lemon water." I shook my head.

"You change that much?" he asked.

"Someone had to." I pulled my hand to my lap before he could grasp it. The hint of his cologne lingered in my nostrils. He had always been the one to ground me. Until he couldn't.

The drinks arrived. I chugged half the blue margarita before gripping my water.

He pressed his palms on the table. "Can we talk honestly, Josie?"

"Sure."

"What are we doing here? I mean, okay. I'm not the jealous type—"

I snorted and reached for a napkin.

He squirmed. "Listen. Yeah, I didn't like you going out with other guys on me."

"He was the hospice worker, Ted, and he was married. We weren't dating. We were preparing."

"You talked to him more than me."

The inside of my cheeks hurt.

"Josie." He tilted his head and gave me that quirky Ted-look that always got my affections. His hair flopped over his eyes, so I reached to fix it. I probably shouldn't have done that.

"Remember that time at Ruby's on the pier?" His smile faded as he recalled something I no longer wanted to see.

"You'll have to be more specific." He never could say everything out loud.

"That time." He waved his hand around. "You remember. I thought you were gonna choke."

"I didn't expect to swallow a ring in my brownie."

"Why'd you say yes, Gypsy?"

"We were good together, Ted. Until we weren't."

"Could we be again?" He pulled the ring off my finger and twisted it gently between his thumb and forefinger.

Our server appeared with the food. "What a beautiful ring."

"Thanks." Ted grasped my left hand tight and slid the ring on. "Been a long time coming."

"That was unnecessary." I whispered loudly after she left.

"I didn't lie." He had a way of turning the truth just enough to either amuse or annoy me, and I couldn't decide which emotion I wanted to invest in right now.

I tugged on the ring. He put his hand over mine and his brows furrowed. "Don't make a scene, Gypsy. Not now. Let's evaluate."

I stared out the window and let his words echo into me. What was I doing here? What did we have to evaluate? Why was that ring still on my finger?

Too many thoughts tried to filter through the noise. Martin, Ted, the break up, the funeral, the stolen laptop, Greyford. Why was Ted the one breaking my emotional dams? I didn't want someone to care for me, or the opportunity to screw things up again. Or worse, make them work. I especially didn't want any of it with him.

But maybe familiar pain with Ted was better than unfamiliar loneliness when thinking about something else ... someone else.

Nothing sorted out. Martin always said I had a way of dumping the fridge into the omelet.

I ignored him as he watched me process. Seriously, what was I doing here?

"Congratulations!" I heard a man say. He approached with our server. "I'm Jeromy, the manager. I understand you just got engaged. What a fine couple. We'd like to help you celebrate. Your meal's on the house."

Ted grinned and shook his hand. "Well, thank you. See that, babe? C'mon. Give us a celebratory kiss." He leaned across the table, but the food was in the way. The heat nauseated me. "We'll fix this." He slid to his feet and pulled me into his arms, kissing me more than I wanted to be kissed by him. At first.

The surrounding patrons clapped and cheered, and Jeromy slapped him on the shoulder. "Treat her right."

Ted loosened his hold. "I intend to."

I stood in a state of embarrassment and anger. And then horror.

Rain! He was halfway between the door and our booth, his motorcycle helmet in his hand. He fisted his other hand and stared at Ted. "Yeah. Treat her right. If she'll let ya."

"Rain. Wait." I chased as he pushed his way outside.

We were three rows into the crowded parking lot before he turned back to me.

"Congratulations," he spewed.

"This isn't—we're not—Ted is just being Ted." I shuffled half a step closer.

"And from the looks of it, you're just being you."

"What does that mean?"

"It means, what is this, Penny? Love the one you're with?"

I bit my finger. "How did you find us?"

"Us." He sneered and waved his cell phone. "I didn't know you still had Toni's car. I tracked the GPS and went in for her, not you. This was a lucky bonus."

"You stalked her? What, does it run in the family?"

"Knock it off." He straddled his motorcycle.

My mouth puckered around unspoken obscenities. "Can I help you?" I said in my best white girl, street thug manner and pulled my hair to distract the copperhead from surfacing.

The engine roared, reminded me of the screaming baby on the plane. Reminded me I wanted to cry, scream, kick, and fuss. Reminded me I couldn't.

His voice echoed its anger. "I'm done taking care of you."

"I didn't ask you to take care of me," I yelled. "I don't want you to take care of me." It was a lie and by the squint of his eyes, he knew it.

"What do you want, Gypsy?" Ted sauntered up and dropped an arm over my shoulders.

My teeth hurt. "I am not your babe. I am not your Gypsy. You get it? We're done."

"Then why'd you call him?" Rain asked. "And why you still wearin' his ring?"

My throat closed and my head buzzed. I ripped the ring off and threw it to the ground.

Ted retrieved it as Rain sneered and put his helmet on.

Ted stood tall. "Thanks. I'll take her from here."

"Take her, then." Rain kicked his bike and revved off.

CHAPTER TWENTY-TWO

NEW FORGET-ME-NOTS CAME TO LIFE IN MY crafted orange glass, next to the unlit candle.

I pulled out my cell phone and messaged Douglas. *Talk.*

He showed up twenty minutes later with two coffees, and we sat at a table tucked in the corner of the pool patio. "You got twenty minutes." He tapped at his watch. "Go."

"Why?" I asked.

"Why, what?"

"You know what. No warning. You show up at Rain's, and bring Ted with you. How did you know I'd be there? Or was that the point?"

"Slow down, Penny. It ain't like that." He kept eye contact and took a slow slip.

"You were going to flaunt Ted in front of Rain whether I was there or not, weren't you? I can't believe I thought—"

"You do a lot of thinking without a whole lot of processing, Penny. What would it serve me to do what you're saying? I took a chance you'd be with Rain, and since it was late, I figured he'd be at the Manor."

"Why didn't you call?"

"I did," he said. "But Rain has a habit of not answering when he sees my name on the Caller ID, and your voicemail was full. That's all there is to it."

"That's all?" I squirmed and made a mental note to clear the voicemails.

He reached to inspect my bracelet. "I see some Toni influence here. That girl always had good taste. Couldn't run her boutique without it. Hold on." He pulled something out of his wallet, set it on the table, and pushed it toward me. "Take it. Been carrying that one around for a while."

I inspected the silver Mardi Gras mask charm. "Why?"

"'Cause, it suits you. 'Cause you're collecting charms and that's a good one to have. It'll remind you, down here in N'Awlins, people hide more than what you think they do. And maybe it'll remind you it's okay to be yourself and take the mask off once in a while."

"Thanks, but I mean, why do you have it in your wallet?" I clipped it to my collection.

He leaned back. "You could say they're my own kinda mojo. Been holding onto that one a few months. Glad to have someone to give it to."

"What's the deal with you and Rain?"

"What's the deal with *you* and Rain?" he retorted. "Or that Ted fella?"

The charms jangled in my silence. I raised my coffee without drinking.

"There ain't no deal, Penny. We're cousins. That don't mean we're friends." He studied his coffee and chomped his toothpick. "I get it. I'm not a member of the Vernon Rainier Fan Club. And maybe in some ways I ain't tried as hard as I could to mend things. So." He tapped his finger on the table. "You're fresh to the city, to the situation. What do you think?"

"You both say maybe things have been misinterpreted. After all this time, why don't you both just come together and try to work things out?"

"Do you think we've misinterpreted each other? Him and me, I mean."

I stared at him. "I don't know."

Douglas gave me a sideways grin. "See, now. I don't believe that."

I fingered the Mardi Gras charm. "I think there's a lot of hate between you two, and I think you're okay with it like that. I think Toni got caught up in it and you used her to get back at Rain for whatever. I think I wish this coffee had Kahlua in it."

He stood, looked at his watch, and held out his hand. "Come with me."

"What?"

He smiled. "Some place I wanna show you."

"Don't you have to be somewhere soon?"

"Yeah. But this is important. I think you'll find more answers this way."

I couldn't stop fidgeting with my bracelet.

Douglas parked in the back lot of some brick building and circled around the front of the car, hand over his hip holster, his eyes scanning the area before he opened my door.

The barrage of faint music greeted my ears as we passed a few employee-access doors, then through a small crowd who nodded and gestured to him in recognition.

"Sit." He pointed to a row of chairs in the back.

"Uh-uh." I started to push past him.

He put a finger to his lips and pointed again. "You don't get to talk right now. You get to listen."

He ignored my sideways glances.

The crowd came in, found their seats. Some said hi to him, and tried to introduce themselves to me. I knew what was coming. I'd been here before. I wasn't about to be friends with these people. I wasn't—couldn't be—one of them. Not again.

He looked at me now and then—a concerned, it's-going-to-be-okay look. A familiar connection began to tug at me.

Then came that awful question. "Would anyone like to share?"

Was he asking me? I froze. The rules hadn't changed: You can't share if you'd had a drink within the last twenty-four hours. I remembered that from my first meeting. My many first meetings.

How did he know? Or was he guessing? Was I that transparent? I wasn't about to tell him. I didn't want to talk. I wanted to drink.

I raised my motor-fuel coffee and halted midway as he walked to the rickety podium.

"Hey. I'm Douglas. I'm an alcoholic."

I tried to listen, but my heart pounded too loudly for me to understand.

Three years and some odd months of sobriety. Everyone clapped politely.

I closed my mouth and swallowed.

He spoke to everyone. He focused only on me. "I was married. Made a mess of it, of course. Cheated on her, blamed it on the drink. I could do nothing wrong, and she could do nothing right. Thought I was hot stuff, man of the house. She saw the façade. All I saw was how others hurt her, and I was going to be the one to rescue her. But she didn't, didn't need to be rescued. Except from me."

I bit my lip. Douglas's words created a recognition in me.

He went on about the differences between care and control, and it was eerily familiar. Like a mass-marketed guide for anger management distributed to police nationwide.

"She ended up leaving me for a better life. Thing is, the drink was just a symptom. Not the cure. It took me taking her to rock bottom with me, before I got it. Before I sobered up. So, I lost my wife. Lost my family. Dang near lost my job. But I'm sober now." He exhaled with a laugh. "Man, these steps are hard."

The rest of the meeting blurred, but before we left, he made sure to point out the sign near the door.

What you see here
What you say here
When you leave here
Let it stay here.

Jones's Pub was a strange place to go after an AA meeting. Douglas ordered a water, and a rum and Coke. I took one of each, too, to make him comfortable. To make me comfortable.

"Why'd you order that?" I pointed.

He turned the glass, studied it. "The moment I make a

conscious choice to sip this drink that's in my hand is the moment I lose everything. Keeping it here, just out of reach, makes me a better man than I used to be. Any time, any day, things can change. But I'm the one who has the power to react, or resist." He pushed it to the opposite corner of the table and pulled his water closer.

"Does your partner know?" I asked.

"Denton? I never volunteered this information, if that's what you mean."

"I mean—"

He waved me quiet. "I know what you mean. Truth is, I can't say for certain. He's a smart guy. Got a good head on his shoulders. He's got a knack for getting to what's buried."

"How long you been partners?"

"Close to four years, now."

I tried not to do the mental math, tried not to figure out if Chase was around when ... I noticed my foot was tapping.

He noticed, too. "Penny."

"Yeah."

"Meetings aren't just about not drinking. They're about having a safe place to speak your mind. A place to be when you, or the world, ain't safe. You know this, yeah?"

I kinda hated that I wanted to trust him and tell him things. "Yeah." I took another sip of water.

He sipped, too. "I can't be your sponsor."

"Wasn't asking you to." I played with the perspiration on my glass and cursed my predictability.

"Nah, not outright. But I think maybe my watching out for you might make you think it. I told you before, I'm here for you. But if you need to work your steps—"

"Stop. I'm not working any steps."

"I can see that. But then I hope you can see that's another reason I can't be your sponsor." He finished his water.

I swallowed air and blinked.

"C'mon, Penny. You don't really plan on sticking around. You're gonna start these steps—or not. Get restless, and move on before you finish. Isn't that what you do?"

I glared, hatred and anger, embarrassment and recognition, boiling on my tongue. "You sound like Ted. I didn't realize y'all were becoming best buds."

"It's not like that, Penny, and you know it. Hey, if you're searching for absolution, you got it. Okay? Whatever it is you done, it don't matter. I'm fine with it. No judgments here."

I bit my fingernail.

He pulled my hand down. "Stop that. And stop seeking validation. You'll never find it that way. Especially when you want it to be at the bottom of a drink."

"What have you got on Rain? Or against him?"

His eyes penetrated mine. "We haven't been able to find enough evidence to arrest him and make it stick. We also haven't found anything that clears him. Or anyone, for that matter."

"You really think she—Cheryl—is dead, and he killed her?" It was the first time I'd said it sober, out loud. The words were chased up with bile and I chewed ice to quell the fire. "He's innocent," I said. But did I really believe it?

"No one's innocent," he said. "But if he's not guilty of this, I'll do what I can to make amends."

"Step Nine."

"Knowing your steps ain't the same as doing them." He studied my glass. "So. Are you?"

"Doing the steps? Not lately." I swigged some rum and motioned for another one. Was that relief or disappointment when he didn't fight me?

I waited until the waitress left. "And if he did it?"

"Then we get you out of there, sooner even. And deal with him."

"How did you find the baby?" My vision blurred as I stared down.

I heard him clear his throat. "There, uh, there was a family place. Thought if she was really trying to get away from him, she might start there."

"Where is it?" I asked.

Before he could answer, his phone buzzed and he held a mumbled conversation.

"Duty calls?" I asked when he hung up.

"It does." He stood. "You good? You need a ride or something?"

"I'm good."

"Atta girl." He patted my shoulder. "Get dressed up, go out, do something fun. But be careful. You can be a very successful alcoholic here in N'Awlins. It's just awful hard to be successful at the recovery part."

He took the rum from my hand and set it out of reach.

CHAPTER TWENTY-THREE

THE SHADOWS REACHED THEIR LONG FINGERS, trying to hold on to the day before the sun recanted its presence. The lights competed with the sky and a different bustle took over. I inhaled the twilight. The wind smelled like patchouli. It excited and terrified me.

Hesitation and determination. Both clamored inside. Everyone said, "Trust me." But there was no one I could really trust.

So, I took everyone's advice, and ignored them all.

The unfamiliar store greeted my wallet and I walked out with a new dress. One with no strings, no memories, attached. The copper tulle peeked out from under and around the folds of cocktail length black and orange florals.

My phone buzzed with a weather alert. Another tropical storm had intensified, and Hurricane Odessa was on a path to the Gulf.

The safety of California was still at least a day's flight away. Before I bought the plane ticket, there was one more item on my New Orleans bucket list.

The cab deposited me in front of the green shutters of Pat O'Brien's. One more Hurricane couldn't hurt, especially since I looked the way I looked and felt the way I felt.

I took a seat at the bar and ordered the drink of New Orleans, along with strips of fried catfish and a cup of gumbo. The glass was tall, curvy. I caressed it to keep from imbibing too quickly. The orange-red flow reminded me of the tumbler I'd crafted, and the mojo bag over my heart.

The place was larger than I expected, filled with active people. I stared at the immense collection of steins hanging from the high rafters and was thankful the South didn't often have earthquakes.

I never cared for so many strong drinks before NOLA. I took another swallow and thought long before not ordering another. I was angry and anxious and didn't want to recognize why. My journal pages recalled themselves as I considered triple X's and unanswered prayers.

A shadow moved next to me. "Hey."

"Ted?" Not fair. He wore that purple pinstripe shirt I'd always loved on him.

I stood on my toes to reach him before remembering to be mad. "Are you following me?"

"Happenstance, Gypsy. I was in the corner and saw you walk in. Bucket list, remember?"

"You're always showing up," I said.

"Better than always leaving." That cursed smile invited me. "Truth?" He continued. "I've been trying to find you. Went to a few places I thought you might be at."

"Why didn't you call?" I tapped my phone.

"Would you have answered?"

I let my silence be my answer.

He put a twenty under my glass and extended his elbow. "Walk and talk?"

I chugged the dregs of the Hurricane and let him escort me outside. My heel almost caught in the cracked pavement, and old memories brought new hurts. I yelled as I tore the shoes off and started walking again.

He pointed to my bare feet. "I don't recommend walking around like that out here. Something 'bout sepsis."

I wanted to stay barefoot. I wanted to prove him wrong. But my wound wasn't fully healed. And that would prove him right. I held his arm and slipped the shoes back on. "Better?"

"Sure enough," he said. "You hungry?"

I pointed toward Pat O'Brien's. "I've reached my limit." In more ways than one.

"Babe, it's New Orleans. Can we at least go somewhere and talk? Really talk?"

"As long as it's not a bar."

"There's no harm in sitting in a comfortable booth and having a beer with dinner."

Of course not. What harm could there possibly be with me in a bar with my ex-boyfriend and his award-winning smile?

I didn't pay attention to where we were going. I barely paid attention to Ted. I needed closure. I wanted to be alone. I guess it was safer that I wasn't. Could I trust him to keep me from ending up in old habits?

"Trust." I snorted.

"What's that?" He put his hand on my arm, drawing me out of myself.

"Nothing. Thinking out loud."

"Well, think out loud in complete sentences, would you, Gypsy?"

Ted was always good at taming my fire. Except when he was part of the kindle. Was he now? If not, at least he was here. Available. And that meant he was about to bear the brunt of all things wrong. I sucked air through clenched teeth and stopped walking. "People are ... You don't even ... And the worst is—"

"Babe." He grabbed my hand and unsuccessfully tried to pull me out of the crowd.

People wove around us, gaping at the storm about to arrive.

He stepped close, the charmer trying to subdue the copperhead. His movements, his demeanor, were all calculated to prevent a dangerous strike.

I wasn't having any of it. I tore the shoe off my foot again and stood, lopsided, waving it at him. "They lied. They all lied. Everyone lies!" Foul language and incomplete thoughts poured their vinegar in and out of me.

He let me fling words until I raised to strike him. He battled for my shoe and stepped closer. We struggled but he pulled me in, like a dance I didn't want, and whispered in my ear. "Breathe, Gypsy." He wrapped his arms tight around me, a fierce embrace I couldn't escape.

He countered each step and push I made. It was an angry tango. I wanted to scream. My body tensed with aggression when I couldn't fight his movements and instead found us wrapped together, leaning against a wall like sidewalk lovers.

My new dress fluttered and stilled. I couldn't relax. The best I could do was stand still, cement in my veins.

Ted's arms, still strong, were no longer tense. "Better, babe?"

I rested my cheek on his shoulder and took in the neon city. Rain was right. I was always ready for a fight.

Would Uncle Martin approve of my making new memories with an old boyfriend? Could Ted be my new story?

"How 'bout that restaurant?" He followed the sidewalk.

"The restaurant?"

"The one we talked about, from that magazine. The one that started our whole bucket list. What was the name, do you remember?"

My heart stuttered. "I was actually thinking of someplace else."

"No way, Gypsy." He took my hand. "You got me to come all the way to New Orleans for you. You can go to a restaurant for me."

"We're not—this isn't ... You get that we're not together any more, right? This isn't our trip, our bucket list. I don't even know what you're still doing here."

He stopped walking. "You don't?"

"Ted. This isn't a date." I dropped his hand.

"Yeah." There was that familiar gaze. "I know."

"Because we're just two friends who happen to be in the same area."

"Who used to be lovers, and haven't seen each other in a really long time."

I chewed the inside of my cheek. "Used to be."

He tipped his head to meet my eyes, and reached for my hand again. "Used to be? You called me to come here, Gypsy. That can't be coincidence or mistake."

"Ted."

He raised his hands. "Can't blame me for trying. Okay, Gypsy. I know this isn't a date for you."

"Better not be for you, either." I pretended not to notice he was stroking my ringless finger.

He let my hand go. "Now. What's the name of that restaurant?"

"Restaurant D'Arcy is in the French Acadia. It's owned by Vernon Rainier."

"I don't—" But suddenly he did. The realization crept over his face. "Oh."

I waited, forgetting to react, forgetting it shouldn't matter. I was tired of forcing new memories into old thoughts. I started walking.

"Josie, wait." He caught up and walked backwards in front of me. "Somewhere else, then. We had more than that on the bucket list. Hotel Monteleone. The Carousel. C'mon, Gypsy. You're looking like all that. And I'm looking like all this."

An unwanted chuckle emitted. "Not a date?"

"Not a date." He stuffed his hands in his pockets and offered his elbow.

We navigated through the crowd and arrived under the intricately carved white front. It reminded me of the alabaster tomb at Greyford. Which reminded me of Rain. Which reminded me I didn't want to be reminded of him.

I pulled Ted close to the wall, wrapped my hands around his neck, and drew him into a kiss.

"What's this, babe?" He pulled me back. "You should run away more often."

"Ted." I punched his chest.

"No, I mean it. I like not dating you."

I turned away before he could not-date-kiss me.

We entered the extravagant lobby and absorbed the air of elegant history as we made our way to the Carousel Lounge. A part of me had hoped to experience this with Rain and maybe Toni. I needed balance. I reached for Ted's hand and held tightly. He gave me a squeeze and a smile. I hated myself for using him, but he was using me back, so didn't that make it okay?

The Carousel spun us around slowly as we sipped our Vieux Carres and enjoyed samplings from the Bar Bites Menu. Whenever the bartender checked on us, he shared his stories of the Big Easy. It was indulgently delightful, and everything Ted and I had thought it would be.

"We should stay here."

I took another bite of my shrimp pot sticker. "In New Orlins? We're already here."

"Not New Orleans. Here. In the hotel."

I set my fork down. "Ted."

He put his hands on my thighs. "C'mon, babe. *This* was on our bucket list. Let's do it."

"There were a lot of things on our bucket list."

"Let's do them all."

"Not all, ba—Ted."

He grinned at my slip. "Why not? You're not not-dating anyone else, are you?" His enthusiasm was contagious, and I didn't want to remember why I thought I should say no.

A slow smile crossed my lips as he bent in for a kiss.

"I'm sorry." I backed up.

"Stuck on him? I'm not stupid, Josie. I know it wasn't me you wanted to be kissing earlier. I know it's not me you want with you, here and now. Or later. But he's not here, now, and I am. And I don't want to give you up again."

I didn't want to move. Rain was exhilarating and new, but I didn't have to explain myself with Ted. Had I been wrong to leave him? We couldn't go back to what we were, but we could move forward. We could go home. To Anne and Chris. To my house. I could make new memories with my past. Right now, that was better than the maybe-yet-to-come memories of what I was no longer sure could be my future.

I turned my sight to the neon world outside the window. Was that—? A woman stopped and peered in. Did we make eye contact?

Her red lipstick captured my attention. What was she saying? "Orange?"

"Momma Tristan?" I mouthed.

She laughed her approval. "Orange embraces change." At least I think that's what she said.

"What?" Ted leaned into my line of vision and followed my gaze.

I flitted a glance at him and when I returned it to the window, she was gone.

"So?" He patted my thigh and whispered. "What do you want to do?"

It was over.

Anne held my hand as we sat in the green folding chairs. Chris stood nearby, politely greeting the people I didn't want to say hi to.

Tears fell from my unblinking eyes. I wanted to watch them lower the coffin. I wanted to see how deep the hole went. I wanted to jump in it and be buried with Martin. I shook my head.

Chris bent to my ear. "Someone wants to say hi." He squeezed my shoulder. I recognized the squeeze. It wasn't encouragement. Chris's encouragement came through talks and thumbs up and text messages.

This was a warning. A warning to stop me from doing something stupid.

Like lift my head, smile, and say hi to the man I'd hated for the last two years.

He knew me so well.

CHAPTER TWENTY-FOUR

MY PHONE BUZZED BEFORE I COULD ANSWER
Ted. *Where y'at?*

I texted back. *I'm sorry.*

It took five minutes for the reply. *Let's talk.*

It took me three seconds. *French Market Inn. Bring dessert.*

I opened the door. He was dressed differently than I was used to—mussy hair, jeans, and an untucked shirt. Fatigue weighed on him in equal balance with irritation and reserve. He still took my breath away.

I stepped aside and let him in. He set a food container and bottled waters on the side table before turning to me.

"Penny." He came close and I let him hug me. With my bare feet, he was even taller. I could smell the garlic musk I loved so much.

"Hi, Rain."

We took our treats to the courtyard. It wasn't the same privacy we'd had at Greyford, but it was mine to share with him. And I didn't need heels to enjoy it.

The pavement glistened with residual moisture and the air held a tangible vibe.

The cleaver tattoo peeked from under his rolled-up sleeves. I wanted to review his skin for more tatts, to find ones I hadn't seen yet. I wanted to know their delicious stories, his stories.

"Glad you messaged me." It was a private, pleasing award from him.

I wanted to savor every moment, every taste, but his demeanor shifted and he cleared his throat.

I fidgeted. When he didn't stop me, I fidgeted more. It was no use. He wasn't going to still my hands no matter how much he saw them move. I withdrew them to my lap.

I couldn't tell if he was patient or irritated. The shadows flickered their tree branches across his face. He was so beautiful. Oh, how my love of artificial night light made everything more appealing.

His arm was over the back of his chair. "I took off the extra security."

"Yeah?"

He chuckled. "Worst thing to happen was you stealing—sorry, borrowing—my car. And since that happened with them on duty, what was the point?"

I smirked and took a bite of bananas Foster.

What was it about him that kept me coming back for emotional punishment? I'd done a good job—a *great* job—of locking away these feelings. I didn't want to feel this way again. I didn't want to know hope and a future. I was content being automated and getting through life one day at a time with no expectations.

I was. But not now. Not here. Not in New Orleans.

And it was his fault.

I let a single tear drive its crooked path down my cheek.

"What are we doing, Penny?" He put his spoon down. We looked at each other forever, and I willed myself to find the answers in his eyes. It was almost a game of Blink, and I didn't care who won. I only cared that I wouldn't lose.

"Tell me about Cheryl." I wanted to scream it at him. Tell me everything. Tell me what went wrong, and what you did to try to fix it. Tell me you don't do those things any more. Tell me you never did. Tell me this part is the nightmare. Tell me the dream is next.

"She was beautiful and fun."

Why did he think I would want to know that?

He gripped his spoon and his cheeks tightened. "My cousin had an affair with my wife and got her pregnant. Is that what you want to keep hearing?"

The noise in my ears, in my head, was a strange sluggish roar and the patio was a little crooked. I held onto the table.

He continued with an anger directed at his past.

"You knew, and yet you stayed with her." I didn't mean for it to sound so accusatory, but I couldn't swallow the words.

"Forgiveness, Penny. I couldn't leave her." He paced behind me, and his voice grew louder. "Maybe I should have. But I couldn't. I knew it was happening, and I didn't stop it. I knew when she was pregnant the first time. I knew it every time she went out with no real plans, when she told me I wasn't man enough to keep her home."

"And then she came back to you." Why was love so hard to understand? Why did it have to be mixed up with pain and hate, anger and confusion?

He rubbed his heart. "Char was mine, Penny. She was my baby, my girl. She would have been my life."

Few thoughts made sense. I waited for him to circle in front of me.

His mouth twitched. "Cheryl said she would change. I believed her."

"You hate starting over." I whispered to no one.

"Because of her." The contempt was hard to miss. "She always wanted to start over, do it better." He drained his water bottle. "But we never got better. Penny, believe me when I tell you I would never hurt you. Promise." His hands were strong, comforting, as he stood behind me and rubbed my neck. "Come back to the Manor," he said. "You can have your own room. I just think ... We've got the start of something here. Something good. If we're going to move forward, you need to stop moving away."

I kissed his hand, grateful he couldn't see my face. What he was asking terrified me.

One more question. "Did you love her?" The same words I'd cried before, the same daggers I'd dug deep under his skin.

"Too much."

That's not what I wanted to hear, but anything less would have been a lie, and I respected him through my hatred.

I swallowed. "I'm not ... I don't know how ..." I stood and threw up my hands. "Forget it. I'm not any good at this. Forget the full disclosure. I don't wanna do this. I don't wanna know any more."

The stone was cool under my feet. I swayed and willed it through my body to ease my temper.

"You were always good at keeping your eyes closed, Gypsy."

Rain pivoted with fury.

"Ted! What are you doing here?" I stopped him two feet from Rain.

He eyed me, then Rain. "I didn't think you'd run back to him so quickly after our date." He wiped his mouth. "Hell of a kiss for someone you didn't want to be kissing."

I heard Rain step behind me.

The patio closed in on us like an underwater cage, but I was the only one drowning.

"Ted." I put my hands on his chest. "Please."

He placed his hands over mine. "We're fine, Gypsy. Trust me."

Trust him. How often had he said that? How often was that the trigger for him to lie to me more?

"No." The tension roiled around us.

"No?" He stepped back, an over exaggerated shock on his face.

"I think she's asking you to leave," Rain said.

"That's not what I heard."

They stood nose to nose, flexing, steaming, not saying a word.

I took in the bull fight about to happen, slipped into my flip-flops, and grabbed the dessert. "Clean up the mess when you're done."

CHAPTER TWENTY-FIVE

THE GRAVEL PATH LED ME IN THE HUMID DARK-
ness, and I wished the fireflies were trying to keep me company rather than avoid me.

New Orleans was more than voodoo, liquor and characters. She was peaceful, welcoming, and still filled with wonder.
The birds sang unfamiliar tunes and the willows reached for
me with the breeze.

This was the New Orleans that was good for my soul.

I climbed the steps and rang the doorbell. "Girlfriend," I
shouted. "Open up. I have news. And I brought leftovers."

Leaving my suitcase at the door, I walked around the
verandah twice, sent Toni a text, and used Rain's key to let
myself in. I clicked the kitchen lights on and filled the tea kettle with water. But where did he keep the tea?

Earl Grey. Lemon Verbena. Dandelion Root. The higher
shelf held more boxes and tins. I climbed on a chair and reached.

And in the back, a small, unmarked box. I nudged it to
the side, sifting through more options.

The chair wobbled as I stretched, and I wildly clutched

for anything to grip. Containers clattered down. As my nerves settled, I shook my way to ground level.

The box had spilled open, vomiting its dusty contents onto the floor. A baby jar of loose-leaf tea. A gold band. A dried cluster of Queen Anne's Lace. A separate ring with the stone missing. What were these doing in the kitchen? Fabric— an empty mojo bag? A small bottle of some kind of liquid. A pocket lighter. Photos.

I leaned against the cabinet and filed through them. Rain in a tux and Cheryl in her wedding gown. Lou in a rougarou costume, holding the head, as Cheryl mocked fear. Cheryl and Douglas laughing together. Cheryl and Toni in front of a bayou cabin. Cheryl holding her pregnant belly. Cheryl. In each one, her face was partially X'd over.

I'd wanted him to hate her, to want to leave her in the past. But these photos. These damaged, vandalized remnants of her memory showed how much emotion he'd invested. Hatred wasn't the opposite of love. Apathy was. And the anger in this box certainly wasn't apathetic. It was full of whatever it was he tried to hide, and whatever it was I'd hoped didn't exist. I wanted to ignore it, to come up with other reasons, but the evidence was right here. He still felt for her. One way or another. Was his prayer for her to die? I traced invisible X's on the deconstructed mojo bag, and peered at the stiff flora. A tiny, off-white gathering. But it wasn't Queen Anne's Lace.

My hands shook. The box, the photos, the jar. They all tumbled out again. I stuffed it all back into the box, stuffed the box back onto the shelf, and stuffed the moment away as the tea kettle screamed.

I kicked my flip-flops into the grass and sat on the verandah. The untrustworthy tea bag never made it into my cup
of hot water.

Headlights froze on me before they turned into the garage.
I bit the remaining tip off my fingernail.

Footsteps. I couldn't see who it was, and told myself I
didn't care.

Rain stopped at the bottom of the steps. I searched
him, saying nothing. Wanting to ask everything. Wanting to
already know the answers so I wouldn't have to.

He held his side. His sloppy shirt was ripped, and dark
stains speckled his sleeve and abs. Without a word, he opened
the door, set my suitcase inside, and disappeared.

After a moment, a wrenching sad tune from the piano
captured my soul. Impromptu jazz. A vaguely familiar tune.
He had played something similar during my first days at Greyford. It haunted my rest then, and it haunted me now. It was
a lonely music, but with a touch of hope. I pictured him running fingers over the keys, not caring if they stumbled, gazing
into the distance as he saw things no one else could. I pictured
the sadness on his face, and I wanted to comfort him.

I didn't know until this very moment the games I'd
been playing. It came on me like morning dew giving way
to warm sun.

I was in love.

With a murderer.

I laughed out loud. To myself. To the fireflies. To the music
behind me. I fidgeted with my bracelet and moved my wrist so

it could dance. The soft plinks joined the wind chimes that hung from the eaves above me.

The mojo bag weighed heavy on my neck, over my heart. What had Momma Tristan said? It attracts more of the same. So far, it hadn't brought any fortune or clarity my way. Still, not wearing it would be a choice to break the spell, to give up hope. I wasn't sure how much of me believed in hope anymore. And how much of me believed in habit. Maybe it was my fault. I'd not given it a name, an identity.

I should have bought a voodoo doll instead. At least I could manipulate it instead of waiting for it to get to work.

I stepped inside, ignoring Rain because to not ignore him would mean to acknowledge things I wasn't ready for. Things like Ted, my feelings, his wife. Our hurts, confusion, anger, happiness. Magic. Love.

I strode into the kitchen, retrieved a six-pack of green-bottled beers, and went back to my perch. Old habits were about the only thing I could handle right now.

The piano stopped. Rain's head lifted as he watched me.

The quiet bit me. I spooned the dessert and wondered if I should wait for Toni. I texted her again.

The cap wouldn't twist off the beer. Another curse sailed through the silence.

I heard the piano bench scrape gently on the floor. Southern blues music flowed loudly from the stereo. The screen door closed and from the corner of my eye, I noticed his jeans and bare feet come closer.

He sat next to me like I wasn't even there. I guess I deserved that.

He tucked the six-pack behind him, and took my unopened

bottle. Without a word, without acknowledging me, he opened it, took a chug, and set it between us.

My thoughts flew as fast as my heart beat.

His cheek was grazed.

"Ted?"

He shrugged and flexed his knuckles. They were red and a little swollen. His index finger was cut and spotted with dried blood.

"Save me any?" He pointed to the carton.

I passed him the last of the bananas Foster, and he scraped the container clean.

When I reached for the beer, he intercepted my hand. I tried to turn away. He tucked my hair behind my ear and guided me to meet his eyes. Sliding closer, he brought up his other hand, and my face was wonderfully captured in his palms. His lips teased me before touching.

This was kind of lovely. Kind of fulfilling. This was kind of wonderful and I hoped Toni was at her apartment with no plans to come over any time soon.

I took his wrists and gently pulled them to my lap. "Tell me more."

His smile disappeared. "Why?"

"Because I want to understand you. Because I came here seeking a friend, and I think you came home for the same thing."

His gaze captured unseen history on the lawn. "Is that what we are, Penny? Friends?"

"Hey." I leaned into his eyesight. "Not just."

He pulled his hands away. "Cheryl loved Marilyn Monroe. Trips to the beach. Her special tea. She could be the life of the party. Until the party was over."

"Oh." I didn't understand, but the conversation didn't invite questions.

"She'd disappear for days, weeks, on end. I'd be worried sick 'til she'd call and tell me to pick her up at some dive near the bayou or across state lines. She'd be a wreck. Crash the car. Swallow pills. Whatever she could. And then she'd tell me, never again."

I was a bird mesmerized with the story of a snake.

"It was a game with her. How far would she push me away before I'd turn around and help her? I thought if I loved her enough, she could love herself and stop. I sought help. Asked her to speak with a doctor. She said she did, but she got worse. She was putting Lou and Toni in danger. You can only save the ones who want to be saved."

I stared at the beer. "I'm sorry. Forgive me."

"Forgiven. Penny, I'm no saint, either. There are more than a few things I'm not proud of. I learned at a young age I'd have to parent my older brother. When our folks passed on, it was hard. I'm not complaining, don't misunderstand. I did what I needed to, to protect Lou. But then Cheryl came into our lives and at first she was this refreshing whirlwind."

"A hurricane," I offered.

He smiled. "I wouldn't say that. A hurricane is a thing you see coming. Cheryl. She exploded on us. It was like one day she was good, and the next, she chose crazy. I've told you all this but there's something more. There's a reason Douglas is still pursuing this."

"What?" The air hadn't suddenly chilled, which made the sensation on my neck all the more prickly. Did he know I'd found his box?

"That day she disappeared. We'd said a bunch of stuff. She threw a vase. Knocked some furniture around. And I was afraid."

"Afraid of her?"

"Afraid of what I might do. I'd never lost control, not really. But Douglas already had me on record for his assault. His history with Cheryl, it colored him at first. If she said it, he believed it. And the other cops did, too. She knew how to push, and she would. One argument, instead of walking away, I barricaded us in the bedroom. Locked the door and asked her to stay. Just to talk. I wanted her to see what she was doing to us. Douglas convinced her to press charges for domestic violence and kidnapping."

There were too many words in my head. "Oh," was the only thing I could say.

He took a long drink. "She dropped the charges. We went to counseling. But Douglas still had the department keep an eye on me. Anyway, I thought things had calmed, smoothed over. But that last day, I knew. She'd tried to change, but some part of her was never going to. We were in trouble. I was in trouble. So, I left. Went to the hotel to cool down. And I never saw her again. No one did."

I placed my palm over his heart. He dropped his head and covered my hand with his.

"I need to know. Char was so little. And I wasn't there to help her be born, to take care of her the way a dad should. I need to know she didn't hurt. I need to know she's in a better place."

We were statues, willing life where there was none. I needed his happy ending.

But there wasn't one.

He sat close, his eyes searching me for a response. Our feet were good together, his larger toes near my smaller ones. My foot twitched and accidentally nudged his.

He smiled sadly.

"I'm sorry," I said.

"Now you know."

I pursed my lips. "I hate full disclosure."

His head tipped lightly in agreement.

I reached for the beer. This was not about getting drunk. This was about finishing, so I could make a new start. He didn't stop me. I gulped half, stood, and allowed it to take effect as I made my way to the grass. My flips were around here somewhere, but I wanted the cool blades instead. I shuffled around, pointed the bottle at him.

"I'm sorry," I said. "For everything." I spread my arms. Everything. Everything that happened. All the things I wasn't a part of, couldn't save him from. For my actions that brought up his past. I needed him to forgive me. Maybe it would help me forgive him. Right now, I just needed him to need me. So, I pushed the dangerous, dark thoughts out of my mind, and ignored their violent tug.

I danced and pointed again.

His smile turned crooked and he clasped his hands in front of him. "Careful of the chiggers."

"You've said it." I ignored his warning. "You're not perfect. I'm not perfect. Let's embrace these facts, shall we?"

I couldn't tell if he found me delightful or insulting.

I paced a large, slow circle, humming to myself, sipping occasionally. I pretended he wasn't there, watching me. I thrilled at the touch of the grass between my toes as my feet slid through it.

"Drawing a crop circle out there?"

I forced a smile to embolden the ounce of courage trying to grow into a pound. "Join me."

He leaned back, his palms pressing on the verandah, his body illuminated by the porch lights.

I clambered up the steps, reached behind him, and pulled another bottle from the carton.

A disapproving challenge crossed his face as I opened it and flicked the cap onto the porch before returning to my crop circle. One way or another, I would leave my mark on New Orleans.

"Penny." He stood near, a shadow of a New Orleans god and demon.

I continued my circle.

He took another step. "Why? You're so self-sabotaging. Why do you have to destroy us before we even start? Can't we take what we have, and put the good on top?"

"Are we starting, Rain? Because I don't know. Every time I think we're stepping up, one of us steps back."

He touched the graze on his cheek. "I'm trying to protect you."

I swayed and stared at his rough face. "From what? And who protects you? Who takes care of you?"

His lips tightened. "I do the taking care of, Penny."

"Sounds like a lot of responsibility, and kinda lonely."

"I don't have time to think about that."

I stepped closer and repeated my quest. "Who takes care of you? What are you protecting me from?"

"From this, Penny." He spread his hands wide. "You come

down here knowing nothing, passing judgment on everything, and trusting no one. Before you go asking a bunch of questions and finding information you don't want to find, you better be sure what you're doing. You know Douglas hurt Toni. You know he and Cheryl hurt me. And yet you still ask about him, still reach out to him."

My voice tried to hide. "To get his side of the story."

"We're not the same story told different ways. We're different stories. You get that?"

"And he's different with me. I don't see what you see. I'm sorry, but I don't." Given that my second beer in half an hour was in my hand, it would not be smart to mention the AA meeting Douglas had taken me to.

Rain held my shoulders and brought his face close. "You're right. I do these things because I want my name out there. I admit it, Penny. I want the good press. I'll do whatever it takes to protect my family. I don't want people thinking poorly of me, my father, or grandfather. Or Lou. He can't help he has autism, but you'd be surprised at who wants him held accountable for every little slip I make.

"You don't know what it was like to see my name—my parents' names—dragged through the mud so long ago. You don't know what I'm still up against, trying to keep this legacy going. You think I want it to be this? Crime and violence and death? A missing wife, and people whispering everywhere I go? You know nothing, and you never admit when you're wrong. You don't how hard I've had to fight for all of this. To keep Lou safe. To keep Toni safe. I put up these walls. I'm the strong one. I do the protecting. Then you show up and I'm supposed to let these walls down, supposed to ..."

My hands sweated. "You're not supposed to do anything, with me."

He was breathing hard. "Can't we just be us? No past. No ghosts. Just us. Right here, right now. Let's start over. Can we do that?"

"You don't believe in start overs." I hoped the darkness hid my eyes. I had to turn away. I whirled gently, letting the breeze dance with my dress. The music carried through the air like electrons seeking a place to bond. I was lost in my own moment when there was a tug on the beer.

"Aw, Penny. You're my hurricane, aren't you?" Rain closed his hand around mine, still holding the bottle, and put his other hand around my waist. "I want you. I don't mean ... You belong here, Penny. I want you to stay."

My toes reached for his and we swayed to Van Morrison's "Someone Like You."

I tried to tip the bottle for a last taste, but he pulled it up and drank it for me. He bent his head and again our lips met. He tasted like caramel and beer. He smelled like life, like home. I buried my nose in the crook of his neck.

I wanted to step into his shirt, under his skin. I hated myself for wanting him, needing to be the air he breathed. I wanted to be with him always, to be this close and closer, and never be away from him. "I'm scared."

"I know," Rain spoke low. "I am, too."

He brought his lips to my ear and whispered lyrics while leading me in a slow waltz. The lawn played with our feet and lightning bugs lit up around us.

"New start?" His breath tickled my cheek.

I nodded. I couldn't speak, couldn't open my eyes. Couldn't

break this heavenly spell. We let the magic carry us through countless songs and kisses. The cooler the night grew, the warmer he was. Nightingales joined our melody.

A distant noise interfered, an engine hummed itself to quiet and two birds flew from the garage. I was lost in contentment and took a moment to realize Rain had straightened.

"'Bout time you came back, girl!" Toni called out.

"Penny Josie's here," her companion eagerly announced.

Rain squeezed my hand has we separated. "Hey, guys."

Lou walked up with an enthusiastic smile. "Rain. Penny Josie's here."

"I see that, bud."

Toni joined us. "Got your texts." She motioned toward Rain. "Got his texts, too." She winked. "Figured one of you had things under control."

"Thanks," I said.

"Penny Josie. Toni made gumbo for dinner and we ate all of it."

"Yeah? Sounds good."

"It was. Did you have gumbo for dinner?"

"No, but I had bananas Foster."

"Weren't no trouble." Rain grinned.

"Something was." Toni cupped his chin and turned his face toward the porch light. She stepped back and let out a whispered curse. "What happened?"

He pulled her hand away. "Nothing. Little misunderstanding between me and a piece of furniture."

I wondered which piece, and how much it would cost me.

"Who won?" She tried to brush the dried blood from his shirt.

"It was a tie." He looked at me.

Toni glanced at me. "You knew about this?"

"I–"

Another noise intruded. Wailing sirens and many tires on gravel.

"Rain?" I asked.

"Not sure." He stepped in front of me and Toni.

Lou mimicked his protective stance.

I wanted to move to the safety of the raised verandah but couldn't leave Rain's shadow.

Blue and red lights cast flickering ghosts on the leaves and the Manor, reflecting eerily off windows and bird ponds.

I turned from the brightness of a high-beam flashlight.

"Who is it?" I put my hand on Rain's arm.

"Rain." The gruff voice called out.

"Douglas?" I peered toward the silhouette.

"Step back, Penny."

A half-dozen or more uniformed officers made their way inside the Manor as Douglas, Detective Chase, and two more cops paced outside. One held up two documents.

"Douglas, what is this?" I asked.

"No cops." Lou raised his voice. "Rain, no cops."

Rain called to Toni and she faced Lou.

"Look at me," she pleaded. "Look right at me, Lou. It's okay. It's gonna be okay."

An officer pulled out cuffs and approached Rain.

"No, no, no." Lou wailed and moved past Toni. "You leave my brother alone!"

"It's okay, Lou. Stop." Rain tried to command his screaming brother.

Douglas strode between them. "Easy, Lou. Ain't nothing gonna happen. I'm truly sorry for this."

"Sure you are." Rain's eyes flashed the heat of his anger.

"No cops!" Lou flailed at his cousin.

"Penny." Rain tilted his head toward Lou.

I forced my way to Toni's side and together we tried to pull Lou away as an officer cuffed Rain.

"Lou." Detective Chase stood in front of him. "You gotta calm down and not make this worse. I'm sorry, Lou. I am. But you're gonna be taken care of. You hear me? You're gonna be okay."

Douglas was shouting. Rain and Lou were shouting. Toni and I tried to protect the brothers but were pulled into the melee as diligent officers forced Rain and Lou apart.

Screams flew with fists, pleadings for obedience went unheard. I'd never needed to get into a catfight more than in this moment.

Toni reached for Lou, his hands pummeling his own arms and his humming screech reaching an unearthly volume.

An officer held me back. I met Rain's gaze, tears in both our eyes.

CHAPTER TWENTY-SIX

DENTON CHASE SAT ACROSS FROM ME IN THE harsh, bare room. "Veronica Lynch is missing."

"Who's that?"

"She's one of Rain's students. You know her as Ronna."

"Ronna?" The shy Krewe member Rain was so proud of? "I don't understand. Where is she? What does this have to do with Rain?"

"We think she found something, some information or evidence."

"About what?"

"There's a guy we've been after a while. Preys on young girls. It was a pretty quick arrest, thanks to Ronna's help. She really took a risk. This evening, she vanished from the safe house, after exchanging several text messages with Vernon Rainier."

"Rain was with me this evening."

He put his hands on the table. "All evening?"

My legs slid from under the chair. "Why do you think he has anything to do with it?"

He stood akimbo against the wall. "We found a burner phone and traced it back to one Rainier purchased a while ago. Looks like the two of them have been texting each other quite a bit lately."

"That doesn't make sense. Why—"

"The officer protecting her was assaulted. Rain sent a text he was coming for her, and he can't account for his whereabouts earlier this evening. Penny, he was in a fight. There's blood on his clothes, and he's got bruising. It's only a matter of time before the DNA comes back to the officer. He's close with these kids, this Krewe of his. But he didn't start it to be altruistic."

"What does that mean?" What did any of this mean?

"This isn't his first or second run-in with us. The guy you're so enamored with has a history, a rough one. He has a record of domestic violence. This thing with Ronna. Well, I hate to tell you, but it appears they were having an inappropriate relationship. She may have discovered some things about his past, about his wife. And now she's missing."

Nothing made sense. A low, crushing noise started and I couldn't hear him. The room shifted its gravity. Denton gave me a funny, concerned look. The walls tilted sideways as I heaved over the trash bin.

Greyford had been legally ransacked.

How different from the first time I'd entered. A sickening, frightening feeling now grew in my belly. The New Orleans black magic had finally reached me, and left its fiery tentacles clawing at the inside of my stomach.

Toni and I surveyed the interior carnage as Lou wailed in his garden room.

I couldn't believe Douglas had let this happen, after he assured Lou he'd be okay. Vases broken, glass shards on the floor. Books and papers askew in every room. Furniture overturned, drawers upside down. It was pandemonium of the worst kind.

"Where's my suitcase?" I called out.

Toni peeked through the kitchen galleys. "I put it upstairs, in Rain's room."

I found it at the foot of his bed, the bed of my nightmare. The zippers weren't as I'd left them.

I closed the door, knelt down, and opened the case. Everything seemed okay. My T-shirts. The other dress. Those shoes. My hand fell in relief onto the pile and stopped on something firm. I shifted through a layer of clothing until I found it. A box.

Not just any box.

His box. His I-killed-Cheryl-with-poisoned-tea box.

Toni knocked and opened the door. "Where y'at?"

I slammed the suitcase closed and jumped up. "Getting ready for bed."

"You can sleep? Good for you. I'm gonna make some tea. Want some?"

I tried not to glance at my suitcase. "No, thanks. Not now." And probably, not ever.

"Suit yourself." She closed the door behind her.

I scurried back to the floor, back to the suitcase.

He must have put the box in here when he came home, when I was on the verandah falling in love with him and drinking away my ghosts. My hoodoo candle peeked from between a pair of socks. I pulled a folded paper from inside it. It was his handwriting. Strong, bold.

Sorry.

–R.

Sorry? Did he even know what for? Or was this some blanket apology to get him out of whatever trouble he thought I knew about? *Sorry.* I choked on the word. Crumpled the paper. Straightened it. And tried not to crumple it again. The box lid came off without a fight. Everything inside was as I'd last seen it. I stuffed the note between the photos, put the lid back on, and buried it deeper in my suitcase.

The candle had less than two layers left. I wiped a lonely, tired tear, all the more tired knowing I wouldn't sleep, and made my way to the bathroom.

I glimpsed my horrible self in the mirror. My dress was misshapen. The flip-flops had done little to protect my feet from dirt and police station filth. My make-up had either worn off, smudged off, or been kissed off, except for around my eyes. I was an embarrassed and horrified night-girl raccoon.

After a good cleansing, I sat in the basin and let the shower spray its warmth over me. I was too tired to stand, too tired to cry. So many thoughts fought for attention, so many concerns and unanswered ideas.

My mojo bag emitted a strange, wet fragrance. I'd forgotten to remove it before my shower. Was it damaged, too? In the marble-enclosed steam, I closed my eyes and counted.

Ooonnnnne.

I forced myself into a rhythmical slow exhale. *Repeat.*

There wasn't much I could do from the sanctuary of the bathroom, but I relished the protection as long as I could.

Frantic mumbling rose from the foyer. I pulled on capris and my Beatles T-shirt before hustling downstairs.

"Lou, open up." Toni rapped on his potting room door. "He's okay. You know he's okay."

Banging and pounding answered her. "No. He didn't come home. He had bruises and blood. You saw. He's not okay. Nobody's okay."

Toni raised her hands and eyebrows.

"Lou?" I leaned my head against the door. "It's Penny. Open up."

The pounding subsided. "Penny Josie?"

"Yes."

Pound. "Police stations are bad."

"I know. Hey, you wanna open the door so I can see you? I like seeing you when we talk."

Pound. "Why?"

"'Cause I like your face."

No pound. No hum. The lock clicked and the door opened. "Penny Josie."

"Hi." I waved.

"Hi." He waved back. "This is my face."

"It's a nice face."

"You have a nice face, too," he said.

"Thanks."

I hadn't realized Lou and I were almost the same height. I could meet his eye without shifting. "Can I hug you?"

His smile dropped and his hands stilled. His eyes wandered for a short second before his head gave a singular bob.

I cautiously stepped close and put my arms around him.

He awkwardly brought his arms up.

I wanted to hug him tighter but didn't want to scare him. The flood of joy and protection I felt for him overwhelmed me and I stood back.

"I don't want to go to the police station," he said.

Toni stepped closer. "You don't have to."

He stiffened. "I don't want to be the rougarou anymore."

She tried not to touch him as she guided him into the foyer. "You don't have to. How 'bout we get a good night's sleep and think about the rest of this tomorrow. Is that okay, Lou?"

He swayed. "I don't want to cancel the party. Rain has to be home for the party, so if we have the party, he'll come home. I don't want to cancel the party. I want Rain to come home."

I wanted to put my hand on his shoulder, or hug him, or wind back time to stop his hurts. But how far? Hours ago, before the police showed up? Six years, before Cheryl died? To his childhood, before he was teased for being different? To the womb, before he *was* different? My frustration caused my fists to clench.

"Are you mad at me?"

"What? Oh, no, Lou. No." I shook my head. "I'm mad for you."

"I don't think anyone's been mad for me before. Except my family. And Toni." He shuffled away, his body a controlled seizure of hums, pats, and nods. Halfway up the stairs he called out. "Penny Josie. Do you want to sleep with my Ninja Turtle tonight?"

How could I refuse such an endearing hero?

The plush toy warded off any interference as I drifted to dreamless restlessness.

I woke, holding the ninja turtle like a treasure, and thankful it had worked. The manor was eerily still, and I recalled Rain's description of the day Cheryl disappeared.

After a somber stretch, I paced to the landing and sur-veyed Lou's open door and the foyer. I heard a light clatter of dishes as the aroma of chicory greeted me good morning.

Toni sat at the island and pushed a hot cup in my direc-tion. We eyed each other without words through several sips.

"Where's Lou?" I asked.

"In his room."

"It's empty."

She set her cup down. "What do you mean?"

"I just came down. His door was wide open. He's not there. You didn't notice?"

She nodded toward the Great Room. "I fell asleep on the sofa. I haven't been upstairs this morning."

We rushed out of the kitchen and scattered through the Manor, calling for Lou.

Eternity passed in the blink of an eye until we regrouped at the base of the stairs.

"Where is he? What happened?" I asked.

"Why are you asking me? You were the last to see him."

"Don't put this on me, Toni."

She ran shaky hands through her hair. "No, no. Not again."

I grabbed her. "What?"

"I think he's run away."

Our arms hung limp. "Why? Has he done this before?"

Her face contorted. "When Cheryl ... Rain was inconsolable. Lou's autism slows him but doesn't stop him. About a week after Char passed, Lou showed up at the boutique with a suitcase. Said he was moving in with me 'til his brother got back. I asked what he meant, and he said Rain hadn't come home the night before. I tracked Rain down at the Acadia. That was the only other time he'd been gone overnight without telling anyone."

"And since you take care of Lou, he figured he should go to your place? But you were here last night. We both were. So why would he leave?"

A knock on the door interrupted us. Toni stepped aside as Cedric and Teegan entered, followed by a half-dozen more members of the Kitchen Krewe.

"Money Girl, you still here?" Cedric greeted me.

"Yo, Tones." Teegan whistled. "This worse than a hot mess in here."

"What are you doing here?" Toni tried to steady her voice.

Cedric strode to the center of the foyer. "Man, my brother's in lock up. Again. He called my daddy when he saw Chef Rain in there, and Daddy said Chef Rain been too good a influence for me as I ain't yet been in lock-up. So, he sent me to get Teegan and come over here to see what you need."

"That's right," Teegan said. "We got a party to prep for."

"Party?" I crossed my arms and leaned against Lou's door jamb.

Cedric turned. "The Halloween party we doing for our fams, that's the party."

"Right." Toni closed the door. "Guys, listen."

241

"Aww, no. Uh-uh." Teegan interrupted. "I know that 'listen.' No way, woman. Don't you be tellin' us the party's canceled."

"Please, Miss Toni," Georgina said. "Ronna's gone and I'm worried sick, liable to get in all sorts of trouble by myself."

Two others agreed.

"Man," Teegan said. "My moms bought herself a costume already. I ain't telling her she can't wear it."

Cedric shoved him. "Yo momma gots to wear costumes every day, man. No one wants to see her as is."

"Don't be talking 'bout my moms like that."

The boys play-scuffled until Toni got between them. "Go into the kitchen and get some food. I need to talk to Penny."

When the foyer was empty again, she spoke low. "We could use their help around here."

"Are you serious? We have to cancel the party."

"Wait." Her bracelets jangled as she reached for me. "These kids, their families. They're willing to move forward with the party. We should give them the opportunity."

"And it doesn't hurt Rain's reputation if he has all this community support, right?"

She scowled. "This isn't that, Penny. This isn't façade. This is hope. This is setting the example for the ones who watch us whether we want to be watched or not."

"Hope is a four-letter word." I said it more to myself than to Toni.

"We're not doing this for ourselves," she said. "It's for them, the kids and the community. Rain didn't ask for the spotlight. He hates it. But it comes with the territory because of this place. Because of who he is and what he does."

"Then why not move? He could leave this place a[n]
a new start."

"Sugar," she said. "We can't all up and leave h[o]
because we want to."

Her words cut me, and she knew it. I fingered my r[

"I didn't mean that, Penny. In a way, I envy you bein[g]
start over. I know it's a mess. I don't mean the Manor. B[
here, roots run deep." She paused. "We need to find Lo[u]
Ronna. And we need to clean, and we need to have thi[

I surveyed the shambles around us. "We could [
some look for them and some start cleaning."

"That's my girl!"

"What do we tell the Krewe?"

"Yo." Teegan stood near the galley doors. "You [
nothing."

Concern crossed Toni's face. How long had he bee[n

Cedric pushed his way past Teegan. "We ain'[t
ladies. Let's say we gots our ears to the ground and [
things. Them rumors 'bout Chef Rain already star[t
we ain't having none of that." He waved his cell phon[e
Krewe got his back, man. He ain't let us down, we ain'[t
him down."

Toni and I glanced each other.

"That's right, that's right." Teegan approached us[
usher. "Now you two ladies go get yourselves cleaned [
do what you got to do. Tell us what we need to do. My [
she own a cleaning business. I'm about to call in som[e
she owe me."

Toni reached for his phone but missed. "You do[n
to do that."

243

He smirked. "Oh, I know, but she owe me big time. Don't worry. We ain't letting anyone outside the family see this mess. We know what we gotta do. And she keep her mouth shut, too. She don't want me calling my auntie for anything."

I pulled Toni aside. "They haven't said anything about Lou."

"Let them focus on the party. We'll find Lou."

Georgina and the others circled closer. "You ain't gotta be quiet. We all know. We ain't saying nothing, but the rest of the Krewe is out looking for him. I bet he's back before Chef Rain comes home."

"How did you ...?" Toni gaped.

Teegan puffed out his chest. "We told you. We gots people on the inside, too."

"Not that inside." Cedric knocked him. "We just saying we gots all y'all's backs. The Krewe's not wanting to stop, so we gonna do what we can to keep it going. That means cleaning the Manor and bringing Lou home without letting the cops know. Most of us pretty good at hiding stuff from them already."

The Krewe chuckled in agreement.

I peered outside. Odessa, still a day away, was already bringing a darkness with her. Lou hates storms.

"I have a better idea," Toni said. "You get the word out. The Halloween party just became a hurricane party. Finish here, get your people together, get some belongings, and head over. Your families, too. Anyone who has vehicles, pick up the others. No Krewe left behind."

"You mean it?" Georgina brought her hands to her chest.

"I mean it. But not a word about Rain or Lou."

Toni and I faced each other, a slow appreciation creeping upon us. We smiled—a weak, things-might-be-getting-better-if-nothing-else-goes-wrong smile. She picked up her keys from the side table. "Can you guys stay here? And stay out of trouble?"

"Where you going, Tones?" Teegan asked.

"To find him."

CHAPTER TWENTY-SEVEN

RAIN'S VEHICLES GREW SMALLER AS WE DROVE away. We should separate, cover more ground. But I didn't know the area. Toni moved the BMW cautiously down the road as we peered for any sign of Lou on the sides, in the ditches, anywhere. But he was nowhere.

We drove in silence. Where would he go? How long had he been gone? What was his safe place? I had no idea.

And then I did. "He likes the blue sea."

"It's too far to the Gulf."

"But not the hotel."

The BMW accelerated as Toni wove through traffic. The city's stormy decorations imprinted their turmoil and my head swam as we reached the valet. Strung lights danced and dazzled in the breeze, a humid kiss on my soul separating nature from unnatural.

She tossed her keys to the attendant and we raced inside. Through the lobby, past the restaurant, into the long hallway. I crashed into the storage doors, waiting for her to key in Rain's code.

The doors clicked as we pushed them into the darkness. Toni flicked on the lights and I waited for my eyes to adjust. There were the same stacks of colors he'd shown me. The Tiffany blue napkins. The circular tables. But nothing was set up where a little boy—or a little boy in a man's body—could hide.

"Why did we think he'd be here?" I asked myself aloud.

"Rain brought him to the Acadia a lot. He'd sometimes stay here whenever Cheryl ... Anyway, he'd bring Lou here, too. He loves ordering room service. Sometimes he makes something up to see if Rain would fix it. Always does." She stroked a blue tablecloth. "Momma B passed in the hotel. 'Bout eight years now. She'd be so sad."

"Did she know? About Cheryl's problems?"

"I bet she had suspicions, but like everyone around here, hoped for the best. It's what we do. N'Orlins ain't a place to hold on to the ugly. I wished I'd known who Cheryl really was before she and Rain got together."

"I wish I'd known her," I said.

"Cheryl?" She turned quickly.

"No." I almost laughed. "Momma B."

"She'd have loved you, sugar. You fit right in."

I disagreed.

"Momma B was the best. Took care of all Rain's friends, momma to us all. Did her best to keep us outta trouble. She was always our safe place. Wherever she was. We had a problem, didn't matter what was on her plate. She'd drop it in an instant and come help. She was always helping us put the good on top." She shook herself from her memories. "We gotta find Lou."

The mojo bag clung to my damp skin. I gripped it through my shirt and squeezed, sending thoughts to it through the nerves tingling in my fingertips. I willed it to tell me where he was. "Where else would Lou go if he thought the rougarous were after him?"

Toni's thoughts were on her face: concern, anger, love. Recognition. Fear. "Follow me."

The windshield wipers distorted the view. A perfect harmony with the mess we were in.

Familiarity joined my thoughts as she drove her car past rundown buildings and onto a muddy path. "We have to walk from here."

I stepped out of the car. "To where?"

She pointed past the Tupelo. "The remains."

I couldn't see what she saw. I trusted her to lead the way.

The mud plucked at the soles of my shoes, and I reached for balance, pulling and leaning myself along the path until we reached charred wood in a haphazard shamble.

Toni stopped. A curse flew from her throat. "I hate the bayou."

Dust mites and cobwebs filled the open spaces between fallen planks.

"What is this place?" I asked.

"It was Rain's bayou cabin. His granddaddy built it as a resting place for when they'd come fishing or boating."

The cabin from the photo.

"What happened to it?" I toed a charcoal remnant.

She licked her lips twice before answering. "It was after Cheryl left. After Char ... Rain came back in a fit. Never seen him like that before or since. He was beyond reaching. Nothing I could say or do would help. He said he wanted to make sure Cheryl wouldn't be able to hide out here again."

"Toni. What are you saying?"

"This is where all the bad is caught."

I squinted. "What do you mean?"

"We had some good times here over the years." Was she ignoring me, or so lost in their past she hadn't heard me? Her foot drew squiggles in the muddy trail. "This is where Douglas found Baby Char."

Vomit raised and lowered within me.

"Rain burnt it down. Wanted no memory of Char's birth like this. Said there was no good to put on top of this, and I agreed. But I didn't think he'd do anything like this. Don't know how he managed it without harming the bayou, but he did. Left it as you see it."

"But, our boat ride."

"He doesn't mind the skiff, Penny. In fact, he loves it. Finds his solace with it. But the cabin. The place his wife birthed and abandoned his baby. That's a different story."

"Why would Lou be here?"

"He wouldn't."

"Then why ...?"

"Because." She paced in front of the water. "None of this makes sense. Rain arrested after all this time? Lou gone? And Ronna. We know Rain didn't take her."

"Right." I said. "But she's still missing, too."

"Unless she isn't." She grew animated, excited. "Hiding isn't the same as gone missing. What if—"

Her words filtered through me. "Lou would go someplace he knows, or with someone he trusts."

"And he trusts Ronna."

"Occam's Razor," I said. "They're together. But how?"

Toni clapped her hands and brought them to her face. "We can't go to her house and tell her folks anything. They may call the cops. Douglas would find out."

"So." I bit my lip. "Where are they?"

"And how do we help Rain?"

My phone buzzed with a text. "Can you drop me somewhere?" I asked Toni. "I need to take care of something I think can help. You keep searching for Lou, and I promise I'll let you know as soon as I have more information."

"You running again, Gypsy Firecracker?"

I perched on the damp park bench in Jackson Square. "Not this time."

Ted held out a cup from Café du Monde before he sat next to me. "I got you something." He pulled my hand to him.

"Ted." I tried to retreat.

"Relax, Josie." He fingered my bracelet.

I drank my coffee and waited.

"There you go." He patted my hand and nudged it back to me.

I raised it to observe the new charms.

He smiled. "Think of me when you see that carousel. Don't forget, life goes 'round in circles, and I'm always here for you. When we're not dating. And even when we're not-not dating."

"And the horse?"

"To remind you to relax and take a step back. You go full force through life, Gypsy, like a racehorse, and the rest of us are pulling the reigns to bring you back. You keep racing, you're gonna pass up a whole lot you won't ever see. Stop once in a while and evaluate."

"Or I might surprise you and actually win the race." I dropped my hand to my lap.

"Hey." He leaned into my eyesight. "What's got you?"

The coffee steadied me. "Rain's been arrested. They're saying he kidnapped some girl. Really it's because they think she knows something about Cheryl's death, but she's missing."

"Cheryl's missing? Not dead? How do they know?"

"Not her. The girl. Ronna. She was talking with Rain, then went missing."

He sucked in a low whistle and muttered. "That's messed."

"Tell me about it."

"Goes to show, you don't always know a person."

I choked and glared. "You think he did it?"

Ted squinted. "You think he didn't? C'mon, Gypsy. You're not that stupid."

I hated when he suggested I was stupid at all, let alone when it was possibly true. I readied to dump my coffee on him. After another sip.

He shifted back comfortably, and I hated him for that, too. "So?"

I swigged the latte. "I need you to talk to Douglas."

"Why?"

"The fight you had with Rain. They're saying that's the time when he took Ronna. But if you say he was with you—"

"And get myself arrested for assault? What are you thinking?"

I leaned back and closed my eyes. "Not about myself."

I could feel him draw closer. "You chose him, didn't you?"

"I didn't choose anyone. I chose me."

His breath was on my cheek. "Liar," he whispered and kissed me.

My eyes flashed open and I pulled back. "Stop."

"Why? We're here. In our place."

"This isn't our place."

"It was until you came here without me. Face it. You don't want to let go. Not really."

"Not wanting to change isn't the same as being happy the way things are."

"Aw, Gypsy. Stop being afraid to move forward." He stood and extended his hand. "Come on."

"Where?"

"If I know you, and I do, you haven't eaten since this whole thing started. And you're no good at making decisions on an empty stomach."

I brushed his hand aside. "Yeah."

Douglas and Detective Chase slid into the booth across from us.

"What'd you do?" Ted grimaced at me and balled his fist.

"I'm hoping, the right thing," I whispered while studying the menu.

"You eaten at the Clover Grill before, Penny?" Douglas asked. "I highly recommend the special club sandwich and beer batter onion rings." He motioned to the waitress. "Usual, Iris. Times four."

She acknowledged the order and slipped behind the counter.

"You got information?" Chase asked.

Ted set back. "You don't waste formalities, do you?"

Douglas pointed to the window. "Big city out there. We're pretty busy."

Ted sneered and bit his cheek.

"Nice knuckles," Douglas said. "I take it you're the alibi?"

Ted put his hands under the table and cocked his head at me. "You need an alibi?"

"Ted." I wanted to pull the words from him, make him tell the truth. But the one thing I was learning here in NOLA is that truth is relative.

"Naw, Penny. It's fine." Douglas rested his arm on the table and waited.

I fumbled with the charms on my bracelet as thoughts broiled in my head.

Ted shifted his attention from the detectives to me. "So, we're all having lunch like it's nothing."

"It's something." I hissed and turned away.

"If it helps," Denton said to me, "I know you're not involved. At least not as far as hiding evidence. There are bigger things to consider."

Ted shook his head. "What evidence? Gypsy, what's he talking about?"

I squirmed.

Douglas added his encouragement. "Penny, you're a kind soul. The kind that don't deserve to get messed up in a thing like this."

I raised my head and slapped Ted's charms on the table in front of him. "You're right. I have to go."

Ted reached for me, but I twisted away. "Where you going, Gypsy?"

Denton tossed two twenties on the table and followed me outside. I heard Ted scramble to keep up.

Iris hollered from behind the counter. "What about your food?"

"Donate it," Douglas said.

"Hold on." Ted stopped us on the sidewalk.

The wind threw light rain spittle against us.

"Gypsy. Firecracker. This doesn't make sense. Can't we stop and evaluate?"

An unwanted smile curled my lips.

"*In vino, veritas?*" He stepped closer and breathed in my ear. "Don't leave me yet."

"You don't need it," Douglas said.

"What?" I asked.

"The drink. You're doing fine, you know. You're holding it together, and I'm impressed. I know that don't matter much, but I am." He tapped my bracelet. "And you're doin' okay."

I closed my eyes. Inhale. *Ooonnnnne.* Exhale. *Ooonnnnne.* Inhale. *Ooonnnnne.*

Ted was close. I smelled his sweat, cigar and sea-breeze cologne. My fingers curled and uncurled in a rhythmic desire to be held, and my heart pounded in the irregular heat. The stench of alcohol and filth rose from the gutters. I heard Douglas's jaw work his toothpick. It all permeated into me, under my skin, into my marrow. "No." I opened my eyes. "This isn't about us."

"No, honey, it's not." Douglas took a half-step forward. "It's about family."

Ted stiffened. "Thought we were family."

My jaw hurt from tension. "When? When you left me to bury Martin on my own? When you decided wine was always a better healer than, say, patience and love? We were never family, Ted. We were just sometimes-lovers. Right now, I can't believe we were ever even friends." I turned to the detectives. "He *was* with Rain last night. They fought. It was at the French Market Inn patio. They broke some furniture that I'm prob'ly gonna have to pay for. They prob'ly got it on security camera or something. Get his statement, put him on a plane. I'm done." I paced and returned. "Can someone take me to the Acadia?"

Denton followed me through the hotel, into the kitchen.

"That's bad business, bringing him around here." Chef Ben greeted me.

"I'm only helping her out," the detective said.

Ben exaggerated his turn toward me, ignoring my companion. "Whatcha need, sugar? You and Toni okay?"

"We're okay, Chef." I wanted to make comforting small talk but didn't have time. "We're getting the Manor ready for the party."

"Honey," he said. "They set evacuation orders half an hour ago. You need to get out of here by tonight." He pointed between me and Denton. "Get some sense into her, would you?"

Denton tipped his head. "Not everyone can leave. So, let's take care of the ones who have to stay."

The kitchen was full of cooks. Ben shifted focus now and then as a waiter came in and went back out with a full tray. "We open the doors for shelter," he said.

"I know," I said. "And Toni said you'll do it again. But the Krewe's been working hard, and they—we—don't think their efforts should be in vain. They're gathering their families as we speak."

"Well, then." Ben's gaze moved from Denton to me. "What do you need?"

CHAPTER TWENTY-EIGHT

SLEEP ELUDED US ANOTHER NIGHT. AND SO DID Lou and Ronna. Were they together, or was that wishful thinking? Why hadn't we heard anything? Why hadn't they reached out? Something was still terribly wrong.

The storm was creeping over but the worst of it was still some distance away. While Toni and the Krewe were gathering people and supplies, I had another errand to take care of.

"Miss Penny. How are you?" Momma Tristan's eyes searched me for signs of hoodoo.

I fingered my lanyard and she smiled. "I need a few candles."

She raised her eyebrows and turned to her shelf. "And for what purpose are you needing to invoke the flames?"

"We're preparing for Odessa. May as well bring some good mojo as long as the candles are needed."

"Juju." She faced me. "Mojo is your bag. Juju is what they bring. The bag, the candles, you. You all have your own juju. So, I ask you again, what juju you be needing?"

I sighed. "Do you have anything for time travel?"

She laughed and put several candles in a large bag. "I give

you nine, for protection. You put them near the main entrances and windows and your place will be safe."

"What if there are more than nine windows?"

"Put them at the doors first. At the windows, garlic."

"Garlic?" I smirked. "I'm not trying to ward off vampires."

She chuckled. "Garlic staves off more than the undead. It stops many evils from entering. What you think makes your mojo bag stay pure?"

I couldn't help myself. I lifted the bag and sniffed it. Nothing. I shrugged.

"Where you staying?" She held my mojo bag and sprinkled fresh oil on it.

The scent reminded me of Rain. I wanted him back, and the life I felt when I was around him. Wasn't this mojo supposed to help me change direction?

"Just outside the city. Greyford Manor."

She almost dropped the bag before she set it on the counter. She took a step back, waved her hands around, and started to murmur.

"What are you—"

"Shh." She motioned to the herbs and poured several scoops into a paper bag. She folded it over, bowed her head, and murmured more. "Here." She set it with the candles. "You take this. You sprinkle it at the entrances. You burn some in a glass bowl at the doors and windows. Not with a gas fire. No lighters. With a true flame. Use a match or a stick. Smudge the ashes around the openings. The same with these candles. Use only a true flame." She put more candles and two bottles of oils with the herbs into my bag. "I'll not take money from you for this. Go." She waved her hands. "Go."

The scent of coming rain refreshed me as I walked to the verandah. The peacocks shrieked their welcome and birds sang from their bath as I sat on the steps.

Momma Tristan hadn't told me when to light the candles or burn the herbs. Was I supposed to wait until everyone was here? Or before they arrived, so nothing arrived with them?

"Evil is evil," I told myself and placed a candle near the door, hoping I'd have time to light it before the storm came.

The heavy bag lightened as I removed candles and placed them near doors and shook a few drops of the garlic oil at each window. I inhaled the scent, something kind of wonderful, like patchouli and a home-cooked meal.

I didn't believe in the juju. But I welcomed the distracting task.

Ben would soon show up with food and bedding, and the Krewe would be here to help. But so would their families. And with them, perhaps questions I couldn't answer.

Best thing I could do was whatever kept me out of trouble, and out of the way.

I was sprinkling oils and herbs in front of the bedrooms on the landing when the front door opened. "That you, Ben?" I called.

It took a second for the reply. "No."

A small clump of dried whatevers fell from my fingertips to the floor.

I was glad it took forever to dust my palm and fold the bag. But I also hated it. My hands smoothed my hair and shirt, and I leaned over the railing.

Rain stood in the center of the foyer and lifted his head toward me.

I took the stairs as quickly as I could and raced to him. I stopped two feet from him, not sure what to say or do. How I wanted to reach out, hold him, let him hold me, run away. Together.

His expression was an unreadable mess of hurt, fatigue, anger, and worry. "Where is everyone?"

What did he know? What should he know? "They let you go. I knew they would. How are you? Are you hungry? What do you need?"

He clamped his lips and nodded. "Well, I'm not to leave town for a while. Where's Lou?"

I tried not to fidget. "Toni." Was it a lie if I didn't say "with?"

He made his way into the kitchen. As he pushed through the galleys, he turned and motioned for me to follow him.

I went to the fridge and poured two glasses of sweet tea. "What are you hungry for?"

"What's that?" He pointed to the candle by the verandah doors, and sat on a stool at the island.

"Momma Tristan." I tried to play it off. "We changed it to a hurricane party."

He looked at the ceiling. "Quiet 'round here."

"Yeah." I stopped my fingernail from raising to my mouth. "The Krewe's on their way. So's Ben."

"Ben?"

"With supplies."

"Right."

"The party must go on," I quoted Toni.

"It's an image thing."

"Yeah. She said." I decorated the island with sandwich fixings.

"It's not for us." His voice was flat, automated. Had he slept since they took him? "If the Foundation loses support, the kids lose support. These kids. You should have known them before. I can't let my past affect their futures."

"Yeah," I said again. When I set the sweet tea in front of him, he captured my wrist and pulled me to face him.

"Did you tell them about the box?" His eyes were dull, a sleepwalker's stare.

I stiffened, but didn't try to pull away.

"I know you saw it, Penny."

I bit my cheek. "No. I couldn't. It doesn't make sense to me, but it isn't mine to share."

He subtly swung my wrist, and sipped his tea with his free hand. "It's not mine, either."

Confusion swatted the happiness in my thoughts. I stilled my arm. "I don't believe you." There. I said it.

"Promise," he said.

"Rain." I walked to the counter. "I saw it. I saw everything in it."

"And what did you see?" Was he trying to hypnotize me with that low voice, those still eyes? Because it was working. I was being drawn back to him.

I waved my hands around, hoping they'd help me find the words I needed. "The mojo bag you took apart. The diamond ring you destroyed. The photos all messed up."

I saw his jaw tense and his eyes narrow. "Can't you let it go, Penny?"

I reached for my tea.

He whispered my name and intercepted my hand. Our
fingers interlocked and I laid my head on his shoulder. He no
longer smelled like I remembered. He smelled dirty. Sweaty.
Tired. I didn't care. It was the best scent I'd ever known. It
was him.

Our breathing synced and I knew if he stopped, I would,
too. If he were no longer here, I no longer wanted to stay. His
New Orleans was no longer just a place. She was a living thing,
living around me, in me. I was a part of her now, too. And I
would leave my mark as much as she'd left hers.

With my hand still in his, he pulled my chin until our lips
touched. His fingers explored the absence of Ted's ring.

He lowered his chin and our hands, and released me.

"Rain?"

His head pushed into me as he wrapped his arms around
my back and pulled me tighter. He lifted his head and sought
me with a look I hadn't known I'd missed.

I knew no other kisses before this. Gentle. Fierce. Passionate. Needing and personal. It was him I was fully kissing, and
I let him fully kiss me.

We only breathed when we had to. The motion of his
hands on my neck, my back, my arms, was all the life I needed.

I stepped back.

"Penny, what is it? What's going on?" He walked into the
foyer and tapped on the piano keys.

I caught his arm. "Rain, I need to tell you something."

"Tell me he's safe."

I nodded. I didn't want to lie, but needed to get my footing before we talked more. I walked him to the Great Room.
He had one arm on the rest and one on the back of the sofa.

Oh, how I wanted to lean against him like before, to have him tell me nothing else mattered. To give back to him some of the strength he'd given me.

"Cut to the chase, Penny."

I closed my eyes. "Lou got upset. He, he ran away or something."

He gripped the back of the sofa. "What do you mean, 'or something?'"

"We went to bed. When we woke up, he was gone."

He stood quickly and ran and wild hand through his hair. "Who else knows?"

"Toni and the Krewe. Sworn to secrecy." I stood to reach for him, but he backed away. "You should see these kids, Rain. They—"

Expletives peppered the air. "What did you do to my brother, Cheryl?"

I fell against the cushions. "Cheryl?"

"Penny," he said. "I meant, Penny."

Fear crept its tentacles around me. He wasn't thinking clearly, but what did that mean? What could I do?

Light thunder rumbled and the smell of rain intensified.

He walked to the wet bar.

"There's something else," I said.

He was exhausted. I didn't know what the past two days had been for him, but he didn't need more piled on. He abandoned the bar and slumped into the easy chair, his forehead buried in one hand. "What else is there?"

Martin was in the ground. The medical equipment was gone. The house had been put back to how it was before tragedy entered its doors. Nothing would be the same again.

Anne held my hand. "Been a hard week. The busyness is over. There's no worse moment. I don't care how far down the road it is, if you need me, you call me."

"I know."

"See you at Sunday dinner?"

We hugged.

They left.

And I tried to cry but couldn't.

The walls didn't change no matter how long I stared at them.

CHAPTER TWENTY-NINE

"IT'S NOT JUST ABOUT RONNA'S DISAPPEARANCE."

Rain slowly lifted his head. "Ronna." I'd not seen such tender fear cross his face before.

"Denton said she was an informant or something."

"Yeah." Rain sat back. "She had some street past. Her old man ... Anyway, she was getting over it. I'm so proud of her fight. I want to give her a way to succeed."

"You have," I said. "You are. But they made it sound like she ... Like she ..."

"Penny, we don't have time for you to be delicate. Just say it."

Something sour crept into my mouth. I spit the words out. "The night you were arrested, Douglas left the police station. Detective Chase interviewed me and said Ronna found information that you hurt Cheryl, and that's really why they arrested you. They said, before the arrest you found out where Ronna was hiding so you tried to take her, but she fought back and that's why you were battered. I tried to tell them it wasn't true, but since you have prior assaults on your record—"

"They figured this was that." He walked to the wet bar. His back was to me. No matter how loud my thoughts were, he couldn't hear them.

He held out a glass but I waved it away. He shrugged, set it on the mantel, and paced.

The rain picked at the window and I glanced at a candle. I should have lit them all a lifetime ago. I should have flown to Cincinnati. I should have stayed in the desert.

He shook his glass and the ice danced. "I didn't mean it."

"What?"

"When I called you Cheryl."

"I know."

"Penny."

My fingernail found its way between my teeth.

He stood in front of me and tugged my hand. His thumb rubbed over my fingernail before letting go. I waited for the smile that didn't come. "We need to find them," he said.

I met his stance as the door opened.

"You're home!" Toni rushed her affectionate attack.

He turned from her and put his arm around me. "Where's my brother?"

"Rain. I—"

"Did you find him?"

She lowered her head. "Rain, I'm sorry. Nobody seems to know anything about Lou or Ronna. But I didn't let everyone know they're missing. We have to be careful."

He slammed his fist on the wet bar and threw his glass at his great-granddaddy's portrait. "I'm so tired of keeping quiet! So tired of keeping up appearances, doing the right thing. Douglas and Cheryl. Lou. Keep the family secrets. Keep the honor. But don't let anyone know when you need help." He gripped the wet bar as his seething subsided.

Toni caught my eye and encouraged me toward him. Before I could reach him, he turned toward us.

"Why aren't we out there?" he asked.

Strong thunder answered with a brutal rain.

"That's why." She pointed to the window. "Rain. I know you don't want to hear this, but he could be anywhere. And it's only the few of us searching for him. I think the best thing is to get the Krewe and their families here, all together. At the least, no one else can go missing and blame it on you."

We followed him into the foyer.

"Rain?" I asked.

"Yeah. Okay." He turned to Toni. "But you think Douglas isn't gonna use this against me and try—"

She put a hand on his shoulder. "Then you'll fight him again. Later. Right now, the important thing is to find Lou and Ronna."

"He'll take everything from me. From Lou. The kids. Everything."

Two loud thumps startled us into silence. Rain motioned for us to stay calm as he opened the door.

"Boss!" Chef Ben entered.

Rain clapped his shoulder, and Toni directed the hotel attendants where to put the makeshift beds and extra bath supplies.

The Manor was an orchestrated assembly as people brought more supplies.

Teegan and Cedric parked next to the delivery van.

"Chef, you're back." Teegan greeted Rain. "Thanks for doing this. My moms be bringing the fam over later. Sure glad we don't have to cancel our party."

Cedric pointed to the clouds. "Second best reason in New Orleans to have a party."

I stepped from the verandah and let the rain fall on my face.

I wanted to slip my shoes off. To feel my crop circle under my feet. To feel Rain reaching for me.

He called from the door, keys in hand. "Penny. I gotta look for him. Come with me?"

We dodged the falling sky as we made our way to the Escalade.

Odessa pushed against us, but Rain pushed the gas harder.

My brain tried to tell me it was regular time passing, but my heart was certain the rest of the world had taken a Prozac and was moving far too slow and caring far too little for the situation.

New Orleans was a neon ghost town. Rain navigated seen and unseen forces as we headed further into it. We stopped at a red light with no traffic. He gripped his watch and flexed his jaw.

The windshield wipers were like CPR, giving my body a rhythmic focus.

Getting from here to there was a blur of boarded windows and scurrying leaves. Halloween décor was tossed about in a dangerous dance. Pumpkins dared suicide under the tires.

"It's unnatural," I whispered.

Rain concentrated on the drive. "It's exactly natural."

"I thought hurricanes weren't supposed to have lightning and thunder."

"Not supposed to," he said. "Doesn't mean it doesn't happen."

I studied his profile. His five o'clock shadow was days old. His clothes were jailhouse sloppy. He was beautiful.

Had Ted searched for me with such intensity? Did Rain feel this way when Cheryl called him to her rescue?

We left the vehicle at the valet station.

"Why don't you send them home?" I admonished.

"They're volunteers," he said, racing ahead. "Their families are here."

We entered the lobby. The buzzing melee took me by surprise. Families grouped around luggage and trash bags. Dogs on leashes barked at cats in cages. Older children ran a chaotic game as toddlers clung to their mothers. Homeless people clustered in a corner and eyed us with suspicious thanks.

"Toni and I came here earlier. He's not here."

"I know." He put a protective arm around me and led me to his kitchen office. He closed the door and handed me a bottled water.

"What are we doing here?" I asked.

"Something I need to get." He keyed open a lower desk drawer and took out a locked box.

"No," I said. "Rain. No."

He holstered the pistol. "I'm not taking any more chances." He grabbed an extra mag and box of ammo with one hand, and reached for me with the other. "Put these in your bag til we get back in the truck."

I complied out of fear. Out of adrenaline. Out of something like love. "I hate New Orleans." I gripped my defunct mojo bag and almost prayed.

"I know you hid the box in my suitcase."

"What's that?" Rain asked, driving fast.

"The box with the tea and the photos. You put it with the note in my suitcase before they arrested you. I know you put it there. I don't care. I'm here, Rain. I'm here with you. No matter what."

He glanced sideways at me. "I don't know what you're talking about. Can we not do this now?"

We were going to die soon. Best to clear this up so it was one less haunting we'd have to deal with. "I got your apology. You said you were sorry, and gave me the evidence. Rain, I get it. You did something bad, really bad. But ... we can start over."

He took his eyes off the road for almost too long. "Penny. I swear to you. I didn't put that box in your suitcase. I told you, it's not my box. I found it, like you did. Years ago. Just before Cheryl died."

"Then who's is it?" Horror hit me. If it wasn't Rain's, who's could it be?

"I don't know. Cheryl, she ruined the pictures. I saw her do it, so I took them away. I don't know how all that stuff got together in that box. Promise."

"Why did you keep it?"

"Guilt? Helplessness? I guess I always thought someone needed me to keep it safe."

Our voices were screaming over the storm.

"Someone?" I shouted. "You mean Lou?"

"I don't know. Maybe. Or I thought, maybe, Cheryl used him to kill herself. And I couldn't let him go to prison for that."

"What about your note to me, your apology?"

He focused on the drive. "I was apologizing for fighting

with Ted. For not trusting you, for not being honest with you before that night. I wanted to ..." He trailed off, his attentions going to the storm. He reached for my hand.

I heard a scream—my scream—as the SUV spun. Rain gripped the wheel at all angles, his feet going to the pedals as best they could. Left. Down. Up. Right. Beams of light. A hard jarring against my side. White impact.

Darkness.

"Penny!" The voice disturbed me. I needed to sleep. Sleep? No. That's not right. "Penny." A hand tapped my face and I moaned. A curse. Another pat. Another plea. "Wake up. Are you okay?"

"My foot hurts." I whispered and licked my lips. The cut. The infection. Wait. This wasn't that. This was—what was this?

"Open your eyes, girl. C'mon. Wake up." The urgency forced me to comply.

Panic fused with the mass of metal and dead airbag drowning me. Rain cursed the broken seatbelt entwined around me.

"Rain." I couldn't reach him.

"Don't move. I'll get you out. You okay?" He was moving fast, in and out of the SUV, tugging on the bent door, pushing a branch from the window.

"I'm fine," I said, not certain it was true.

He leaned over me.

"Rain! Your head!" The blood trailing his cheek wasn't a small amount.

He continued to work the seatbelt until it released and I fell into him.

I gasped for air and couldn't stop.

He pushed buttons on his cell phone, and grimaced. "No service." He shoved the phone into my backpack, slung it over his shoulder, and reached around my waist.

The rain spit its awful daggers upon us.

"Can you walk?" he shouted.

"I don't know." I said. "I don't know where we are."

He peered into the wet night. "I can't see."

We waited as Odessa roared around us. The mangled SUV offered no shelter. My heart was louder than the thunder.

"We'll make it," he yelled. "Promise."

I clung to him and drank the storm.

How much time passed? Seconds? Hours? Odessa backed off her attack.

A faint light flickered, vanished, reappeared. Two. Headlights. Heading toward us.

Rain turned, his arm tight around me, and kept his eyes on the vehicle. He raised his other hand and yelled.

The car crunched to a stop and the side window rolled down. The driver leaned over. "You need—Penny?"

"Douglas?" I gripped Rain's hand. "What are you doing out here?"

"Safety check. Get in. I'll take ya home."

Rain didn't move.

Douglas cursed. "The Manor's just down there. The whole area's lost power. You'd never find it in this mess."

Rain helped me into the back seat, held the backpack in his lap, and murmured his thanks to Douglas.

"You two okay?"

Rain looked straight ahead. I had nothing to wipe the blood with.

CHAPTER THIRTY

A TUMULTUOUS PARTY HAD OVERTAKEN THE Manor. Generators hummed their electricity to dim lamps against the barricaded windows, and my candles flickered vicious protections about us. The Kitchen Krewe was sharing their edible creations. The smell of garlic mixed with pumpkin soup and bay leaves. Ben and his team had rolled in folding tables and set up a magnificent display. A long buffet was established in the Great Room. High, round cocktail tables populated the foyer. A bartender served up drinkable hurricanes to the adults and Shirley Temples to the kids.

I wanted to appreciate it, but it made me sick. How could this celebration take place when Lou was stilling missing, and the storm still raging? Would his likeness soon be on billboards and hotel walls?

Toni helped us to Rain's room before anyone could ask questions. She closed the door, flicked on a lantern as I sat on the bed and Rain tossed the backpack next to me.

"What happened?" She dampened a cloth and wiped his face.

"I don't know." He sounded bewildered. "We didn't have a chance to find him." He was broken. Toni wiped a tear from his cheek and handed him an electric razor.

He saw my reflection in the mirror. "How's the foot?"

I winced as I tried to rotate my ankle.

"Let me see." He knelt and took off my shoe. Odessa dripped from my sock as he pulled it off.

"Can you walk?" he asked.

I stood and fell back onto the bed, shaking my head.

"Might be broken," he said.

"What do y'all need, sugar?" Toni asked.

"This isn't happening," I said. "There's a hurricane? And a party? While Lou and Ronna are missing?"

She sat next to me. "We're not doing this for ourselves, Penny. It's for them, the community. It gives the Krewe something to look forward to, and their parents a reason to be proud. This is N'Orlins. Don't you know yet? We always believe things will get better, that life is more than this one tragic moment. It's always restarting."

I watched Rain as he quickly shaved. "He doesn't believe in starting over," I whispered.

She leaned into my eyesight. "Maybe he just ain't recognized his reason yet."

The rain stopped. An unsettling quiet came upon us.

"Rain?" I asked.

He pulled the curtain away from the window. "Everyone downstairs. Now."

"What is this?" I tried to stand.

"Eye of the storm. We gotta move."

CHAPTER THIRTY-ONE

RAIN TUCKED HIS PISTOL INTO HIS HIP HOLSTER and pulled his shirt loosely over it. He brought his cheek next to mine. "You're okay."

I gripped the crutches and followed him and Toni to the landing.

The candles danced below as children bobbed their battery-powered lanterns. Ben had inspired an indoor trick-or-treat and the squeals told us it was well received.

Costumed people were everywhere. Standing, sitting, lying. We made our way downstairs past a race car driver, three versions of the same Saints quarterback, a cop, and a barmaid. My heart scrambled when I saw a peacock queen holding court over three Teenage Mutant Ninja Turtles. Monsters and ghosts flitted about.

Glow-in-the-dark bracelets, necklaces or headbands were on nearly everyone. Cooking fuel canisters gave an eerie light to the food tables.

The coffee was cold, but it was coffee.

Adults gathered around the kitchen table and island, and talked in hushed tones. Playpens with sleeping babies were tucked against the walls. Rain put a gentle hand on my back. I leaned against his shoulder and wondered if Lou would soon be another ghost for him.

"The writer." Momma Tristan appeared. "You almost have your story."

I shook my head. "Rain, have you met Momma Tristan?"

"We've met once or twice."

She considered him. "Yes. Yes, I know you. And I know about you. You keep doing good, no matter what. It's not what others say about you, it's what your heart says. And yours is a good heart."

"Thank you," he said.

"What are you doing here?" I asked.

"I come with my sister." She raised her hands. "Come to make sure the end is only the beginning. You know about hurricanes, yes?"

"I know they're destructive in general, and I know this is a bad one."

"Destructive, true. But they also unify. Look around you. They bring people together. The make a community where there wasn't one, and they strengthen when there is. They wash away that which isn't strong, and leave a new foundation. Hurricanes are a cleansing force. Destruction doesn't have to mean death. It can be a renewing. A new start."

Did Rain shift at that last statement? Momma Tristan continued. "Yes, they leave damage and debris, but that which is left has been washed, put through the turmoil, and remains on solid ground. You have a strong foundation here, writer.

Don't forget, it's not always where you came from, or where you're going. But who it is that goes with you."

Warmth enrobed me as Rain squeezed my hand.

"Mr. Rain?" A tired woman approached.

"Barbara." He greeted her tenderly. "It's so good to see you." Rain turned to me. "This is Ronna's mother."

"Ronna." I gasped and hugged her. "Oh, Barbara." What could I say that wouldn't bring more attention to this silent situation? I chewed my lip and hugged her tighter.

Momma Tristan stepped forward. "She is my sister."

I stepped back and considered them together. "You're sisters?"

Barbara reached for Rain's hand. "I want to tell you what a nice thing you be doing for the kids, for all of us here."

Too many emotions clouded the tear clinging to his eyelash. He casually wiped it away. "I didn't realize you two were related."

Ronna's mom continued. "And where is your brother? My diamond talks about him all the time, says he come to the class now and then. I'd sure like to meet him."

"He's around here somewhere," I said before Rain needed to lie. "I think I saw him go upstairs a little while ago." If days could be considered a little while ago.

We excused ourselves and went back to the foyer.

I parked myself against the stairwell and surveyed the gathering. Adults hid concern behind drinks. Costumes decorated people of all ages. Young children were either asleep or scouring their candy loot.

The Grandfather clock chimed midnight and the group shouted their Halloween celebration.

Toni laughed as Rain squinted at her. "Don't do it," he said.

She twisted her mouth playfully.

"Toni." His head turned with the warning.

"Happy birthday, Rain!" she shouted.

"It's your birthday?" I asked.

He motioned for my silence, but it was too late.

Barbara and Momma Tristan came through the galley doors. "It's Ronna's birthday, too." Barbara sniffed.

Chef Ben led the group in soft song.

Toni grinned as Rain gave his polite appreciation.

The peacock queen strutted over and took off her mask. "Happy birthday, Chef Rain." She turned to Barbara. "Momma, Auntie. I'm here."

"Ronna?" Rain and Toni surrounded her. "Where have you been?"

Barbara embraced her. "Oh, my diamond. Are you all right? Are you hurt?"

Rain turned her back to him. "Do you know where Lou is? Is he okay?"

The generator sputtered and the lights grew dimmer. The storm crashed hard against the Manor, and the wind screeched to get in.

"Momma," Ronna pleaded. "I'm so sorry."

Douglas approached her with a quick step and a strong arm. "Ronna. You're safe."

She pulled away and whimpered. "No. You're a liar!"

Momma Tristan grabbed Douglas's wrist and eased Ronna out of his grip. "You stop with that girl and all them girls. You let them be now, you hear me?"

"What are you going on about?" he asked.

"She tell me all about you, those men. So many broken girls you think you can—"

"This is police business," he said.

"But it's not your business," Detective Chase pushed through the gathering.

"C'mon, Den," Douglas faced his partner. "I'm just looking out for her. He tried to snatch her. I need her side of the story. That's why—"

Ronna stood tall. "No, it's not true. I'm sorry, Chef Rain. He told me I had to tell them about a box, and that I knew you killed your wife."

"The box." I gasped, and tried not to stare at Rain.

Douglas uttered words I'd not heard in R-rated movies. "Yes, the box. The one I put in your luggage for safe keeping. I trusted you to do the right thing, to bring it to me so I could finally put him where he belongs. But you didn't. Because you love him. Like I loved her. Like she loved me." He faced Rain. "In the end, she thought she loved you. But I knew better. She lost my baby but did everything to keep yours. That should have been my baby." He spread his arms. "This should be mine."

"Greyford?" Rain glared. "Is this still, after all these years, what you're about? She scratched those photos. She couldn't..." He paced, rushing a hand through his hair down to his neck. He stopped in front of me. "She couldn't stand the sight of herself. Hated herself so much, she asked how I could stand to look at her. She couldn't forgive herself, didn't believe I could. We tried. She wanted to. I took those damaged photos from her because I didn't want her, on her good days, to be reminded of her bad days."

The adults ushered children out of the way. Sleepers were roused and moved. Two of the costumed Ninja Turtles stood and removed their masks. No surprise: Cedric and Teegan.

Lightning flashed, thunder boomed, and rain shattered its hard daggers around the house. But it was the wind, the roaring, screaming noise mimicking a train or crashing plane, that terrified me most.

"Hell of a storm," Douglas said. "Come here, Ronna. We need to finish our conversation."

The third Turtle stood and unmasked. Georgina. "You leave her alone!"

Barbara pulled Ronna to her. "It's okay, baby." She smoothed her hair and kissed her tenderly. "No one can take you from me again, diamond. You're safe now. I'm so proud of you."

Douglas huffed. "Your diamond? Your little whore diamond? She's fake. She's trash. She's broken, and I know just how. She's—"

"Stop!" A costumed rougarou removed its head. "You're wrong. She's not those things, ever. She's my friend!"

"Lou?" Rain's bewildered gaze fell on the man. "You're a rougarou?"

"Oh, Rain. Did I do something bad? I was just trying to stay safe, and Ronna, she—"

Rain rushed to his brother, stopped short of embracing him. "No, bud. You did good. Did you take care of her?" He talked to him like a child, but respected him like a man.

"We took care of each other."

"Are you okay? Where have you been? And why are you dressed like this?"

Lou grinned proudly. "I'm okay. I keep telling you. The rougarou isn't bad if you don't deserve it. And the Krewe helped me see that I'm not bad anymore, so the rougarou won't get me."

Rain gazed on the Krewe members closest to him, patted shoulders, put a tender hand on Ronna's cheek. "You all took care of Lou?"

They nodded and smiled. "He's one of us," Cedric said. "We ain't gonna let the boy down."

"But how ...?"

Lou puffed out his chest. "I didn't want to stay here without you, so I was going to go to the jail. But I knew Douglas wouldn't let me so I was going to go to Momma's room at the hotel instead. Ronna found me outside and since she was hiding from Douglas, we went to ... to ... Ronna?"

Ronna patted his arm. "I knew I couldn't go home, couldn't tell anyone just yet, so we went to my auntie for help. And tonight, I texted Teeg and Cedric to let them know we was okay and on our way here. They got the costumes for us so no one would see us come in."

Momma Tristan hugged her sister and niece. "It was after Miss Penny came for the candles. I knew then I had to come to the Manor before the storm hit."

"Rain." Lou pointed. "You hurt your head. And Penny Josie hurt her foot again."

Rain touched his forehead. "Yeah, bud. But I'm okay now. We're okay."

"I'm okay, too. I had to hide from the rougarou at first. Douglas said it was coming for us, and if I didn't hide it would get you too, just like it got Cheryl."

Douglas glowered. "I never said that."

"You did." Lou shrugged. "You gave me more tea for Cheryl and told me to make it strong. So, I did. But first she and Rain fought. Then you came over and she drank her special tea and fell down and you took her away. But you always told me special tea is bad for anyone else and I should never drink it, so I haven't. Ever."

Rain looked sick. "What's he saying, Douglas?"

Douglas turned. "Nothing. He's stupid. You can't trust a thing he says."

Rain focused on Lou. "What else did he tell you, bud?"

"He told me to put the rest of the tea and herbs in a mojo bag, and if anyone asked, tell them the rougarou did it. But no one asked, so I didn't have to lie. It wasn't the rougarou, and it wasn't you. It was me. But mostly it was Douglas and even though I don't like him, he's family and he said that means I can trust him. So, I don't have to be afraid."

Douglas edged toward the door. "Lou. You don't know what you're saying. That never happened."

"Yes. It did. But Rain always tells me to face my fears. You hurt Ronna and I don't want you to hurt anyone else. So I'm going to listen to Rain. Even if it hurts me because I know he wouldn't mean it. But I think you mean it even when you say you don't."

Rain dropped his hands. "Douglas."

Ronna stepped forward, her cheeks damp. "It's true. I don't know 'bout all that Cheryl stuff, but I know he's a liar, and he hurt me."

He turned back to Douglas. "What did you do to Cheryl?"

His cousin gave a dark chuckle. "Too bad you missed the cremation. It wasn't anything fancy. Oh, wait. You're the one who started it."

Toni went pale. She gripped Rain's arm and he struggled to keep her standing.

"What are you saying?" Detective Chase asked.

Rain's eyes turned on me, but there was nothing in them. "He's saying, I burned her when I burned my cabin."

A sick, disgusting smile appeared on Douglas's face. I wanted to show no reaction. I needed to vomit.

Ronna cried out. "He said her body was under some bayou thing, a fishing cabin or something, and if I didn't want him to hurt my momma or the twins, I'd have to do as he said. And he said I had to lie about you. I'm so sorry, Chef Rain. I know now it ain't true. I know you didn't kill no one."

Denton stepped closer. "What have you done?"

Douglas set one foot at an angle and pointed at Rain. "Why don't you ask him? He had the perfect life, perfect wife. Perfect alibi."

Denton brought his voice low as he spoke to Ronna. "Will you swear to all this?"

She looked at her mother, Rain. Lou. "Yes, I'll tell whoever I need to. That man ain't no good cop. He's mean, and I ain't do those things no more, no matter what he say."

"Good enough for me." Denton pulled out his cuffs.

"Den, c'mon." Douglas backed up on the foyer steps. "You can't believe them. I'm your partner."

"Yeah. You're my partner. And you're everything they said you were."

Douglas's gaze changed from confusion to realization to crazy hatred. "It was you. You're the one they sent to investigate—" He reached the door and stopped.

"How dare you!" Toni paced the short distance from us to Douglas.

He cocked his head. "Aw, darlin'."

"Don't you ever!" She slapped his face hard. "I trusted you! We all trusted you!"

He leaned close, spitting his words on her. "You never trusted me. None of you. If you had, you wouldn't have left me. She wouldn't have—"

"You killed my wife," Rain growled.

Douglas shifted his focus, and put a hand on the door knob. "Your brother gave her the tea. He killed her. I saved your baby. You can keep your precious plantation. Your daddy's land. Your idiot brother. And this." He gave Toni a shove and opened the door. "I'm done with you all."

Rain lurched forward, a full attack that hurdled both him and Douglas outside.

Denton chased after them as violent water flew from the absent sky. Fists and limbs threw macabre shadows on the verandah as the extinguished candle rolled violently.

Toni, Lou, and I forced our way through the horrified crowd to the doorway and tried to make sense through the storm. Lou's humming was all I heard. I couldn't understand Toni's words.

A faint discharge sounded with the thunder and one of the shadows collapsed.

CHAPTER THIRTY-TWO

"THREE MORE WEEKS, GOOD AS NEW." ANNE PAT-
ted my shoulder with encouragement. "You'll just have to take
it easy for a few more days."

"I can't believe you and Christopher came all the way out
here for my broken ankle." I slipped myself from the hospital
bed into the wheelchair.

"Who cares about your ankle?" She laughed. "We came for
the food. Besides, he's enjoying getting to know his counter-
parts out here."

I followed her gaze into the hallway where Chris and Denton were having an animated discussion. Christopher peered
into the room. "Hey, hon. You'll never guess what they call
Internal Affairs out here."

"I'm guessing it's not Internal Affairs," Anne replied.

Toni picked up my bag and crutches. "Public Integrity
Bureau."

"So, it's true? What Douglas said?" I asked Denton. "You
were—"

"A rat?" he said. "Not quite the way we see it. The PIB mission is for transparency in how officers of the law deal with

the public. Douglas had raised a few flags recently. Once is a mistake, twice is a consideration. PIB approached me some months ago to ask if I'd be willing to check it out. Wasn't hard to see him starting to unravel, and it was either him or the ship."

Toni kept her hand on his arm. "Won't you get in trouble with the other cops?"

"Not the ones who get it. And that's not really the point. Someone had to stop him."

"What's going to happen now?" I asked.

Toni scowled. "They're keeping him out of Gen-Pop for his own safety. Court date hasn't been set yet."

"And his shoulder?"

"Through and through," Denton said. "He's got a nasty scar. But he's alive."

"Thank goodness," Toni said.

"You care?" I asked.

"Only that I'll get the chance to testify against him."

Anne leaned over my shoulder. "How 'bout we change the subject? You ready to leave?"

"You have no idea."

A nurse pushed the wheelchair through the sliding exit. I inhaled the moist, fresh air.

Rain parked the Ghost and walked around to open my door.

"There it is." Toni handed me my belongings.

"There what is?" he asked.

Her lips turned as she brought her gaze from him to me. "Just a little recognition. We'll see you for dinner." She left with Denton and Chris.

Anne hugged me then followed them.

The nurse retreated as I stood on my crutches and leaned into Rain.

"I have something for you," he said.

I stroked his arm. "I don't think I need anything else."

He laughed and clipped a hurricane charm on my bracelet, then opened the door.

As he sat behind the wheel, he turned to me and pulled on a lanyard around his neck. "Also, I think this was yours."

"Fred," I squealed.

He quickly tucked it back under his shirt. "Hey, you're not supposed to see it. Probably shouldn't have shown you the lanyard. It belongs to me, now. And it's not Fred anymore."

"It's not?"

"New owner, new name."

I sat back and chewed my smiling lip. "So, what did you name it?"

He pretended to think. "I think Savor is what I'm looking for."

"Savor." I mulled it over. "And how's it working for you?"

He leaned over and kissed me. "I think it's working just fine, boo." He hooked a finger around my lanyard. "You name this one yet?"

"Unity."

"I want to ask you a question." He sat back. "I was wondering how you felt about helping around the restaurant. Maybe share your skills with the Kitchen Krewe?"

"I'd have to think about it," I lied.

"Fair enough." He started the engine but kept the car in park. "Did I tell you I'm changing the name?"

"Why?"

"Been thinking it's time to start over."

My heart fluttered. "To what?"

He gently tugged a strand of my hair. "I was thinking, maybe, Embers."

I gasped in joy.

He put his hands on the wheel and looked at the side mirror. "Wanna get a drink—coffee—and talk about it?"

"How 'bout beignets and chicory?" I giggled.

"Like you live here." He moved into traffic. "One more question."

"What's that?" I couldn't imagine being any more elated than I was in this moment.

His fingers wove around mine. "You wanna fall in love?"

THE END

Mais Chers,

Thank you for reading through NOLA. This project has been near and dear to me for seven years, and I trust you have fallen in love with the characters as I continue to do, over and over.

This is my first novel, which is apparent as it took me seven years to get here. Yet it took just a blink. Writing is a tricky sport. There are rules, but depending on your learning platform, those rules change. Bend. Even disappear.

When I first began NOLA, it was a glimmer of a short story, perhaps a murder mystery. It soon became apparent this story cannot possibly be told any place other than the Crescent City, and my idea for a location-mystery genre was born. Then my editor pointed out my flair for romance, and here we are. The Big Easy lives and breathes her own majesty through these pages, shaping the adventures and hearts of Penny, Rain, Toni, Lou, and the rest. The location herself is such a character, and I'm delighted to share New Orleans with you.

I wrote the beginning eight times before my mentor told me he refused to read any more until I finished the entire story. Most writers will do that: write out a rough draft. Clean it up. Write it again. Clean it up again. The process is wonderfully excruciating. I settled on writing it the best way I know how: Just tell the story the characters showed me. How often I yelled at my computer or walked away. And returned. Some scenes took weeks, others, minutes.

There's a magic that comes with giving so much of one's self in a creative work. Is NOLA autobiographical? Perhaps, a little. Perhaps, in a backward sense. In writing the character of Penny Jo, I realized I am more like her than I first recognized. I allowed her to grow in confidence, and she showed me what life can be like when you dare greatly.

I thought finishing the book would be painful. A hard goodbye to these characters, this place, I have lived with for so long. Instead, it's just the beginning. NOLA is not leaving home, not saying goodbye. She's coming home to stay. A permanent piece of my heart, and, I hope, your book collection.

As you enjoy your beignets and chicory, I ask that you consider posting a review on Amazon, Goodreads, and your social media sites. Reviews are the currency of authorship, and I welcome your authentic feedback.

I'd love to connect with you at MollyJoRealy.com.

Savor the journey,
Molly Jo

— CAPTAIN —

ABOUT THE AUTHOR

MOLLY JO REALY IS AN AWARD-WINNING WRITER, editor, social media ninja and author coach. Nicknamed the Bohemian Hurricane, she encourages people to embrace their unique talents and gifts to come alive and celebrate life every day. She has been featured in children's magazines, on blogs and devotional websites, and her short stories have earned her awards and scholarships from nationally acclaimed writing programs.

Her unique style makes her a favorite speaker at writing and marketing seminars.

She is the founder of New Inklings Press, and curator of *The Unemployment Cookbook: Ideas for Feeding Families One Meal at a Time.*

Recently rooted in South Carolina, she celebrates with her family, her cats, a good cup of coffee, and an addiction to pens.

Her favorite quote is from Isaac Asimov:
I write for the same reason I breathe.
Because if I didn't, I would die.

You can find her on:
Facebook, Twitter, Instagram,
and her blog, *FranklyMyDearMojo.com*

Post Office Box 81031
Simpsonville, SC 29680

Visit us online at
http://www.NewInklingsPress.com

Made in the USA
Columbia, SC
03 July 2019